TRAIN ROBBERY!

McCoy ran down the aisle, kicked away the gun and checked the wounded man but found no more weapons. He stepped over him and looked out the small window toward the next car. A gunman stood there guarding the entrance to the express car. His two buddies were probably inside trying to blow the express car's big safe.

As Spur watched, an explosion jolted through the two cars. He saw the connecting door to the express car slam open and knock the guard off his feet, dumping him into the area between the cars.

Spur jerked open the door and leveled his Colt Peacemaker at the gunman who tried to sit up and raise his gun.

"Drop it, dead man," Spur said.

Also in the *Spur* series:

SPUR

MINT-PERFECT MADAM

DIRK FLETCHER

LEISURE BOOKS   NEW YORK CITY

A LEISURE BOOK®

February 1990

Published by

Dorchester Publishing Co., Inc.
276 Fifth Avenue
New York, NY 10001

· 1 ·

May 5, 1874, Near Sacramento, California:

A shot slammed over Spur McCoy's head where
he crouched in the end of the railroad passenger
car. He lifted up and snapped a round at the man
who left the rear seat and tried for the door. The
round jolted through the running man's side and
punched two large holes in his aorta, dropping
him gasping to the floor as he started to bleed to
death internally.

Half a dozen people in the rail car started to
peer over the top of their seats.

"Stay down!" McCoy barked. "There are still
three more of them."

He could see the man he had shot sprawled on the floor next to the connecting door to the railway express car. The robber's gun had skittered two feet from his hand.

"Help me, somebody!" the robber's anguished plea stabbed through the clicking of the railroad wheels on the rails.

McCoy ran down the aisle, kicked away the gun and checked the wounded man but found no more weapons. He stepped over him and looked out the small window toward the next car. A gunman stood there guarding the entrance to the express car. His two buddies were probably inside trying to blow the express car's big safe.

As McCoy watched, an explosion jolted through the two cars. He saw the connecting door to the express car slam open and knock the guard off his feet, dumping him into the area between the cars.

McCoy jerked open the door and leveled his Colt Peacemaker at the gunman who tried to sit up and raise his gun.

"Drop it, dead man," Spur spat.

The man kept lifting the six-gun until it was almost pointing at Spur. Spur McCoy's .45 bucked in his hand and the round cut into the gunman's right wrist, breaking both arm bones and angling up the arm ten inches before it exited near his elbow.

"Bastard!" the robber roared.

His six-gun flew from his hand and fell between the cars. It bounced along on the railroad ties underneath the car.

The train began to slow.

"You need one more round?" Spur asked.

The robber shook his head. He sat up holding his broken right wrist with his left hand.

"How many more in the express car?" Spur asked.

The robber looked up and snorted, then looked away. Spur tapped the robber's broken arm with his boot toe. The miscreant bellowed in pain, tears streamed down his face and he glared at Spur.

"Two of them, and I hope they kill you!"

Spur stepped to the open express door and looked in. Smoke had been coming out the top of the door since the blast, but now it was almost clear. He looked around a stack of mail sacks in the middle of the car where the safe sat bolted and welded to the rail car frame itself. One man was leaning inside a big safe, the other was looking in Spur's direction with a sawed off shotgun.

The robber lifted the scattergun and pulled the trigger just as Spur lunged behind the steel outer door. Buckshot peppered through the open door and dug into the mail sacks. A roaring blast and blue smoke from the black gunpowder filled the car.

Spur looked in the express car from the floor level. He was hidden by more of the mail sacks but he could see the gunman's legs. At once he aimed and fired and in one motion was on his feet, weapon aimed at the same area.

One robber had taken a round in his shin. He pivoted to the side and hit the floor. He tried to turn with his shotgun but Spur sent another round into the robber and he doubled over and lay still.

"Just you and me left, badman," Spur shouted. "You in such a hurry to get rich you want to die with all that money in your hands?"

Two hands came over the top of the heavy safe door that had been shielding the last robber.

"Not me, no sir. Don't shoot. I'm just the

3

dynamite man. I ain't the boss of this bunch." The man stood, his hands over his head.

"Come this way slowly," Spur said.

The train had almost stopped. When Spur could see the man plainly, he spotted the revolver in a holster at his side.

"Drop that iron on the floor, do it easy. Do it now."

The gunman eased the weapon out of leather, bent and skidded it on the floor. It didn't discharge.

A man ran up the steps of the passenger car and Spur could sense someone behind him.

"Don't move, mister," a voice said. "This is a shotgun aimed right at your back."

"Hey, not him," another voice said from behind. "He's the one who stopped the robbery!"

Spur couldn't look away from the robber. "Friend, behind me, easy with the scattergun. I'm on your side. You want to do something helpful, put the shotgun down and get in the express car and check that fourth robber. He might be dead and he might not be."

Spur let his breath out when he heard something touch the floor.

"Yeah, okay. I didn't know who was who," the man stated as he stepped past Spur.

"Not yet! You come between me and that robber, he could get away. Just stand still."

Spur moved into the express car and frisked the robber, found a hideout derringer which he pushed in his own belt. He took a knife from the man's boot and then tied his hands behind him with a piece of twine from the express car workbench.

The railroad conductor checked the last robber.

He came back looking a little pale. "That one back there is dead, and there's a dead one in the passenger car. Two dead and two alive. They get anything out of the safe?"

"Where's the express car clerk?" Spur asked.

The railroad man searched the car and found him behind some boxes. His throat had been slit. The railroad man threw up.

A half hour later the blood and the mess was cleaned up, the three bodies stowed in the express car, and the car locked from the outside until they could get a new expressman to straighten out the situation and sign for everything.

The conductor came by and thanked Spur for his help.

"Sir, it isn't often that we have a passenger who jumps into a situation like this and actually prevents a robbery. The Central Pacific owes you a great deal of thanks."

Spur shook his hand and went back to the car behind the one he had been riding in. He sat down in a seat that had been turned to face the one behind it. It gave more leg room if there was no one sitting opposite.

A young woman sat on the window side riding backwards. Spur sat on the aisle seat facing front and stretched out his legs luxuriantly.

"It does seem to make it easier riding, doesn't it?" the woman said. She was about 23 or 24, with soft blond hair falling gloriously around her shoulders. She had been reading a book but now put it down.

"Yes, I can use a little extra room."

"I hear you're a hero."

"Afraid not. Just at the wrong place when the robbers came in."

She watched him with unwavering blue eyes. She was attractive, well formed, and wore an interesting outfit that fitted tightly across her breasts.

"You killed two of them. Is that. . . ." she looked away. "Is it hard to kill another human being?"

Spur met her gaze and appraised her a moment. Her gaze never left his.

"It isn't hard at all to kill, when you know that the other person is about to kill you. It's the ages old law of the jungle, kill or be killed."

The girl shuddered. "It seems so . . . so drastic."

"Miss, I hope you're never in such a situation." He smiled. "Indeed I do hope so. Now to more pleasant things. What are you reading?"

"Hamlet."

"Ah, yes, the moody Dane. Do you suppose William Shakespeare actually wrote it?"

"Oh, I'm certain of it. One of my teachers told me all of that talk was just so much baloney. He said not to believe it until someone proved that another man wrote the great Shakespearean works. That's good enough for me."

"But you wouldn't argue about it?"

"No. It doesn't change the great writing, does it? I can't walk up to him and thank him for doing it, so it matters little to me exactly who did the writing."

"I remember a young lady I'd like to introduce you to sometime if I had the chance. Speaking of introductions, my name is Spur McCoy."

"Oh, nice to meet you, Mr. McCoy. I'm Laura Grandifar. Are you going to San Francisco?"

"Yes, and you?"

"I live there. I'm coming home from college, actually. I graduated and now I have to figure out what I want to do."

"Then you're not married?"

She looked up quickly and smiled. "No, and I don't see any wedding ring on your hand, either."

"Just never quite got around to it. Have you lived in San Francisco for long?"

"All my life until I went back to Boston to college. Where is home for you?"

"Almost anywhere these days. I grew up in New York City, not so far away from Boston. When do we get to Sacramento, do you know?"

"The conductor said about two in the afternoon. I still like to get off there and take the riverboat on down to San Francisco. Have you ever taken the boat?"

"Several years ago," he said.

They talked for another hour and then came to the outskirts of the bustling little town of Sacramento, which was growing by leaps now that it was the state capitol and the transcontinental railroad went through it in both directions.

"I'm hoping you'll ride the boat. Besides, I have a cabin and it's quiet and peaceful. We could talk. About Hamlet, or anything."

"It takes a lot longer to get to San Francisco that way," he said.

"I know, that's part of the charm." She put her hand on his shoulder. "Spur McCoy, I would really like you to ride down on the boat with me. It could be a . . . an interesting trip for both of us."

Spur smiled. "I think I might just do that, Miss Grandifar. Yes, why not?"

He found his suitcase where he had left it in the other car and returned to help Laura Grandifar with her two suitcases and carpetbag.

"This will be my last trip across the country for

a while, I hope," she said. I've done it four times now."

She watched him. "I'm glad you'll be taking the boat."

"It should be fun. I haven't been on a boat ride for a long time."

"Good, then you can help me with my bags. The staterooms aren't big. I reserved one just for the fun of it. There are only six, and I like to get one for the privacy. There is so little here on the train."

She watched him from her light blue eyes and he saw the hint of a smile on her pretty face.

"I'll be more than pleased to help you with your bags, Miss Grandifar."

"Please, call me Laura. May I call you Spur?"

An hour later they settled in the small stateroom on the riverboat headed for San Francisco. It was on the upper deck, had two portholes that looked out on the river, and a couch and two chairs.

She sat on the edge of the couch and frowned. "Spur McCoy, I really want to see you again after we get to San Francisco, but that might be a little hard. I'm sure mother has a series of balls and teas and parties all arranged for me. She's frantic about getting me married since I'm 23 already and have no prospects. Oh, dear. I'm sure she'll have a dozen young men lined up just waiting to sweep me off my feet."

She laughed softly when he looked up surprised. "No, Spur, not because of my dazzling beauty. You see, I'm the only child of Wilbur D. Grandifar of the Grandifar millions. I'm a poor little rich girl, and I can't help it."

She motioned to him. "Sit over here, please. We have several hours to relax and get to know one another, and I hope it will be as pleasant for you as I'm sure it's going to be for me.''

He sat beside her, so close his thigh touched hers through the dress. At once she leaned over, caught his face in her soft hands and turned it to hers to kiss him.

It was a firm, willful kiss, with the promise of much more to come. She closed her eyes and when she opened them, she leaned away from him and smiled.

''Does that shock you?''

''Not at all, it pleases me.'' He put his hand up on her breast and rubbed softly. ''Does that shock you?''

''Not at all,'' she said smiling. ''It pleases me greatly.''

He kissed her and his mouth came open as he explored her open mouth as well. After the long kiss, his lips left hers and worked down her throat and her chest until he covered the point of one breast. He blew his hot breath on it through the fabric, then kissed it and reached for the buttons that kept the front of her dress closed.

He opened one button and kissed her lips lightly. Her pale blue eyes glistened.

''I like unwrapping pretty packages, and nice lady, you are the prettiest package I've seen in a long, long time.''

Her hand slid over to his crotch and rubbed a long hardness she found there.

''Oh, you have some sort of swelling down there. Is it painful?''

''It won't be for long. I have a notion that you'll be able to help me relieve the pressure somehow.''

He unbuttoned more of the fasteners and when he was halfway down, he slid his hand inside the dress, under the short silk chemise she wore, and put his hand around one of her pulsating, hot breasts.

"Nice," he said.

"It feels better than that. It feels glorious." She bent and kissed him, then stood and pulled the dress off over her head. The chemise followed and she knelt on the bed, her full breasts bouncing and swinging and jiggling from her abrupt motions.

"Marvelous!" Spur moved forward and kissed each swinging orb, then pulled one of them into his mouth and chewed on the delicious pink nipple.

As he did, she began unbuttoning his shirt, pulled his string tie, and helped him slip out of his town jacket. She sat on the bed bare to the waist and covered only with a light petticoat and some fancy underpants that he had caught only a glimpse of.

When she had his shirt off, she ran her fingers through the blackhair on his chest, then bent and kissed his nipples, biting one until he yelped in surprise.

"Figured you'd want to know how it felt," Laura said smiling.

They lay on the narrow couch and soon he pulled her over on top of him. They both were clothed from the waist down. He pulled her up until one of her breasts fell into his mouth and he laughed as he munched away.

"I'm glad you're not married," she said suddenly. "I was afraid you were. One professor we had swore he was single. Then I saw him come down the reception line at the dean's tea with his wife on his arm. The bastard!"

Spur caressed her breasts until she began to

breathe faster, then he pulled down the slip and ran his hands up and down her long, slender legs. She gasped when his hand reached her crotch, but he passed above the treasure trove and went down her other leg.

"You first," she said and rolled off him. She undid his shoelaces, pulled off his shoes, then worked on his pants.

"Why are men's pants so hard to get off?" she moaned.

"So we won't get raped so often," he said.

She stuck her tongue out at him.

A moment later he was naked on his back and she knelt beside him.

"Oh, my!" She grasped his erection and pumped it once while watching him, then let him pull down her Pansiar silk underwear. Laura was a real blonde, with a glistening blonde muff. She lay on top of him and grinned.

"I think we're getting serious here, folks. Say, did I tell you the joke about the door to door salesman and the rich man's daughter?"

"No, I don't think so."

"Then the joke's on you, because I forgot it. You figured out that when I get nervous and a little unsure of myself I start talking a lot. Did you notice that? I bet you did. Are you—"

He pulled her face down and kissed her, then pushed her over on the couch so she lay beside him and moved his hand down to her crotch. She spread her legs and he found the soft, wet place and she groaned in anticipation.

A moment later he went between her white thighs and eased into her.

"Oh . . . oh . . . oh . . . delightful! Yes. So good and marvelous. I think I'll just stay this way for-

11

ever, you up there and me down here, and you inside me and all hot and wonderful."

"You're talking a lot again."

"Not nervous now." She laughed softly and shook her head. "Now I'm talking because I'm so thrilled and glorified and feel so perfect I almost can't stand it."

She began to move her hips and clutch at him with those talented interior muscles.

"What are you thinking about?" Laura asked suddenly.

"Thinking that this is the most wonderful way I know to take a boat ride. How long does it last?"

"I'm not sure. Sometimes I sleep. But this is so much better, just a thousand times better. Now poke me, back and forth. I like that best."

After a dozen strokes he realized that she hadn't climaxed yet. He slowed and then stopped and reached between them to find the tiny node that should do the job. When he touched it she looked at him.

"No, no, please don't. If it happens, it happens. If it doesn't, then we can try again."

"But it should always happen, even if it takes a little help. Won't take but a minute."

"No, Spur. Please. Go ahead, finish. I'm fine. Really."

A moment later it was too late for him to stop and he climaxed and grunted out the male ritual of spasming and resting and then coming away from her.

They lay there holding each other.

"Why?" he said.

She looked at him. "Why did you invite me into your stateroom?"

"So we could do this. I'll be home soon and

things will close in around me."

"You don't have to let your parents run your life."

Laura laughed softly. "You don't know my mother. She is the social leader of San Francisco. If she isn't on a committee, it isn't worth being on. She runs most of them. Puts her people on the rest of them. If Sarah Grandifar doesn't like your little charity function, you might as well forget trying to have it."

"That bad?"

"Worse. She's got at least a dozen parties all lined up for me. I just know it. She didn't want me to go back to school for the last year. Said I should get married and raise a family. I don't even know if I want to get married. Maybe I'll be the virgin queen like Victoria."

She scowled at him. "Don't say I'm not a virgin. I'm probably as much a virgin as Victoria was." She laughed. "I really have no business telling you my problems."

"I asked you to, remember?"

"Nice man. I knew you were a nice man. Sometime let me tell you about a man who is not so nice. But not today. You're going to San Francisco on business?"

"Yes. I work for the government in Washington D.C."

Laura looked up. "How fascinating. What kind of work do you do for my government?"

"I'm not supposed to say. I'm a kind of a trouble shooter."

"I saw you shoot trouble this morning. You shoot good."

"That wasn't what I meant."

"I know. I have some brandy in one of my bags.

Would you like a short snort before we make love again? I'm going to do my best to wear you out before we dock in San Francisco."

They found the brandy and since there were no glasses, they both had little nips from the bottle.

Suddenly, Laura laughed. "If dear mother could see me now, sitting here naked with a handsome naked man and nipping at brandy from the bottle, she would shit her drawers! I mean she really would."

They both laughed.

"Laura, I'm going to plan on seeing you after we get to San Francisco. I want to know more about you. Maybe even meet your family. Your father has retail stores?"

"Papa has everything, owns everything. One day he said he had a piece of everything in town except the United States Mint."

"Good. Right now I want your address, somewhere that I can send you a note or come by and see you."

Laura hesitated. "Why not? I can tell my mother that you're a high government official who saved me from a terrible fate when you stopped the train robbery." She giggled. "Yes, that's what I'll tell mama. She'll probably faint at the very idea."

· 2 ·

The San Francisco United States Mint was established in 1854 to provide coinage and currency control for the fledgling state of California which had joined the union in 1850. Now, in 1874, the Superintendent of the mint was Martin Jefferson, a 20 year employee of the government who had worked with the Treasury Department and for the minting operation his whole career.

For the past 12 years, Jefferson had been the head man here and had received an excellent rating during his infrequent evaluations.

Jefferson was a tall man, with broad shoulders that had stood him in good stead on the Harvard rowing crew. He was 46 years old, wore a full beard and moustache, and used spectacles to assist him in reading and checking on new coinage.

He covered his fine pot belly with an expensive suit and vest. Right now his mouth was set in a firm, hard line, and his forehead wrinkled in a frown as he watched the man across his desk.

"Yes, Philander, we have a small problem, but it isn't a crisis. I told you before, just relax and go about your ordinary business. It was an accident. The San Francisco police have told us that. The family believes that. Even Edmund Pickering believes it. Now just settle down and get ahold of yourself. Nothing has changed."

Jefferson spoke sternly with a touch of harshness to the number three man in the mint, Philander Knox, a man of 44 years who was small and thin, ascetic, clean shaven, had thinning gray hair and a touch of a squint when he looked at a person. His hands were not sure what they should do and at last he folded them in his lap where he sat. His nose was slightly red from too much sun one day recently and his ears were unusually large. He took a long, deep breath and pushed back into the chair.

"I know I should try to relax, but it just seems as if everything is going to come crashing down around our ears. Now I am more certain than ever that he sent the letter. If Redfield did say what we think he did, there will be trouble."

Jefferson slapped his hand down hard on the table. "No! You will not say such a thing again, and you will not even think it. I am in command here, and everything is running normally.

"If he wrote the letter and if he mailed it, and if it reaches Washington, it probably was opened by some new clerk and routed to his immediate superior and then on to his. By the time it gets through the chain of organization in the Bureau of the Mint, we could be retired.

"If worst comes to worst, remember that the Secretary of the Treasury is William A. Richardson, my second cousin. Best thing President Grant ever did was appoint Bill to Treasury."

Philander Knox squirmed in his chair. His boss always intimidated him, had for all 12 years. Not that it hadn't been a fine decade, and they all had done very well. But by nature Philander was a cautious soul, a man who looked both ways before he stepped on a sidewalk. He would walk a block out of his way to go around a person who might speak harshly to him, and he accepted authority with no protest whatsoever.

"Then you don't think—" Philander began.

"Look, I'll say this once more. It's been a month since we think he sent the letter. It's been almost a month since the funeral. If anything was going to happen it would have by now. I'd guess in six months we'll get a routine inquiry from one of the assistants to the director. Now forget it. Is everything ready for the Saturday night party?"

"Yes, of course."

"Good. Now get back to your office and relax. You might take off an hour and go see Molly Brown. A visit down there always seems to relax you, Philander."

For the first time the small man smiled. "Yes, yes, I just might do that. Molly said she was getting in some new ladies."

Philander stood, but Jefferson held up his hand. "There is one more thing we need to touch on. Patricia doesn't seem excited about her forthcoming marriage. Can you tell me why?"

Philander dropped back in the chair. "Who can understand the younger generation? They are willful, don't obey their parents, and in Patricia's case, she's on the dangerous edge of saying that she doesn't want to marry Alexander." He held up both hands.

"I know, I know. She agreed, and we agreed, and it has been arranged and talked about for three months. All the same, she says she doesn't love Alexander. Her mother explained to her that she will grow to love the man once they are living together and she can appreciate all of his fine qualities.

"Damn! I'll have a talk with her tonight. She hasn't absolutely refused to marry him. I just need to do some gentle persuasion."

"They haven't been together yet, have they?" Jefferson asked.

"Absolutely not! I wouldn't allow such a thing."

Jefferson smiled. "It might be worth thinking about, Philander. The first man to part a virgin's thighs often claims a special place in her heart. It could be something to think about."

Philander was ready to explode in rage, but he didn't. There was too much at stake. He knew it, and Jefferson knew it. The only one who didn't seem to appreciate the delicacy of the situation was Patricia herself.

"I'll have another talk with her." Philander stared hard at his superior. "Martin, you've got to assure me that you won't let Alexander touch her unless I give my approval."

Jefferson scratched a match on the leather sole of his shoe and fired up a long, brown cigar. "Of course, of course. I just want to make sure this last marriage gets done and we won't have any problem with strangers coming in to our families."

"I agree there. Well, I do have some work." He lifted his brows and walked over to the big oak door that led to the hall and down to the building's entrance.

As he stepped out, a man two-inches over six-feet came in the outer door, looked around and went over to the receptionist beside the armed guard who sat at a sturdy desk a short way from the door.

"Yes sir," the uniformed, armed guard said to the stranger before he could speak.

Philander watched the stranger a moment. He was about 30, must weigh close to 200 pounds, had sandy red hair, a full moustache and long straight sideburns. As Philander watched him, he saw his daughter Patricia come in and wave at him. She went up to the appointment secretary and began chatting softly.

The tall stranger heard the guard and walked up to him and nodded. "Good morning. I'm here to see Redfield Pickering."

The small, dark haired woman sitting near the guard burst into tears, stood and hurried down the hallway. The woman who had been talking to her looked over at the stranger and frowned. Patricia Knox was about five-three with lots of red hair that billowed on both sides of her head like a crown.

Spur looked at the guard.

"Did I say something wrong?"

"Sir, Mr. Pickering is deceased. He was killed in a buggy accident almost a month ago. The young lady was a special friend of Mr. Pickering."

Spur frowned. "I'm sorry I hurt her feelings. I had no idea the man was not alive. Well, then I must talk to someone else. Could I see Mr. Jefferson? He's still the superintendent here?"

"Yes, sir, he's here. Let me look at the appointment schedule."

He moved to the other desk and looked at a leather bound book the woman had been working on. "Sir, I'm afraid Mr. Jefferson's schedule is full. He's tied up with meetings and production schedules for the rest of the afternoon. Could I put you down for tomorrow morning about 11:00?"

"Yes, that'll be fine."

"Your name, sir."

"Spur McCoy."

"The guard wrote the name down. "And the nature of your visit?"

"I'd rather talk to him about that."

"Yes, sir. We'll see you tomorrow about 11:00 o'clock."

Spur nodded, turned and walked toward the door.

He stood on the street a moment later watching the first of the afternoon fog rolling in on the gentle on-shore breeze from the Pacific Ocean. It would soon be a dreary, foggy day. It would not be a sunny day in San Francisco.

He turned when he heard footsteps behind him. The redheaded girl who had been inside talking to the tearful one walked toward him with a purpose.

As she went past him she said the words softly. "Please follow me. We must talk about Redfield."

Spur looked the other way and waited until she

was half a block ahead, then he turned and followed the redhead. She was a beauty, young and the tight dress she wore gave her bottom an exciting little wiggle that he would follow for miles, even if she hadn't suggested it. What did she want to say about the dead man, Redfield Pickering? Was he dead because he wrote the letter to the Secretary of the Treasury? Or did he die in a buggy accident?

They walked down a block and turned the corner. She was waiting for him.

"Just walk along casually. A number of people know me." She looked up at him and a dark frown cut across her pretty face. "Why did you come here to talk to Redfield? He doesn't run the mint."

"He sent a letter to the Secretary of the Treasury. He said there were some irregularities here. My job is to find out what the problem is and fix it."

"Good Lord! We need to have a long talk. First the introductions. My name is Patricia Knox. My father works at the mint. He's third in command, I guess. Redfield Pickering was the son of the man who is the assistant superintendent, right under Martin Jefferson."

She looked at him and shook her head. "Gracious, I hope that I'll be able to help. I'll have to try to do what Redfield was trying to do. Have you had your supper yet? We could eat at a small place I know where no one knows me. It's down this way a few blocks."

"Supper sounds like a good idea. And I appreciate any help you might give me. I fully expected to talk to Redfield Pickering."

As they walked she put her hand on his arm and

matched his shortened stride. "Redfield worked at the mint, of course. Most all of us do. But he was smart and brighter than most of us seconds. We call ourselves seconds because we're the second generation to work at the mint. Actually I don't work there anymore, but I used to."

"I've been in love with Redfield since I was 12 but he wasn't interested in me. So we became friends. He told me there were some shocking things going on at the mint that I wouldn't believe."

She looked up at him. "Oh, dear, I'm afraid I'm not making any sense at all to you. But it will all mean something if you just bear me out. You see, I don't think Redfield Pickering died in an accident at all. I think somebody murdered him."

Spur stopped her and tightened his grip on her arm. "Are you positive, Miss Knox? Do you have any proof?"

Patricia shook her head. "Not a bit, but I know he wrote a letter, and I know my father was furious about that. He said it was an act of treason and that just could not be allowed. Then he looked at me and calmed down a little, but there was fury and anger and hatred in his eyes."

They came to a building that held only a small sign directly over a heavy wooden door. He held it open and they went in. Violins played softly in the background. The small room had places for no more than thirty diners with tables for two and four crowded close together. It was a German restaurant.

"Authentic German food," she said, nodding at a waiter who took them to a corner table. It was early, so few diners were there. She looked at the menu.

"The *wiener schnitzel* is excellent here and so is the roast pork with applesauce. I'm going to try the pork tonight."

He had the veal and they both ordered black German beer and a short time later she looked at him.

"What did the letter say?"

"I'm sorry, I can't tell you, but it said there were some problems and the entire mint should be inspected and given a complete audit. Someone is stealing from the mint, stealing the gold or the finished coins. That's easy to figure out. Only money would make my papa so angry. What are you going to do?"

"Find out what happened and fix it."

"Just like that?"

"I hope so. That's my job. What about you? Are you in any danger?"

She laughed softly. "Danger? I'm just an empty-headed girl, what do I know? My family thinks I'm harmless. Right now everyone is trying to persuade me to marry Alexander Jefferson, the son of the mint superintendent as you must have guessed. Alex is not slow-witted but he might as well be. He's dull and not at all handsome, and short and fat and bowlegged. I hate him and I'll never marry him."

"Is this an arranged marriage?"

"Yes, of course, and I'm the last one. There were six of us kids in the three families." She looked up. "I mean the three families of the men who were the top three at the mint. We're social and clannish. So we had three girls and three boys, and the parents thought it would be fun to marry us off to each other.

"One pair is married now. Redfield was supposed to marry Lucinda, but dear sweet Lucy had problems. She kept running away, and tearing off her clothes, and screaming at people. Her parents finally put her in a hospital, a private clinic, where she's cared for. So now that match is gone.

"Daddy says if I don't marry Alexander he'll disown me and my dear sister will inherit everything he owns. Which is considerable. But I don't care. When I marry, it will be for love and not to save the family fortune."

Their food came. The *wiener schnitzel*, a thinly breaded veal cutlet, was delightful. Her three thin cut strips of pork roast with mashed potatoes and gravy and a side dish of applesauce flavored with a dash of cinnamon was equally as good.

They ate in silence for a moment.

"So what are you going to do, Spur McCoy?"

"First I'll look into the death of Redfield. If he was killed to stop him talking to me, there will be a trail and I'll follow that trail to the killers and whoever hired them. That will give me an opening to discover what the irregularities are at the mint."

He thought for a moment. "What I'm telling you must be kept in the strictest of confidence, otherwise you'll be put in danger, and I don't want that to happen. There aren't enough pretty redheads in the world as it is."

She looked up and smiled, said a silent thank you and glowed in his praise.

He took out his purse and a wallet and extracted a thin printed card that had been carefully waxed to preserve it. On the card was his credentials as a member of the United States Secret Service. The card was signed by both the Secretary of the

Treasury, and by the President of the United States. U.S. Grant.

"Oh, my!" Patricia said drawing in an unexpected breath. "You know the President?"

"I've met him from time to time. He sometimes has a special job for me."

"My, how exciting."

"The trick is not to get killed, and right now that's what you should be concerned with. Your people know you were friends with Redfield. They may think he told you what he knew to be true about the mint."

"But he didn't."

"They may still suspect. You must act as light headed and casual as possible. Whatever you do, don't challenge any of the top three men at the mint about the business there."

"I won't. What can I tell you about the mint? I know that place inside and out. We used to play there as kids, then I worked there for two years."

"Not just yet, Patricia. First I want to concentrate on your friend Redfield. What section of the mint did he work in? What was his job there?"

"Let's see, for a while he was in distribution, but then he told me he got promoted into the cutting department. That's where the sheet of gold is put through a large blanking press that uses blanking-die punches and thimbles. Twenty-one blank gold eagles say, are stamped out. The rest of the sheet of gold, we call it a scissel or skeleton, is chopped into small pieces and sent back to the start where it is remelted and formed into a bar and then hot rolled into a sheet for die cutting again."

Spur finished his veal, took a pull on the German beer, and grinned. "You do know about the minting business. You're going to be a big help to me. You say Redfield wrote the letter after he got promoted to the stamping department? That might help. Now, I think it's time I see you home so you don't get in any trouble."

"No, it's early. Besides, I'll tell them I was shopping. As long as I don't flat out refuse to marry Alexander, they let me do about what I please. Within limits of course."

She smiled. "Did I tell you, Spur McCoy, that you've got the cutest little grin? You have. I love to watch it warm up and then spin out over your face. I guess we should be going, though. I'll give you my address and you can send a note there. Seal it, and I'll get it. We'll need to meet again, I'm sure."

He grinned and nodded. "Yes, Patricia, I'm sure. One of my jobs is to make sure you don't have to marry Alexander."

"Knew I was going to like you, McCoy."

He helped her into a hack on the street and she rolled away toward her home.

He knew a little about the mint. It had been part of their training. One thing he remembered was that the precious metals were weighed and checked and the weights proved before the goods were moved. He didn't see how the top management at the mint could be stealing coins or bullion. Everything was counted, weighed, signed off for, double checked and then audited every month.

Where was there a loophole that could let even

one ounce of the gold or silver escape? Still there must be a large one, if these people had killed one of their own family to hush it up. What kind of monsters was he dealing with here?

Spur returned to the hotel he had checked into when he arrived on the boat from Sacramento. It was a favorite hotel of Laura Grandifar, the sleek little blonde from the train and then the stateroom on the riverboat. She said that way she would be able to find him or drop a note in his key box.

When he picked up his key the clerk told him there were no messages. He was slightly relieved. He had work to do, and while Laura had been a delight, his job had to come first.

Upstairs he took his assignment letter and spread it out on the bed. He had picked it up at one of his regular check points on the railroad at Cheyenne. A telegram at Denver told him it was waiting for him at the post office general delivery window in Cheyenne.

There were three pages of closely written script, then a detailed printed account of the minting process, and a rundown on the five top people at the San Francisco mint. How long they had been employed, any problems, their promotion times, and a general evaluation on the top four men. He had read it all. Now he went back over the letter from the director of the Bureau of the Mint, as well as a copy of the letter from Redfield Pickering.

The Pickering letter had suggested, rather than spelled out, what he called, "shocking, unbelievable embezzlement of both raw gold and $20 gold coins." He said such thefts had been going on "for a number of years." He estimated that there could be a short fall of as much as "$40,000 a year for the past ten years."

"There is no way that an audit will shed any light on this problem. It is diabolically clever and sure. It has worked for so long it is nearly standard procedure. It cannot happen without the top three men in the mint knowing and participating in this scheme. That makes it particularly difficult for me, since one of those three is my father."

Spur threw down the papers and stared at them. He had seen the wages these three men made. The Superintendent drew a salary of $2,400 a year. His assistant superintendent $1,800 a year and the number three man $1,600.

The average working man in San Francisco was lucky if he made $400 a year. Spur's own salary was $80 a month, $960 a year. More than twice what the working man on the streets made.

How could someone steal that much from a United States Mint that had armed guards on every door, that had inspections of workers' lunch buckets and their clothing, that had delicate weighing in of all coins, scrap, scissel, and tally sheets kept that had to match?

It was impossible. Yet young Redfield Pickering said it was happening. Twenty pounds of gold a week would make up about $33,000 a year. Would that be easier than stealing the coins that were counted and weighed? He had no idea.

It would be 2,000 of the double eagles to equal $40.000. That would be almost 170 a month that had to be stolen. It just didn't seem possible.

In the morning he would begin to dig into the mystery by learning more from the police reports on the death of Redfield Pickering.

· 3 ·

Spur Mccoy sat across from a man in a trim black business suit in the San Francisco Police headquarters. He had to talk to three people before he at last got to the right man. Spur had just showed the man his identification and the policeman had been impressed.

"Never seen anyone quite that high in law enforcement. I'm pleased to help you however I can. Yes, we checked out that accident," the policeman said. His name was Gale Daniel and he was an inspector for the force.

"Seemed a little unusual at the time, but the more we looked at the situation, the clearer it became. The horse spooked, began running down that tremendous hill and stumbled, the rig came directly over the horse and then both horse and buggy rolled. Have you looked at the hill? We want to ban any buggy or wagon traffic on it because it's too dangerous.

"The buggy broke free of the horse and careened another two hundred feet down the hill, rolling, tumbling. The young man fell out along the way and was crushed by either the horse or the buggy itself. He was mashed up too much to live.

"One witness saw the end of the thing. Ran over to help the kid but he was dead by that time. We inspected the scene and filed our report. You can read it but it says about what I've told you."

"I'd like to read it." Spur went through the three page report slowly, found nothing that hadn't been said and handed it back.

"Thanks for your help, Inspector Daniel. I just don't see how the young man could have died that way. But that's my problem. Would you mind if I talk to the witness?"

The policeman shrugged. "Not with the identification you carry, Mr. McCoy. You can talk to the mayor if you want to. I'll get the witness's name and address for you."

But the witness had no permanent address. He had told the officer he sometimes stayed at a rooming house down on Third Street where it stretched near the bay to the south. It took Spur over an hour to find the place. The landlady smiled when he asked about Stoop Lackwalter.

"He stays here when he has any money, which ain't usual, but lately he's had money. Don't know where it comes from. Says he gets an envelope every week." The woman was tall and rangy, with limp brown hair and pouches under her eyes. She was in her fifties, he guessed.

"He leaves most of his money with me so he don't splurge it on whiskey and wild women." She cackled a high piercing laugh. "One good young woman would stop his heart for good. He owe you money or something?"

"No, ma'am. It's about the accident he saw when that poor young man was killed."

"Oh, yes. He still talks about it. Reckon you could find him at the Blue Pelican, a drinking place three or four blocks down that way on Third."

Spur thanked the woman and continued his quest. The Blue Pelican was a sailors' hangout, rough and ready. He ordered a beer from the barkeep and asked about Stoop. The apron motioned to the end of the bar where a man stood hunched over the mahogany.

As the Secret Service agent moved that way, he saw that Stoop was stoop shouldered, his head, neck and shoulders thrust forward and a permanent hump on his back. Spur leaned against the bar near him.

"Mr. Lackwalter?"

Bleary eyes looked up at him. He blinked. The man was half blind drunk and it was just after ten o'clock.

"Mr. Lackwalter, I need to talk to you."

"Yes sir, yes sir, three bags full." He howled in laughter and then blinked again and looked up. "Thought you said you wouldn't come see me again."

So someone had contacted him. That was probably where the weekly envelope of money came from to keep him drunk for a year. It could be productive. "Yes, Stoop, I know, but we need to talk again. Let's go for a walk."

"Don't like to walk." He reached for his beer.

Spur pushed it away from him, caught his finger and forced Stoop's whole hand back toward his wrist, the way it doesn't bend.

"Oh, damn!" Stoop muttered as the pain increased. "Yeah, yeah, I'll come for a walk."

They went outside. The sun had burned off most of the morning fog and clouds. Two blocks down from the saloon they found a bench and sat looking out over the bay. Only a few short docks fringed the shoreline this far south.

"We think the police might talk to you again. Tell me what you saw."

Stoop grinned, still mostly drunk. "Hell, you know I didn't see nothing. I was passed out at the time. Told them just what you said I should tell them."

"That's right, Stoop. We appreciate it. Do you remember my name?"

"Sure, yep, course. Your name is Jefferson. Never forget that."

Spur's mouth tightened. Jefferson, the same name as the man who ran the mint on Market Street.

"You know how much you get in that envelope each week, don't you?"

"Damn right." Stoop blinked again, raised his brows. "Fifteen honest dollars. Pays my board and room and I get to lift a beer or two." He stared at Spur. "You look different today, Jefferson."

"No, the same. You're drunker this time, Stoop. Can you find your way back to the Blue Pelican?"

"Damn right! You think I'm drunk or something?" He snorted, stood and weaved his way south along the street toward the saloon.

So, the conspiracy and the thefts and the murder

went right to the top, Jefferson himself. After all, Jefferson couldn't ask Edmund Pickering to murder his own son. Pickering probably still thought it was an accident. He might be able to turn Pickering, if he could prove they murdered his son. Yes. But not yet.

He checked the gold watch in his vest pocket. If he could find a cab he would be able to make his 11:00 o'clock appointment with Superintendent Jefferson. He was glad he didn't talk to him yesterday. Now he would take a much different approach than he might have then.

He'd try the old friend approach and be searching for work. He wasn't ready to let Jefferson know his real reason.

A hack came and he got a ride up to Market Street and the mint in all its imposing, solid stature.

This time when he went in the door the guard looked up and nodded. "Yes, Mr. McCoy. Helen will take you down to see the Superintendent."

Helen, the dark eyed small woman who had burst into tears yesterday, looked up, tried to conceal a frown, and stood motioning for him to follow her. Three doors down, the girl opened a door and he stepped into a large office. A tall man lifted up from behind a desk and came forward. He held out his hand.

"Yes, good morning. I'm Martin Jefferson, what can I do for you this morning?"

"Mr. Jefferson, my name is Spur McCoy and I'm from Washington D.C. I just got into town and I love San Francisco already. My uncle told me I should contact you when I got here. You see, I'm looking for some kind of employment, a position of some sort."

"Well, that's commendable of you. Why don't I send you down to the man who handles our employment office? I'm not sure what kind of openings we have right now."

"He said to tell you his name, he's William A. Richardson and he's President Grant's Secretary of the Treasury. I guess the mint is a part of his department from what Uncle Richard said."

There was a visible change in Jefferson when he heard the secretary's name. He brightened considerably. "Yes, of course, we're technically in his group. We're the Bureau of the Mint with our own director. Well, you'll have to say hello to your uncle for me.

"Let me look over our management team and see where we might be able to place you. This is our busy time and it'll take a week or so. In the meantime, you can have a short vacation. Where are you staying?"

"I'm at the Almont. It was highly recommended."

"Yes, it's a good hotel. Well, do you have a summary of your qualifications?"

"Afraid I haven't done that yet. I graduated from Harvard and worked for a couple of years in my father's stores in New York City. Then I worked for two years in Washington as an aide to Senator Arthur B. Walton, the senior senator from New York who is an old family friend."

"Well, McCoy, that is impressive. I've made some notes." He stood. "I'll be contacting you at your hotel within the week. Good to have met you, McCoy."

A few moments later he was standing on Market Street in front of the mint looking for a cab.

* * *

Stoop Lackwalter made it back to the Blue Pelican about two drinks down. He got to a table and held up two fingers.

The barkeep brought him one draft beer. "One at a time, Stoop," the apron said. "The other one will go stale on you. Just whistle when you're ready."

Two hours later, Stoop Lackwalter was trying to play a game of solitaire. The simple game was well beyond his alcohol fuddled mind. He looked up with a slow registering surprise as the barkeep came to his table.

"Stoop, some guy wants to see you outside. He sent in a note with a dollar bill pinned to it. I'm supposed to help you to the door, if you can't make it by yourself."

"Yeah, yeah. Who are all these damn visitors? I'm getting too damn popular. Liked it better when I was just a drunk cadging drinks." He stood, weaved and fell against the barkeep.

"This way, sport, he wants to see you near the outhouse since you'll be needing to use it anyway."

Stoop staggered through the back door toward the outhouse but he never got there.

A large man with a scar on his cheek and one eye drooping stepped up beside Stoop and took his hand.

"Down this way, Lackwalter," the big man said. "I got a man who wants to see you."

"Who the hell are you?"

"Friend of yours. Friend of your friend who gives you money each week so you can afford to get drunk."

Stoop's wary drunken look vanished and he smiled. "Oh, yeah, my friend with the money. Know him, yeah, know him."

At the end of the alley, the big man helped Stoop into a buggy that had side curtains. They turned back on Third Street and drove south into the less populated section, then toward the bay. Soon the buggy was surrounded by high marsh grasses, reeds and some brush that hid the rig. There wasn't another person around for half a mile.

"End of the line, Stoop," the scar faced man said.

"Huh? thought we was going to see my friend."

"You remember what your friend's name is?"

"Damn betcha! Never forget him. Mr. somebody Jefferson. Got bucks, that man. Know him good."

"Not anymore, you don't. Mr. Jefferson wants you to forget him."

"Huh? Why for?"

"Come out here aways and I'll show you."

"Out there? Is it wet?"

Stoop was sobering up quickly. Partly it was the fresh air and the tangy ocean breeze. Mostly it was raw, nagging fear.

"Nope, think I'll stay right here. Want to go back to the Blue Pelican."

"Not possible."

The big man grabbed Stoop by the shirt front and dragged him out of the buggy. He threw him to the ground and kicked him hard in the side. Stoop doubled up into a ball and when he wasn't kicked again, he sat up.

The scar faced man squatted in front of Stoop and his hand made a swift motion in front of the drunk's face. Suddenly blood spurted from both sides of his throat as the knife sliced deeply from one carotid artery to the other. Blood shot out ten feet from the first artery cut.

The killer jumped back and to the side as

Stoop's eyes went wide. He tried to scream but only a bloody, bubbly froth came out. He looked at the big man for a moment, then he sagged forward where he sat on the marshy ground before he fell over backwards. His arms flayed wide, his eyes trying to figure out what went wrong with his perfect lifelong retirement plan with Mr. Jefferson.

Blood poured in a red river from his throat. Within 20 seconds the supply to his brain was cut off and he died by stages. Within a minute, his heart raced and then slowed to a stop as it ran out of blood to pump. Slowly the brain centers closed down and his lungs expelled the last breath in a gush through his nose already covered with a bloody froth.

"Yeah, drunken sot. We won't have to worry none about you talking to the wrong person no more."

The man turned around and headed back for the buggy when a rifle cracked 100 yards away. The man with the scar looked up in disbelief as he jolted backward a few steps. The rifle bullet smashed into his right shoulder.

"Noooooooooooooo" he wailed.

The second high powered rifle bullet hit him squarely in the heart and he died before he fell backwards to the ground.

A pair of low flying water birds dipped away from the foreign sound in their marsh. Twenty feet away from the two bodies, a duck turned its tail skyward and pushed its bill down to the shallow bottom and fed on the green plants.

A hundred yards away there was a creak of leather and the jolt of a buggy wheel as a horse moved a black buggy slowly away from the scene of the double murder heading back toward the more populated sections of San Francisco.

Spur finished re-reading the letter from the dead Mr. Redfield Pickering and put on his jacket. He was getting ready to find an interesting meal. He knew you could get the best foods of a dozen different nations in San Francisco.

A knock sounded on his door. At first he reached for his six-gun, but it was in the gunbelt hung on his bedpost. He had decided not to use the gun while in the big city, but rather to rely on the two shot hideout derringer he carried in a small holster on his belt.

He went to the door, stood at the side against the wall.

"Who is it?" he asked.

"Murphy, San Francisco Police. I have a message for you."

Spur opened the door and saw the clean cut young man with an envelope in his hand.

"Sir, Mr. Spur McCoy?"

"That's right."

He handed the envelope to Spur. "I'm to give you this and then if you wish to come, escort you back to the headquarters. Inspector Daniel has something to show you."

Spur read the note inside. It said: "Come see me for a real surprise in your investigation on Redfield Pickering."

"Yes, let's go."

Twenty minutes later, Spur sat in the inspector's office. In San Francisco, inspector was the second lowest rank in the order of the police.

Daniel stared at him a moment. "Come downstairs, I need to show you something."

They went down to the basement and into a room that could only be a morgue. It was cold. An attendant in a white coat pulled out a drawer that held a body.

Spur looked at the man. "Stoop Lackwalter, a supposed witness to a fatal accident that was really a murder."

Daniel pushed the drawer closed. "First I'm interested in this murder. You go to see him this morning, and this afternoon my men find him with his throat slit ear to ear. Concidence?"

"Not at all. I don't believe in coincidence. I talked to Stoop about ten o'clock this morning. He was half drunk already. His landlady told me he was getting an envelope every week with money in it. Interesting? I told him I was the man who sent him the envelope and he called me Mr. Jefferson.

"Your witness to the accident was bought and paid for. He was a drunk who said that the man paying him $15 a week carefully rehearsed him."

"Then you visit him and he turns up dead?" Daniel asked.

"Exactly. Isn't that curious? Somebody told somebody that a stranger had talked to Stoop, taken him for a walk along Third Street. Somebody decided that Stoop was a risk that couldn't be tolerated. So they killed him."

"Who?"

"The man who paid him to lie to you. My candidate is Martin Jefferson, the superintendent of the U.S. Mint on Market Street."

"And the man killed in the buggy crash worked there and his father works there," Inspector Daniel said, remembering the case. "Yes, I'm starting to see a connection."

"The only thing is, we don't have any proof."

The inspector pulled out another drawer and pointed to a man with a scar on his face.

"Ever seen this one?"

Spur stared at the cold features, the slash that left one eye disfigured. He shook his head. "No. He's the kind of gent who I would be sure to remember."

"We found him near Stoop. Shot twice with a rifle from some distance, probably about 100 yards. We found buggy and horse tracks there. This one still had the bloody knife in his hand that probably killed Stoop."

Spur took a long breath and let it out. "My guess?"

"Say it."

"The scar faced man killed young Pickering and caused the buggy wreck with the dead body inside. They bribe a nearby drunk to tell the cops what they want him to say. Then when their *eye witness* had a visit from some unknown, the powers panicked and told Scarface to silence Stoop. At the same time, the killers behind the whole thing tidied up their personnel and eliminated another witness who could talk, Scarface here."

"Jefferson?"

"I wouldn't even whisper that to my grandmother until we have some proof. I applied for a job with him this morning. I might go to work there next week. I told him my uncle was his big boss in Washington D.C."

"Is he?"

"I've never even met the man."

"Sneaky."

They went back to the Inspector's office and sat staring at each other.

"You had supper?" Spur asked.

A half hour later they settled into chairs at a seafood restaurant on the wharf and enjoyed shrimp cocktails of tiny shrimp swimming in a spicy sauce that had more than a nodding acquaintance with pure horseradish.

Inspector Daniel watched Spur thoughtfully for a moment. "You didn't come all the way out here to check up on the accidental death of a government employee."

Spur dug into a giant lobster claw and dipped the red and white meat into melted butter.

"Then why did I come?"

"The mint. There must be something crooked going on up there at the mint. The death is a wedge to get into the main problem."

"I see why you're an inspector already. Next sergeant, and then quickly a lieutenant."

"So, am I right?"

"Close enough. You work on the murders, I'll see what else I can dig up so you make sergeant quicker."

After the lobster dinner they parted and Spur went back to the Hotel Almont. There was a note in his box with the key. It was in a sealed envelope.

Upstairs in his room, he read the note.

"Dear Spur McCoy. If I don't get a return note from you by six o'clock tonight, I'm going to be knocking on your hotel room door. We have to talk. Mother is already impossible. She had a party the night I got home and had one ready for tonight, but I told her I felt miserable and had to go see a doctor. Now write me a note and deliver it. I need your help!"

It was signed Laura, and the address was the same that Laura Grandifer had given him on the riverboat.

Poor little rich girl, he thought.

Just then a knock sounded on his door.

It was tough work, but somebody had to help this beautiful girl to stay single.

When he opened the door, he found red-headed Patricia Knox standing there looking ill at ease and nearly ready to run.

"I've got to talk to you. I heard papa talking with someone and . . . and I'm not sure that I believe what I heard." She looked at him and then walked slowly into the room, glancing around curiously, but there was unbridled anger and raw terror in her eyes.

· 4 ·

Slowly, unavoidably, Patricia Knox began to cry. She wept silently for a minute, then Spur closed the hotel room door and put his arms around her. She leaned against him sobbing now. He held her tightly and let her cry it out as they stood in the middle of Spur's hotel room.

Three or four minutes later she wiped her eyes and looked up at him. "I couldn't believe them. I just couldn't. For the past eight or ten years we've had plenty of money. I've been in a private school and we contribute to charities and mother and father go to the fancy balls and the San Francisco upper crust social things.

"Daddy and mother were arguing in their bedroom. I usually hurry past, but this time I stopped.

I listened. I eavesdropped on my own parents. That's just terrible. I'm so ashamed.''

She wailed again and he held her tightly, her head tight on his chest and her red hair tickling his nose.

Patricia stopped after a few minutes and looked up. "I bet you think I'm just terrible, coming to your hotel room this way and breaking down. There is no one else I can turn to. Nobody!''

She moved away from him a little. "I didn't hear it all, but papa said that he just couldn't 'walk away from it.' He said it had gone too far to stop now. He said it wasn't just the money, there was more to it now."

She looked up at him. "Do you think my father and the other two men who run the mint are . . . are stealing from it?''

"Is that what you think from what he said?''

"Yes. We lived quite simply for a long time, then one day papa came home and said that an uncle had died in Michigan and left us a goodly sum of money. It was set up so we'd get $5,000 a year for 10 years. That was almost five times what papa was making at the time, and mama was overjoyed.

"That was when we started doing things, and contributing to charities, and mama was asked to join some clubs she didn't think she could ever get in.''

"The money made the difference?'' he asked.

"Oh, yes. If you don't contribute, you don't get in.''

"There wasn't any rich uncle back East?'' Spur asked.

"I'd never heard of one until then. But tonight, papa said that there was no chance that he could invent another rich uncle. So there couldn't have been a rich relative in the first place. Makes you wonder where all of that money came from."

"Patricia, it looks more and more like he and Pickering and Jefferson devised some scheme to steal from the mint. I'm sorry."

Her eyes went wide. "Then . . . then . . . if that's true . . . then they must have . . . Oh, poor Redfield! He must have found out. Do you suppose they killed him? I remember him saying that he would never drive down Hill Street. That's the one that's so steep and where he had the crash."

She began to cry again and reached for him. He held her as she cried, a heartsick, impossible to comfort kind of crying. They stood in the middle of the room as he held her tightly again to try to heal the heartbreak inside of her, but he knew it wouldn't work.

At last she stopped crying and looked up. Her pretty face was red and swollen, her eyes still oozing tears. "I swear to you, Spur McCoy, that if they are stealing, I will help you find out how. Redfield must have discovered it and that's why. . . . I'll help you find out. I know the minting process. I can figure out where the easiest and most unlikely to be discovered spots along the coin making chain are.

"It would have to be the bullion. The coins themselves are closely counted, controlled, weighed and checked by at least six different people. The mint couldn't pass an audit if they were stealing the coins. They are tallied every batch, every day. I'll go home and think about it. Somehow I've got to help my father stop this.

"I . . . I won't even think about Redfield. I loved him so much. Now he's gone and if it's even partly because of my parents, I'll move out and never speak with either of them again."

A knock sounded on the door.

"Oh. Do you expect company?"

"There was a possibility." Spur moved toward the door.

The knock came again and Spur shook his head and opened it.

Laura Grandifar came steaming into the room, a frown on her pretty face, her blonde hair flying around her shoulders and halfway down her back.

"I'm so mad I could just scream at somebody!" she stormed as she marched into the room. Laura stopped when she saw Patricia standing there, tears still staining her cheeks, her eyes red and puffy.

"Oh, I didn't know you had company." She frowned and looked again. "Patty? Patty Knox? I haven't seen you for a year. Oh, darling, has this big ox been hurting you?"

"Laura, no, no, it's just some problem I'm having at home. I needed a shoulder to cry on."

"Darling, I'm sorry. I'll turn around and leave. My small crisis wasn't that urgent."

"No, Laura, I was just about ready to leave. We talked it out. I think I know now what I have to do." She reached out and touched Spur's shoulder. "Thank you. I'll let you know what I decide."

She moved toward the door.

"Patricia, I applied for a job with Mr. Jefferson today. He said he'd tell me next week. I don't know if I'll get one, but it might help."

"Yes, I'll keep in touch." She went out the door, waved, and Spur closed the heavy panel gently.

Laura took off the small hat she wore and dropped it on the bed. "Now that was a strange little scene, a girl crying in your hotel room."

"Just a friend with a problem. Somebody she loved died and she's all broken up about it."

"Yes, that would be Redfield. She used to tell me about him, but he wasn't interested in her except as a friend. I made a try for Redfield myself, but he was too busy working. He was an interesting young animal."

Spur sat on the chair and waved her to the bed. "You said you have some problems with your mother?"

"Oh, just the usual. A dozen times a day she talks to me about how important it is to get married."

"You could go to Europe with your aunt."

"I only have one and she has a broken hip. Besides, she never will travel." Laura grinned and watched him. "It may have been just a silly girl's trumped up anger so she could come rushing up here like a floozy to see you."

"Now that makes sense. It's only been a little more than a day."

"That long?"

She went to him, knelt down on the floor and hugged him around his legs. "I'm shameless." She looked up with an impish smile. "Would you have taken little Patty to bed if I hadn't come?"

"No. She's having a serious crisis in her life right now, something drastic and terrible involving Redfield's death. Besides, I doubt if she's ever made love."

"She hasn't, I'd bet. She hadn't last time I saw her before I left for school nine months ago. We talked about that because she had no one else to talk to. I doubt if Redfield ever got Patty's knees pried apart. He wasn't the type to seduce a girl before he was married. I should know, I had one wild fling with him once and he wouldn't do any more than kiss me."

"You really tried and he wouldn't bed you?"

"Damn right I tried. I wanted him. I was half undressed and had his pants open and then he told me he couldn't do this to me. If I'd told him I'd been poked a dozen times, he would have run away fast. All I could do was promise it was what I wanted, the first time with him. If I'd made it, he would have married me. He would have considered it the only honorable thing he could do. Poor Redfield. His honor cost him a really wild night."

Laura unbuttoned her blouse and watched Spur.

"Sweet Spur, we don't have all night this time. I have to be home by 11:00. Should we try to set a new record?"

Spur laughed and dropped down beside her, kissing her ripe breasts through her thin silk chemise.

"No records, tonight. You may even get home early. First some questions. Is the Knox family firmly established in the social structure of San Francisco?"

"Yes, and their good friends the Pickerings, and the Jeffersons as well. They all run the mint, as I remember. How quaint."

"They all give to charities, go to fancy balls and dances and contribute to causes?"

"Yes. Two of them come from old money families from the East, and one of them had an uncle who set them up for life. Happens all the time. The elite don't care where your money comes from, as long as there's plenty of it. I've known sweet little Patty, Patricia she likes to be called now, for, oh, 10 years. We've sort of grown up together, went to the same private school."

She slipped out of her blouse and lifted the chemise over her head. Her full breasts bounced and he bent and kissed them.

"Maybe tonight's the night," she said in a whisper, then pulled him back on the bed on top of her.

It was three hours later when Spur insisted that she get dressed and head for home. "I don't want you to get locked in your room by an angry father. And I hope your papa doesn't have a shotgun. I've heard they are dangerous weapons in an angry father's hands when it comes to a marriageable daughter."

"No worry there. The fact is it's mama who has the shotgun."

She kissed him once more, adjusted her hat and checked the hall. There was no one in sight. She slipped out the door, said she would get a hack below, and hurried away. Spur watched and saw that the excited little wiggle of her cute little bottom still showed through her dress.

For an hour, Spur worked over the diagrams and printed explanation of how raw gold, silver and copper were turned into coins. He went over the process again and again, and at last came to the conclusion that the only place where there was the slightest chance to steal any of the gold was just after the coin blanks had been stamped out by the blanking die punches.

It was this leftover metal that seemed to offer the best opportunity for thievery. Somehow they must siphon off some of that salvage gold. What did Patricia call it, scissel. That must be the area. He nodded, remembering that Patricia said that Redfield Pickering had been working in that department when he died.

Spur slipped into bed working up a plan to confuse and fool Jefferson so he would not suspect Spur's real reason for being at the mint. Working there might be a good idea. He had to get a job there. Surely Jefferson would not dare to turn him away after the Washington connections Spur claimed to have.

He went to sleep remembering the two beautiful women who had been in his room that night, and how different they were. Which one would he prefer? In his bed or in his life? No contest, for a life partner. For that role Patricia was by far the better, more gentle, more concerned, with much more moral fiber and character than Laura.

But for a bed mate, Spur McCoy didn't see how he could beat Laura. She was a great performer between the sheets. The girl had no shame, anything was fine with her. Spur McCoy grinned. Maybe he had the best of both worlds. He was smiling when he fell asleep.

The regular Friday meeting of the Management Council of the United States Mint, San Francisco, met in the conference room at nine A.M. with Martin Jefferson, Philander Knox and Edmund Pickering all on hand. They sat around the walnut table and shuffled papers for a moment.

Jefferson looked up and smiled at Pickering. "Edmund, it's good to have you back on the team here. We've missed you these past three weeks, but we know that you needed the time off for your personal life and to come to grips with your tragedy. We offer again our complete sympathy and condolences.

"But now it's time to strike forward. Life goes

on, and we must weather these storms and strive ahead.''

Edmund Pickering held up his hand. "Enough, Martin, let's just get on with the matters at hand. I want to plunge back into this work until I'm so tired I fall asleep at my desk. Now what's the first item on the agenda?''

Edmund Pickering was 5-10, sturdy but not overbulked. He had brown hair and a full moustache but no beard. His clear green eyes still carried a hint of sadness. He wore a dark suit and said he would for three months out of respect for his son. Now his fingers drummed the table waiting for the superintendent to move the meeting along.

They worked through some mechanical problems with some of the equipment, decided how the problem should be handled and delegated it. Then there was a vacancy in the receiving room and it was filled by a friend of Philander Knox.

When the regular business was finished, Philander cleared his throat. He looked at the other two, then went ahead. "Concerning the matter of our regular Subtractions, it seems to me that now we should stop all together for a short cooling off period. To put it bluntly, we've been damned lucky up to now. Why continue and perhaps invite some official inquiry?

"Edmund, you didn't know about what we think is a critical letter that may have been sent to Washington by one of our unhappy employees. Evidently someone who was discharged for cause some weeks ago.''

"It's our understanding that a critical letter was written that could bring an official inquiry, perhaps a Bureau audit. You know that we could not pass such a far reaching examination."

"Why wasn't I told of this?" Pickering barked.

"It was about the time of the accident, and we felt you had enough to worry about at the moment."

"I understand." Pickering rubbed his jaw. "Have you seen this letter? How damaging is it? Does it suggest any wrongdoing, any missing bullion or raw gold?"

"Not that we know of," Jefferson said. "But there's a chance we'll get some reaction. I expect we'll receive a routine letter or report in two or three months, but we can't tell."

Pickering took out a $200 pocket watch and snapped it open to check the time. He opened and closed it three times as the others waited.

"Perhaps Philander has the right idea." He looked at them. "We've all done extremely well these past 10 years. This could be a good time to simply retire from our extra activities. None of us really has a need for money. Only the five of us have been involved. That could change. Sturgill in Receiving is past his most productive years. He should be retired. That would involve a new man on the team."

He closed the watch and put it in his vest pocket held there by a long, thick gold chain.

"Yes, I concur with Philander. We should strongly consider quitting entirely, or at least cutting back our Subtraction program drastically. Jefferson?"

"No, I couldn't disagree more," Jefferson replied. "We are in no danger. We have covered ourselves. We have two loyal men helping us who are equally as involved and as liable as we are. We should continue."

He glared at the other two men. "We're in this *together.* We made a pledge years ago to that effect. There is no chance to resign from our small club. No way to quit."

He watched his partners in the scheme but saw them look away without challenging him. He softened his tone. "Of course if we see some official action, we will suspend at once all Subtraction activity. If we eventually face a Bureau audit, my plans are all made in Mexico City." He hurried on. "But that won't happen, can't happen. We've been too careful."

"So you don't think this critical letter will damage us?" Pickering asked.

"Damage us some, but not a lot. There's a chance it will be lost in the bureaucratic procedures in Washington. You know how the main office is back there."

Pickering nodded slowly. "All right, let's play it close to the vest and see what happens. I don't like this news about a letter. Until we know what's in that letter, I'm going to be gun-shy."

"That's it, then," Jefferson said. They stood and went back to their own offices. Jefferson stared out his window at San Francisco. They had done well these past 10 years. He had more money, more power, more influence in the community than he ever thought possible.

But were they near to the point where the whole scheme would explode in their faces like a stick of dynamite? Would it be better to quietly move his family to Mexico City and then just not show up for work one Monday morning? He had thought about it. He already had money on deposit in the Bank of Mexico. He had bought a small house on the outskirts of the city in a pleasant little grove. Once Alex married Patricia she would be off his hands officially.

There was another way, but that would get messy. He wouldn't even think of there being more "accidents" unless one of the other two men showed signs of breaking down. He walked to the gun case on the wall and took down his three hunting rifles. With the care of a man who loves fine guns, he cleaned each one, taking special pains with the barrels and the firing mechanisms. Then he put them back in the rack.

At his desk he unlocked a secret panel in back of the middle drawer and took out a small single edge ledger. He loved to keep records and this book went back 10 years. The first time they tried the Subtraction plan it worked to perfection. That first time they siphoned off two-percent of the scissel, before it was weighed, when it was returned to the receiving department where it would be melted into bars for reuse in the process.

They had been making few gold double eagles then, but there was a continuing supply of the cut up scissel that had been valuable. The first gold they stole that day had been picked up at the receiving station by the superintendent himself. That week they had drawn off a little over eight pounds of gold. It had been melted and sold to a gold buyer who asked no questions and paid the going rate of $20.77 an ounce . . . less the 10% commission for the buyer.

The total was $2,728.44, less the $272.84, to give them a grand total of $2,455.60 left. They had long talks with the two men working the key positions who had to know about the shortage and how it was equalized. They reached an arrangement for both men to receive bonuses each time there was a Subtraction.

Jefferson remembered that night at home. The three couples had gone out and left the kids all at home with friends, and celebrated. Each of the men had $800 in his pocket. It was a bounty they had never expected.

Their wives had to be told and won over. They convinced them that night at the party with a marvelous dinner in the best restaurant in town, some dancing and then when each got home, with furious sexual encounters until they were exhausted, gloriously tired and sexfully delighted. Their wives agreed to go along with the plan.

He had put down in his book each time they made a Subtraction and how much it was and who was paid how much. He had kept a running total, and it was surprising.

He remembered about five years ago the Bureau pulled a surprise inspection and audit right in the middle of a Subtraction operation.

Nance Sturgill had saved them all from going to prison. When the inspector's man came to the receiving department and began checking figures on the returned scissel, Sturgill knew there would be a shortage. He adjusted the scales so it would read two percent heavy and then called the inspector to check it.

It took the inspector twenty minutes to figure out the gold weight and the apparent shortage, matched exactly the discrepancy from the mis-calibrated scale. Sturgill was given a reprimand by the inspector and a note put in his personnel file but no criminal complaint was filed. Later

Jefferson tore up the reprimand in Sturgill's file. That had been the only close call.

Jefferson pushed the book back in the secret compartment and closed the drawer. Maybe the other two were right. Maybe they should slow down or stop the Subtraction for six months. He'd think about it.

Accidents? It would take four more to close all the mouths that could talk. For a moment a cold sweat broke out on his forehead. God, it would have to be four more besides the four men, their wives. He was sure the two workers' wives knew where the extra money was coming from.

Jefferson frowned, rubbed his beard and shook his head. No, not all eight, only those who might talk, the weak ones would be targeted if it ever came to that. Something to think about. Right at that moment, Mexico City seemed like a wonderful spot, but he knew he would change his mind. The feel of that free gold was a sickness that no man could remain immune to.

· 5 ·

Friday an hour after noon, Spur McCoy and Patricia Knox walked along a small park near the waterfront and watched the big ships weighing their anchors and slipping out into the bay with the early tide. He had sent a message to her house earlier that morning and she came for the talk.

"I've been thinking a lot about what I know, and I hate all of it," she said, her green eyes flashing, her red hair constantly in motion as she turned to watch him. "I hate what my father has done. For the past 10 years our whole family has been living a lie, living on stolen money. I hate it!"

She turned after walking another dozen steps and caught his arm and pulled it tightly to her.

"Now I want to do something about it. I know

it will mean disgrace, and father in jail, and mother so mortified she probably will want to move to Chicago or Boise or maybe even Seattle. I understand all that. But I want to help you however I can."

"Good. What we need is evidence, strong, sure, unshakable evidence. An auditor will be able to prove long term losses of the gold taken in and the coinage produced. But that doesn't show who stole the gold.

"I'd like to catch them in the act, but that will be as hard as breaking into the mint and stealing it myself. I know the security and the guards and lockdowns the mint has. I've been in the one in Philadelphia. I'm open to all the help you can give me."

"First, I've worked through the minting procedures, and I see two places where the gold could be embezzled and the theft covered up. Actually, both would have to be used to make it work.

"We talked about the scissel. That's the key. The gold coin blanks are punched out and the scissel is cut up into pieces and taken back to the receiving room where incoming gold and other metals are weighed and recorded.

"After years of doing this, the scissel from say the double eagle punching for 1,000 coins is almost nearly the same each and every time. Say the scissel from 1,000 gold double eagle blanks should weigh 20 pounds. If it showed on the records that a batch came back weighing only 18 pounds, the auditors would be all over that.

"However, if gradually the amount of scissel coming from those 1,000 coins was established at 18 pounds, when it really was 20 pounds, there would be no apparent shortage."

Spur put both arms around her and hugged her. She looked up surprised but pleased.

"Yes! I've been trying to figure out how they could guarantee that there wouldn't be a shortage when there actually was one. That only means that they have to work every time there is a stamping of double gold eagles."

"Not necessarily. They might be stealing from the other four gold coins we produce as well. They all result in salvage. It just depends which one they pick, or maybe all of them. I'd guess that the thefts are not done too often. It might be done over a period of days, then maybe not for a month. The key here has to be the men who weigh the scissel and transport it back and forth."

"How many men would that be?"

"Two, no more. Perhaps one, but probably two, the man who transports the scissel from the blanking presses and the man at the weigh station in receiving."

"Who are they? Do you know anything about them?"

Patricia blinked rapidly and then brushed away some moisture from her eyes. "Yes, I know them, and I like them both. In fact, one of the men has a daughter my own age. She's a friend."

"Who are they?"

"Oh . . . damn! I have to do this. The man on the scales in receiving is Nance Sturgill. He's a tall, thin man with blond hair and must be in his forties. His daughter Christine is my age. The man who works the scissel is Ben Oakmarker. He's short, a little chunky and dark haired."

Patricia hugged his arm against her and he

could feel the swell of her breast. "Will . . . will they get in trouble, too?"

"If they're part of the embezzlement ring they certainly will. From what you've told me, and what I've figured out, I don't see how anyone could steal the gold without the help of these two men."

Spur walked with the redhead back to the street and signalled for a cab. The rig pulled up and they stepped on board.

"Let's drive past the place where Nance Sturgill lives. I'd like to see his home."

Patricia frowned for a moment, then she nodded. "Yes, I understand. You want to see if they are living beyond the means that a regular mint employee should." She told the driver where to go and they rolled along through San Francisco.

Quickly he saw that they were moving into the less affluent section of town. The houses were jammed closely together, there was trash in the street, wash hung from lines in the front and side yards.

They went up a small hill and then along a slightly better street that had a few shade trees and individual houses.

"Just keep going down this street, driver" Patricia told the driver.

She sat close to Spur now and leaned across pointing out the right house.

"There it is, number 315, the white painted one." She frowned. It does seem to be in better repair than the other houses around it." Patricia looked at Spur. "Would you say it was too rich?"

"I'd have to see the inside of it."

A buggy came up the street with a driver up front and Patricia leaned against Spur hiding her face.

"It's Mrs. Sturgill. I don't want her to see me."

When the rigs passed, Spur called to the driver to stop. He watched behind as the other buggy pulled up to the front walk of the Sturgill house. A woman stepped out of the buggy.

Patricia sucked in a breath. "Look at that dress!" I've never seen Mrs. Sturgill wear anything like that before. That dress is like one my mother looked at down at Grandifer's Department store. It cost way too much, mother decided, something like $60 or $70!"

"That would be out of the reach of an ordinary worker at the Mint?" Spur asked.

"Absolutely, that's two months' salary down there."

They watched as the buggy turned and rolled in beside the house where Mrs. Sturgill lived. It was soon out of sight in back.

"They have their own buggy, horse and driver," Spur said. "Seems from our first look that the Sturgills may be spending more than the man of the house should be making at the mint."

They looked at each other for a minute and Patricia let a frown scar her pretty face. "Oh, dear. I was afraid of this. Now I remember the inside of the Sturgill house. It's nice. Now that I think. The furniture is much too expensive for that house. It's a lot like ours in the big house on Nob Hill. It shouldn't be."

"Drive on," Spur called and the rig moved down the street.

"Now, for the tough part," Spur said. "If the top three men are stealing the gold, would it be in the scissel form?"

"Absolutely," Patricia said. "That's the only logical way for them to get it without violating the

63

checks and double-checks and weigh-ins at every step of the way."

"Then how is the gold moved out of the mint? I've heard that employees are searched, and their lunch pails are searched everytime they leave that mint."

"True, it's an inconvenience, but it has to be done."

"Then Sturgill and Oakmarker can't be bringing out the gold. How does it come out?"

"Oh, dear."

He looked at her.

"When I worked there, I remember every day the three top men came in an hour later than everyone else. We reported to work at eight. They came in at nine. And they each carried a leather briefcase. I'd guess they take the gold out of the mint every afternoon when they quit at five. The three top managers were never searched."

"And any one of them could carry 10 or 15 pounds of gold out of the mint in their briefcases every day if they tried."

"I'm afraid so."

"Once outside they melt down the gold, use a form they bought somewhere and pour the melted scissel into ingots. I'm sure there is a buyer of gold in this town who would not ask a lot of questions about the origin of the metal . . . for a price."

They drove back to the embarcadero without speaking.

"I still can't believe he did this. How could my father endanger all of us? We didn't need to be in society. Denise and I didn't need to go to private school and have all the clothes and ponies and the beach house and the country house. Oh . . . damn!"

"I thought you might cry again and I was getting ready," Spur said.

"I almost did, but you don't have to move your arm. I . . . I sort of like it this way."

At the waterfront they let the cab go and walked again.

"I'll want the other man's address, this Oak-marker."

"Yes, I can get it easily from a list. I don't remember it."

"Please be careful. I don't want to put you in any danger."

"They won't even know why I'm at the mint. What are you going to do next?"

"Drive you to the mint, if that's where you get that address. I want to look at Ben's place this afternoon."

She nodded. "Yes, let's do that. Tonight mother has a small dinner party with the Jeffersons and Alexander will be there. Somehow I have to put up with him for two or three hours. At least there will be others around."

They caught another hack and drove within a block of the mint where Spur got out and waited inside a small leather goods store. Patricia went on to the mint and had the hack wait. Spur bought a pair of thin, tight gloves in dark brown and wore them.

A few minutes later, the same hack stopped in front of the store and Spur got back inside with Patricia and they drove away.

"I appreciate your help, Patricia," he said.

"I owe it to everyone, I'm afraid it's a cross I'm going to have to bear for a long time." Then she smiled. "All you really have to do is guarantee that

I don't have to marry Alexander."

"I'll do what I can," Spur said, meaning it.

It was several streets away before they came to the one where Oakmarker lived. It was definitely a cut above the previous neighborhood where Sturgill lived. The house was larger, the lot much bigger, and a fancy carriage sat at the rear of the house.

"It looks like his rich uncle died in the East as well," Patricia said. "The house is too big, the neighborhood too nice and the carriage is out of place."

"So our friend Ben Oakmarker is spending the extra money he's getting. I wonder how much it takes to bribe an honest man?"

"We're going to find out soon," Patricia said.

"They drove back to the waterfront and watched the ships.

"This is one of my favorite spots in all of San Francisco," she said. "Let's walk down to the wharf and get one of those little shrimp cocktails that they sell. I love them."

They bought the snacks in paper cups and sat on pilings along the wharf eating the shrimp with wooden spoons.

Patricia looked up, a tear edging out of one eye. "Now, I think I've had enough of a dose of reality and honesty so I can go back to that artificial and dishonest life my parents have been leading. Please, send me a note if I can help. I'll be trying to find out what I can without anyone knowing."

"Be careful. Remember, the son of one of these three men has been murdered, as well as two more men. Someone is getting desperate to hang on to this thievery. I don't want them suspecting you of any disloyalty to the big three."

"I'll be careful." She called a cab, kissed him on the cheek with her green eyes sparkling, and rushed away in the one horse rig toward her parents' home on Nob Hill past the Customs House and up the slope on California Street.

It was past three in the afternoon. Spur watched the bay waters slap against the pilings. What now? He had been thinking of establishing a watch point on the mint itself. He walked on the far side of the street, past the mint, and decided a two story residence hotel might be a good spot. He went in and found the manager in the basement apartment.

"You want to do what?"

"I'm a detective for a Chicago firm and we're watching a business two doors down from the mint for some unusual activity. I want your permission to go to the roof of your building from time to time and watch from there so I won't be as obvious as standing across the street."

The manager wore an undershirt and baggy trousers. He held a bottle of beer in one hand and shrugged.

"Hell, why not. I could charge you a fee."

Spur reached in his pocket and came out with a quarter eagle, $2.50. He handed the gold coin to the man who nodded twice.

"Yes, fine, you just go up there whenever you want. There's a ladder up the back all the way to the top. It's safe. I had to climb up there last week. Just don't make a lot of noise."

Spur assured him that he would be so quiet they wouldn't know he was there. He went down the alley to the back of the building and found a sturdy ladder.

On the roof there was a false front that would give him plenty of shielding. He sat down and watched the mint. He could see the front door and one side door—evidently where deliveries were made—and where special guarded wagons arrived to take all kinds of sizes of coins to the Federal Banks and to the train for transport all over the West.

Now all he could do was wait.

Below, in the U.S. Mint, they were punching out blanks for double eagle coins. The process went smoothly. The same routine had been followed hundreds, probably thousands of times in the 20 years the mint had been there in San Francisco. It was down to a science, a studied pattern from which there was no need to deviate.

Each time the big blanking presses hissed and punched into the continuous roll of gold rolled to the exactly proper thickness, another sheet of scissel dropped into the salvage cart. The sheet of gold punched in this particular coin was 26-inches long and 13-inches deep. It allowed plenty of room between punchings so there would be no buckling or flowing of the metal from one punching into the next.

The resultant scissel was heavier than visitors to the mint imagined. It dropped into a pristine clean steel lined box on a wheelbarrowlike cart. At intervals, Oakmarker wheeled the scissel to a cutting press that cut the leftovers into small pieces for later feeding into the furnace where they would be remelted.

Oakmarker now opened the bin door and let the

nearly pure gold cascade into his steel lined cart and he wheeled it down a long ramp and up one more ramp to the receiving room.

Here all of the metals to be used in the coins were taken in, weighed and sent to the appropriate section for mixing. The gold scissel was simply weighed and returned to the melting room since it already had the small amount of copper added to it to harden the natural softness of gold.

As always when the double eagles were being blanked, the receiving room was empty except for Nance Sturgill. He grinned at his co-conspirator and lugged the metal box off the barrow and onto the scales.

Sturgill weighed the scissel quickly, deducted two percent and entered the figure on his tally sheet, then picked out enough of the cut gold so the scales equalled his tally. The removed cut up gold scissel went into a small leather bag directly under his tally board in a locked drawer.

The amount of gold in the drawer would vary each time they cut out the double eagles, depending on how many coins were blanked that day. Once, on a nearly continuous operation on double eagles, there was almost 20 pounds of gold and it took two of the ten-inch wide leather bags to hold it.

Today's was a small-to-normal run, and when it was over the tally sheet would show the usual figures for scissel return on that number of coins. Anyone checking records for comparison would have to go back at least 10 years to find any variance on the percentage of scissel from a given number of coins blanked.

Sturgill stole the gold automatically, not really

thinking about it. He had a twinge of conscience now and then but more often he thought of quitting the job, taking his considerable bank account and moving, maybe south to the little community of Los Angeles, or maybe on down to San Diego. He would talk again to his wife about it. He didn't want to stay too long and have the scheme discovered and then have to go to prison. He would not be able to stand it in prison.

He picked out three more chunks of the gold from the metal box, dropped them in the leather sack and closed and locked the drawer. Then he waved at Oakmarker who signed the weigh in record and wheeled the scissel to the corner where he stacked the metal tray with the other boxes, waiting transfer under armed guard to the melting rooms.

By four-thirty they were done. As usual, one of the big three bosses came down to the receiving room. Today it was Philander Knox.

"Good afternoon, Sturgill. Everything going smoothly today?"

"Yes sir, double eagles mostly."

The management men made a ritual of their little tours, inspecting areas here and there on a non-regular basis, but always stopping at receiving.

When no one else was in the room, Sturgill unlocked the hidden drawer, took out the leather pouch, and put it in the briefcase that Knox had opened for him. This was done quickly so if anyone came in they wouldn't be caught.

Knox snapped the briefcase shut and nodded. He felt obligated to warn the man here. "Sturgill, there has been some talk of putting this operation on hold for a while. If so we'll let you know. Otherwise, keep up the good work. You'll get the envelope as usual."

This all was said softly so if anyone were trying to listen they would hear nothing.

Knox nodded, touched Sturgill on the shoulder and walked past him and out the door. His inspection tour was over now and Knox went directly back to his office, then a moment later he walked into Jefferson's office. No one beside the superintendent was there.

Knox set the briefcase on the desk. It held only the pouch of gold scissel.

"Here it is," Knox said.

"Are you still concerned about continuing?"

"Yes, frankly. That letter bothers me more and more. I have a bad feeling about it. We must be extremely cautious in the next few months to see that nothing anywhere in the whole mint gets out of line that could bring down a major audit. We have to be pristine pure and by the book."

"They would have to go back ten years—"

"No, we've discussed this before. If they add up the receiving quantity of gold and the output, and the scissel still in the process, you know it's going to come out about two percent short. If they go to the totals. Now, granted, the last time we had the audit they worked in specifics and never got it down that fine, but they could. The scissel reports are consistent. But a two percent loss in gold is a glaring problem if they get it that far."

"They haven't, and I'm gambling that they won't. Now quit worrying so much and relax. We're still in control. We can take care of everything."

"I read about Stoop in the paper," Philander

said. "You didn't think it was important enough to talk with me about it first?"

"There was no time. Somebody asked for Stoop in his saloon, took him out for a walk and did a lot of talking. There was no other way to handle it. And it had to be done fast."

"Then you had the second man silenced as well. That makes three, Martin. We didn't figure on anything like this when we started."

"No, you're right. But neither did we expect it to last so long or become so profitable. It's at the point now where I can't just fold my tent and walk away from it."

"Yes, but three human lives!"

"We didn't plan that. It just happened. I hope you can control yourself, Philander. We have enough problems right now without making any new ones for ourselves. I hope you understand this, Philander."

"I'll be all right. It was a real shock when I read about it and I haven't had a chance to come in here and talk to you about it before now."

"Things are going to settle down, you'll see, Philander. Why don't you go home early, take Betsy out to a big dinner at a fancy restaurant and relax. Everything is going to be fine. We must have another eight or nine pounds of 99% gold here."

Philander sighed. He stood from where he had slumped in the upholstered chair and nodded. "All right, Martin. But before anything else drastic is done, we have to agree on it. Do you promise?"

"Of course, Philander, just like always. Stoop was an emergency. Everything is just the way it's been around here for ten years."

Philander watched him a moment, then went through the door into the hall.

Martin Jefferson squinted at the vanishing form. He had lied. Things were not as they had been. Philander was turning into a jellyfish. Martin knew he was going to have to do some serious thinking about this new problem, and it was going to have to be done now.

· 6 ·

Martin Jefferson left the San Francisco United States Mint promply at 5:02 as was his custom, walked to the rear of the building where he untied his black horse from the rail, and drove his dark buggy out the alley and north on Fillmore street. Soon he turned and headed for the more industrial part of town near the waterfront.

He stopped in the alley of a small firm that had no name on the rear door. He knocked twice. A small lookout door opened and an eye stared at him, then closed, and the whole panel came open.

"Right on time, sir," the man said.

Jefferson stepped inside, then the man closed the door and locked it. He held out his hand for the leather pouch that Martin took from his briefcase.

"I always try to be punctual, Mr. Halverson. I would expect that you are ready."

"Right, sir, always ready." Halverson was a squashed down little man, no more than five feet tall, with a great bald dome and huge eyebrows. His arms and shoulders were thick and strong like a blacksmith, which he was at one time. Now he specialized in metals and metal salvage, and especially in melting down gold and silver that various blackguards and thieves and robbers suddenly found in their possession.

He didn't know Jefferson's name, the Superintendent had made sure of that from the start. He followed the small man, watched him scour out a heavy iron pot until it was clean, and then put in the handfuls of inch-long pieces of rolled gold. The man never asked where it came from or how it was obtained. He was too smart for that.

When the scissel was in the heavy iron pot, he swung out a sturdy iron bracket over a small forge and pumped the bellows until the fire glowed hot and red in its banked heat. Quickly, the gold in the heavy pot began to melt.

Jefferson knew this was not scientific metallurgy. There was something like one percent copper in the gold mix to make the pure gold tough enough to serve as coinage. He didn't bother to extract the copper. It simply went into the system as a 99% gold bar and was paid for at that rate.

Even after ten years, Jefferson was always surprised at how quickly the gold melted under the intense heat of the forge. It was an efficient system. When the molten gold was ready, the small man put on heavy goggles, heavier gloves, and picked up the thick iron pot with huge metal pinchers and delicately poured the smoking liquid metal into a casting form.

The gold brick would weigh 10 pounds if it was full. This time it was not quite full. It was about eight-inches long, four inches-wide and four-inches high. There was no gold mine imprint on the gold. It was officially labeled as "reclaimed gold" and no requirement was made to say what it had been or from where it came.

As was the custom, the customer never let the precious metal out of his sight during this operation. Now Jefferson sat and had a cup of coffee and a small chocolate bar that Halverson offered. At first, he had thought the man might feed him poison and escape with the gold, but the old thief once said he was tired of running. Now he let the others do the hard work and he obliged them the best he could, and as honestly as he could, asking only for a fair fee.

When the coffee was gone and the chocolate bar eaten, it was time to take apart the mold and reveal the bar of gold. It was still far too hot to handle, but the forms came off and Jefferson nodded as he saw the amount. About eight pounds, he estimated. He flipped Halverson a gold double eagle and the man nodded and grinned.

An hour later, Jefferson drove away from the alley with his briefcase now containing a carefully wrapped gold brick. He left the alley, drove through three darkening streets, and came to another street that had a mixture of residences and small businesses.

Again he drove into the alley and stopped behind the third house from the street. He took his briefcase and walked to the back door where he knocked.

He heard a bolt being thrown and a slice of a face peering at him through the barely opened door.

"Ah, yes, my friend the goldman," the watcher said. "Do come in and sip a glass of fine wine with me."

"Is the bank open?"

"Indeed it is. How is my fine friend, Mr. Halverson?"

"I don't know anyone by that name."

Jefferson watched the buyer. He was always the same. Much talk, without saying much, dressed well, if a little flamboyantly, and had a mop of unruly black hair that flew off in all directions.

"Just as well you don't know Mr. Halverson. The little bastard tries to cheat everyone. I, on the other hand, am as honest and straightforward as the Archbishop of Canterbury, if you're of that persuasion."

"I'd like to make a deposit and a withdrawal," Jefferson said.

"Right this way."

They walked through a storeroom, then into a living room, and toward the front of the house where they went into a study that had upholstered furniture, softly glowing lamps and oil paintings on the walls.

"You have the usual?"

"Nearly, a bit shy this time, but I'm sure your scales are accurate."

"Extremely so. I'm told I should put my thumb on it from the bottom to lift the platform, but never in my life have I done such a thing."

Jefferson handed him the now cool brick. He put it on a scale that read out into three decimal points.

"My friend, we have 8.471 pounds." He did some fast calculations with a pencil. "At $20.67 an ounce, that translates into $2,801.53."

"We're working with 99% purity here again?"

"Exactly. Then we deduct that one-percent, and we deduct my two-percent for transaction your business, and we come out with the three-percent at $84. When that is subtracted from the total, we have the value to you of the gold of $2,717.00. Please check my figures."

"I'm sure it's correct, but I'll take your figuring paper with me."

"One moment while I go see if my rattlesnakes and galley slaves are still guarding my safe."

It was as usual, almost the same words were used each time Jefferson came to sell the gold. Two-percent was the best price he had ever had for it, selling sometimes at five-percent off the value.

The flashily dressed man came back with a bag filled with gold coins. He stacked them in piles of 10 to show that there were 135 of them and some change.

"Agreed?" the buyer said, brushing one hand back through his wild hair.

"Agreed," Jefferson said. He dropped the coins into the leather bag and smiled. "Always good to do business with you, young man."

When the coins were in the bag, he rose to go. His left hand carried the bag, his right was close to the derringer in his suit coat pocket.

The buyer laughed softly. "Keep up the good work, whatever it is, I admire your consistency."

Then Jefferson walked out the back door and to his carriage. He checked to be sure there was no one lurking in the darkness or in his buggy. He stepped in and drove away quickly, working his way across town again to California Street where he turned upward so he could drive to his large house on Nob Hill.

The party was in full swing. He remembered that Wilma had said something about a party that night. He told her he had important business and would not be home until about eight. It was just after that now when he parked in the large area behind the house and gave the rig to the steward who would tend to the horse. He carried his brief-case into the house and straight up to his bedroom, waving to a person or two on the way, but missing most of the guests.

Quickly, he pushed the gold coin filled bag into his wall safe, closed the door and locked it, then pulled the picture back in place to hide it. After washing up and shaving quickly, he went down to meet his guests.

There were about 30 of them, spread around the house. Some still snacked at a buffet, while others danced in the ballroom. He found his wife, Wilma, and kissed her cheek, then moved into the spirit of the party, accepting a drink from one of the extra waiters hired for the occasion. He had no idea what the occasion might be.

He looked for Alexander, but he wasn't in sight. Neither did Patricia seem to be. Vaguely, he remembered something about a planned engage-ment announcement, a formal one, but Patricia had said not yet. She would tell them when the time was right. That worried him.

He spotted Eldridge Grandifar, the man who owned half of the retail stores in San Francisco, it seemed. He went over to him and Grandifar turned and pounded him on the shoulder.

"You promised me another try at beating you at billiards, old man," Grandifar said. "You have that table of yours leveled this time?"

"Let's just go and find out," Jefferson said. "Shall we make it interesting at $100 a point?"

They swept into the pool room with a dozen men trailing along to watch the sport.

Wilma Jefferson fluttered around the party rooms like a setting hen, making sure the buffet was kept stocked and that the waiters provided drinks in a hurry to the men and a few of the women who were drinking. She sipped a brandy as she stood beside the table. Wilma was matronly with a wider waist than she'd had 20 years ago, larger breasts, and a new hair do.

She was in her glory. A social "do" with most of the best people in town. Yes, this was the life for her. Now if that prissy Patricia Knox would just agree to marry Alexander, everything would be wonderful.

She spotted a waiter with an empty tray and hurried over to get him back to the bar for more champagne.

In the guest room upstairs, Patricia Knox stood by the window watching the San Francisco skyline. She had agreed to come up here with Alexander only because he said he had something extremely important to show her.

She turned and sighed. This was starting out to be a horrible evening. Alexander had come to get her at her parents' house, and hadn't let her out of his sight for two hours. Now this strange request.

"Alexander, what in the world is this all about?"

"It's about us, you and me. I want to get married right away, and I thought maybe if I showed you the real me, then you might want to get married sooner."

Alexander unbuttoned his fly and loosened his belt. Before Patricia could yell, his pants fell to the floor showing his white underpants with a bulge in the front.

"Patricia, I want you so bad! I locked the door. We can do anything we want to right here! First we could just look at each other."

She stood there by the window, frozen in place. This was so bizarre it was unbelievable!

Then Alexander pulled down his undershorts and his long, hard penis sprang up. She saw the purple head, the mass of hair and then she turned away.

In a moment, she darted around him for the door. He couldn't move fast with his pants at his ankles. But Alexander lunged at her, caught her around the waist and dragged her down to the thick carpet on the floor.

She hit hard on her shoulder and was on her back as Alexander crawled over her, then lowered his short, pudgy body on top of her. Patricia tried to scream, but one of his hands covered her mouth.

His other hand tore at her dress, ripped buttons, pulled the bodice apart and clawed at her chemise until the delicate fabric ripped and came apart, sagging on both sides to reveal one of her ripe breasts, pink tipped with a large pink areola.

"Oh, god, it's beautiful," Alexander growled, his hand fondling her breast. He pushed her dress aside to see her other mound. He leaned down and kissed one nipple, then the other one.

His hand held her mouth as she clawed at him with her left hand. Her right was pinned under his weight. He ducked her hand and pushed his right hand down to her crotch.

Only then did she realize that when she turned over her legs had sprawled apart and now they were held down that way by his weight. She tried to pull them together, but couldn't.

"Oh, yes!" Alexander chortled. "Tits and all. Now the best part!"

His hand came up her leg under her dress and touched her crotch. She squealed through his hand. Her fingers worked around his face and scratched down his cheek, bringing blood. He yelped in pain. His hand closed around her crotch, digging past her softly silk underpants she had just bought.

Her fingers clawed at him again, this time reaching the bottom of his right eye and pulling down, scratching him again.

Then she felt his hips bucking against her, his long hard penis jabbing at her stomach as his hips and legs drove forward a dozen times so fast she could hardly believe it.

She started to scratch him again. Then she saw him relax and sag in exhaustion. Patricia doubled up her fist and hit him in the throat. She felt something break or give way and Alexander gave a terrible scream and rolled away from her, his hand to his throat.

Suddenly she was free. Patricia struggled to her feet and ran to the door, unbolted it, then looked down at her dress. It was torn beyond repair. She covered herself with the two sides of the buttonless bodice and opened the door.

No one was in the hall. She hurried down to the bedroom where the woman had left their coats and where there was a bathroom with indoor plumbing and a sink and even running water from a tank on the roof.

She closed the door and sat on the bed for a moment, then she began to sob. Her shoulders shook and her hands let go of the cloth she had covered her breasts with. She sobbed and then went to the bed where a dozen jackets and coats lay. She stretched out on a clear space and cried into the bedspread.

After about 20 minutes, Patricia had cried it all out. She sat there wondering what to do. Her mother was downstairs, but how to call her. She knew most of the people there, but she didn't want to let any of them see her this way.

She heard someone leave a room down the hall and go down the stairs. She guessed it was Alexander escaping.

She remembered hitting his throat and hoped that she had hurt him terribly bad. She hated him! She would never be in the same room with him again. He had tried to rape her!

Thelma Mae Pickering came into the room and hesitated. She looked down at the girl on the bed. "Patricia Anne, is that you?" she asked softly. "Don't you feel well?"

Patricia heard the voice, turned until she could see the woman's face. She thought she recognized Mrs. Pickering's sweet voice.

"No, I don't feel well. Could you help me?"

"Of course, darling. What's the trouble?" She sat down on the bed beside Patricia. When the girl sat up letting her torn clothing sag open, Thelma

Mae gasped in surprise and anger.

"Oh, Good Lord!" She hugged the girl to her bosom. Then she stood and went to the hall. "First, we get you out of here and down to Wilma's bedroom. Then, I go get your mother. Who—" She hesitated. "Victor didn't do this, did he?"

"Oh, no."

"Good. Come on. Hold your dress up as well as you can. There's nobody in the hall."

They got to the last bedroom down the hall, and the older woman sat Patricia down on the bed. She sat beside the pretty redheaded girl and smoothed back her hair.

"Patricia, I know this is a hard question, but I have to ask. Whoever it was, did he . . . you know . . . did he rape you?"

"Oh, no. He tried. Scared me to death. I hit him. I don't ever want to go through that again." Patricia held up her hands. "Look, I've got blood and skin under my fingernails. I clawed him twice."

She cried again, and Thelma Mae held her. She didn't have any girls, just the two boys, one boy now that Redfield was gone. When the sobbing stopped, Mrs. Pickering dried off the tears and held her a moment.

"Now, I think I better go find your mother. I . . . I don't want to spoil the party. But I'm certainly going to spoil the party for someone. I saw Alexander come upstairs with you. Was he the one who did it?"

"Yes."

"I thought so. Men, damn them! They think they own a person, even before the ceremony." She reached in and kissed Patricia's cheek. "I'd always hoped that you and Redfield might get married some day. Now I hope you never do marry that Alexander."

"I loved Redfield, Mrs. Pickering. I always will. I'll never even be in the same house with Alexander Jefferson again!"

"Good for you."

Thelma Mae kissed her cheek, then hurried downstairs and found Betsy Knox. She had her fully briefed before they got to the bedroom. Betsy talked with Patricia a minute.

"Honey, you feel well enough to go home?" Betsy asked.

"Yes, of course, mama. He only scared me, he didn't hurt me."

"He's the one who's going to be hurt. Both of those damn Jefferson brats are crazy!"

Thelma Mae laughed but looked around as if hoping no one else heard.

"Thelma Mae, get that new green sweater I wore tonight," Betsy said. "It'll look good on Patricia, and cover up her dress. I'll pin it together and she and I will go out. If it comes up, you tell our hostess that Patricia isn't feeling well and that I've taken her home."

Mrs. Knox frowned a moment. "Oh, yes, and if you can, get a look at Alexander and see how bad those scratches are."

"I . . . I think I hurt him worse than that. I doubled up my fist and I hit him in the throat. He probably can't talk for a while, but he screamed as he lay there."

A half hour later Patricia stretched out on her own bed and looked up at the ceiling. Why couldn't things be simple? Her own father and mother thieves. Her mother had to know about it. Where else could the money have come from? And now Alexander acting like an animal, a stupid, foolish animal. Did he think he could convince her to marry him by raping her first?

Patricia thought for a moment of Spur McCoy and how gentlemanly and tender he was. She thought how he had held her when she had cried, and then how he had put his arm around her in the carriage. That was the way loving was supposed to be. That was the way.

"Anything I can get for you?" Betsy Knox asked as she came into the room.

For the briefest flash of a second, Patricia wanted to say her parents could provide her with a truly honest example and a simpler life, but she didn't. She shook her head.

"Thank you, Mother," she said, and then closed her eyes and drifted off to sleep still thinking of Spur McCoy.

Back at the party, Thelma Mae told her husband what had happened, and Edmund told Philander Knox.

"Now Philander, don't go charging off here until we have all the facts. Let's tell Martin about this, find the boy, and all sit down and hear what he has to say. Then we can decide on some course of action."

"You think Patricia would say Alex tried to rape her if he didn't?" Philander roared. "I want about five minutes alone with that boy right now!"

Martin came in the den on the urging of Thelma Mae and listened to Pickering's account. They looked for Alexander and found him curled up on his bed, his best suit still on, his face showing plainly the marks of the scratches.

Philander rushed at the boy, but Edmond caught him.

"Alex, sit up. We need to talk to you," his father said.

Slowly Alexander turned and sat up, but still held his throat. Five deep scratches showed down his cheek. His right eye drooped where one of the scratches had torn the eyelid. His hands stayed protectively around his throat.

"Alexander, did you tear Patricia's dress tonight and try to force yourself on her?"

He nodded.

"Talk, damn you!" Philander shouted.

Alexander shook his head. He moved his hands from his throat and they saw the ugly bruise and where some blood had seeped through the skin. He tried to talk, but the sound came out garbled and wheezing and unintelligible.

"His throat is hurt," Pickering said. "Thelma Mae told me Patricia hit him in the throat with her fist."

"Get him to a doctor, at once," Philander Knox said. "I want this kid to be able to talk when I kill him."

Martin stared hard at Philander. "You go home and take care of your child, and let me take care of mine. When they both are feeling better, we'll get this worked out. Nothing has changed. We can't afford to let anything be changed! Surely you both can understand that."

He ushered the other two men out of the room and hurried down to the stable behind the house and had a buggy readied. He would drive and fetch Dr. Patterville at once.

The party had wound down. The mood had been

broken, and some of the guests had heard about the trouble. Before long, everyone but the three partners had gone home. Only Philander Knox and Edmund and Thelma Mae Pickering sat in the big living room with Wilma Jefferson. She looked at them, but didn't know what to say.

After ten minutes of staring at each other, the Pickerings left and so did Philander. It was all he could do to contain himself. What he was most interested in now, was if Martin had told Alexander to go ahead and try to seduce Patricia.

"So help me," Philander said, "if Martin did that, I'm going to kill both of them."

· 7 ·

That same Friday night, Spur McCoy sat on top of the second floor roof of the small hotel and watched the mint across the street. At five o'clock, he saw the workers come out the side door and some out the front door. Then two men came out with briefcases. One was Philander Knox, who he had seen before. The other one he didn't know.

A moment later the superintendent himself, Martin Jefferson, came out with his briefcase. He turned as the other management people had and walked down the side of the building to the rear where there was a parking lot and a small barn for horses. Soon he saw the rig drive down the alley and vanish behind another building.

His wait was over. Spur was not sure what he

had hoped to discover by watching. His problem was to establish a trail. What happened to the gold after it was stolen? He had no way to prove the theft unless he could find someone who would testify against one of the big three who moved the gold.

He guessed it would have to be melted down into some other form, then it could be sold on the used gold market. He couldn't follow all three of them at once.

As he climbed down from the roof, Spur worked on an idea that might be practical. First, he had to talk to Patricia again. She was going to have to be his eyes and ears inside the mint until he landed the job there. If he did get it.

The next day was Saturday. The mint would work a full day and with Sunday coming up, it might be the best time to steal gold from the mint. What he needed to know was what scissel would be the best for them to steal, that from the twenty-dollar gold pieces because it was thickest, or that from the one-dollar gold coin? Patricia might have some ideas on the matter. After he found that out, he needed to know when they punched out the right coins, since that was the day that they might be stealing from the scissel.

Spur McCoy had a big supper at a Western style restaurant, then went home and re-read his orders before getting a good night's sleep.

Dr. Patterville had been rousted out of bed by Martin Jefferson. As soon as he heard the name he got dressed quickly. The Jeffersons had been patients of his for 12 years. Now at their house in the middle of the night, he shook his head as he examined Alexander. He knew better than to ask what happened. In the past six or eight years he had answered a lot of calls to repair the older Jefferson child.

"He's had a severe blow to the throat, the larynx. It's damaged, just how much I can't tell. The scratches on his face are superficial and I'll take care of those. The eyelid will take a stitch or two, but the throat is another matter."

He looked up at the father and mother. "Do you have any ice in the house? If not, get some and apply ice or cold water packs on the throat. Start right now. The cold will tend to reduce the blood flow in the area and cut down on blood seeping into the surrounding tissue and help lower and prevent swelling."

"Will he be able to talk again, Doctor?" Wilma Jefferson asked in a whisper.

Dr. Patterville turned and looked at her. "Probably, it depends on how serious the damage is. I saw a man who died once from a blow to the throat like this. His was much more severe, however, and that danger is past with Alexander. For now, don't press him to talk. The voice box is damaged to some extent. It might be like a broken violin that will never make a sound again. But more likely it's just in shock and has been jolted.

"My estimation is that within two weeks he'll be talking normally again. It may happen sooner than that. The important thing now is to keep him in bed, keep ice packs on his throat, and don't try to force him to talk."

All this time Alexander lay there watching his parents, looking from them to the doctor who examined him. He winced and growled when the doctor took a thin, curved needle and sewing thread and put two stitches in his torn eyelid.

"This will heal normally and we'll never know it was torn," Dr. Patterville said. "The scratches should mend as well. One is deep and it might leave the trace of a scar, but on young flesh like this there shouldn't be much scar tissue at all." He finished treating the scratches, putting a bandage over only the worst, then stood and packed away his equipment in a small bag.

"Best if the boy gets some sleep now," the doctor said. They all left the room and his mother turned the kerosene lamp down low and left the door open.

"I'll send one of the help after some ice," Martin said. "I'm sure the ice man can be roused and bring us about 50 pounds."

An hour later the ice had arrived, been chipped, and a soft cloth sack used to hold the chips pressed tenderly against Alex's throat. He had pulled away at first, but then the chill settled into his flesh and the hurt area and the numbing began which killed the pain.

Alexander nodded that it helped and a few moments later went to sleep. Wilma motioned for one of the maids to come and keep the ice pack in place. She whispered how to replace the ice and wring out the small bag when the ice melted. The towel on his chest would catch the drips.

Then Wilma went to the bedroom. It had been a strange, emotional night. She had never seen Philander Knox so furious. Betsy Knox had been tight lipped and angry eyed when she showed Wilma the damage to Patricia's dress and underthings. Amazing.

Before tonight she hadn't been sure that

Alexander had any sexual drives at all. At least that worry was over. Wilma looked at her husband who slept on his back under a light sheet.

She undressed slowly, then lifted the sheet off Martin gently so he didn't even stir. She settled beside him, naked on the bed, and lightly touched his crotch. He stirred but didn't move. Slowly, gently, she aroused him, fondling him, stroking his soft penis gently, watching it rise and harden. Her heart beat faster and her breath came quickly. He whispered something in his sleep, but Martin remained on his back, sleeping.

Now he was fully erect. She moved over him squatting, spreading herself wide, holding his penis upright at the right angle. She gasped as he entered her, then gently she eased down, making him slip into her ready scabbard. Slowly she raised and lowered on him.

He moaned softly. She caught one of his hands, brought it up to her breast and held it there until he began to fondle her.

She lifted and dropped down with a longer stroke now, moving partly forward and then down. Soon she was moving faster and faster until she was riding him like a young stallion.

Martin smiled. "Oh, yeah!" he whispered still in his sleep. Then she sensed him tensing. His hips rose to meet hers and he brayed out a ragged shout of joy and delight.

That was what awoke him. His eyes came wide. He saw his wife bouncing on top of him, her generous breasts rolling and dancing with the motion.

"Oh, god, you did it again," he said and then pumped up as hard and as fast as he could until he exploded inside her, pounding again and again until his load was gone. Then he stopped moving, lying on the bed like a corpse.

She wasn't through using him. She continued her motion knowing that he would soften quickly. Faster and faster she rode him until she dropped flat on top of him with her feet extended near his and a roaring, searing climax rushed through her, sparking every nerve ending in her body, flushing her face and her chest, twisting her body with shattering spasms that rattled her like a penny in a tin can until she at last slowed and stopped and dissolved on top of him, gushing out a pent up breath of satisfaction.

After 10 minutes she lifted away from him. "I was so keyed up, I couldn't sleep," Wilma said. "You suppose Alexander really tried to rape Patricia?"

"Of course. He said he did. She said he did. What more do you want?"

"I'm glad in a way. It proves that he's interested in girls. For a while I wasn't sure. Not that I'm glad about poor Patricia, but she didn't have to fight him. She could have decided it would be all right to be a bride in bed a month or two early. As I recall, you made the same suggestion to me, Martin."

"No, you've got it slightly turned around, Wilma. You invited me over to your house one evening when your parents were away and you came to the door wearing not a blessed thing. I jumped to the conclusion that you might want to get poked right away. Was I wrong?"

"Don't be vulgar."

"We were both vulgar before we had so much

money."

"It's more fun to have money than to be vulgar."

"Sometimes it's more fun to be vulgar because you have money."

"You want to stick me again?" she asked.

"Damn right! You know with me once is never enough. I realize that you could keep going all night."

Later, when they were joined again with him on top, he stopped and caught her face in his hands. "Wife, did you ever get in bed with Redfield Pickering?"

"Martin, what a terrible question to ask."

"So answer it."

She lifted her brows in the faint light from the lamp on the dresser. Wilma sighed. "Only twice. He was seventeen at the time, and curious as all hell. I was his first, and second. It was a kind of public service I did for him."

"You mean *pubic* service. I knew you seduced him, I just wanted to hear you admit it. I swear, you'd open your hole for anything with a cock if you get the chance."

"Not true. That new driver we have. I'll never go near him."

"Damn right you won't! That's why I hired him. He's black and he has both of the social diseases. You better remember it."

When they were laying side by side in the big bed again, she looked at her husband.

"This problem with Alexander, is it going to hurt the Group and our Project?"

"No. The Project is overriding, it is simply too important. We'll smooth this over. Do you think Patricia will every marry Alex now?"

"Not in a thousand years. I saw the way she looked just before she went home. That is one spunky redhead and she's not about to let our Alexander come anywhere near to touching her tight little virgin pussy again."

"So, I guess that's done. Now we have to mend our fences with the Knoxes, especially Philander. I've never seen him so incensed. He had murder in his eyes."

"He wouldn't do that."

"He just might, especially if it turns out Alexander did get his whanger inside Patricia and Philander thinks I encouraged Alexander to try."

"Did you encourage him to try to get her?"

"No, he didn't need it."

"Oh, good lord!" Wilma said. "The girl shouldn't be that sensitive, anyway."

"Wilma, not every female likes to get poked as much as you do."

They lay there without talking and soon Martin drifted off to sleep. Wilma was wide-eyed awake. When she enjoyed sex she did like it to last a couple of hours at least.

Yes, from what Thelma Mae said, Wilma decided that she did like sex more than most women. Thelma Mae said she put up with it so Edmund wouldn't go whoring around. Wilma knew that her Martin had a little floozy he kept somewhere. She didn't care.

She'd had a thing going with the Pickering's driver for about six months. Then he up and quit his job one day and she never saw him again. He had been entertaining, and young, and she brought him gifts every time.

Thinking about Patricia and her brush with

male sex made Wilma think of her first time. Oh, God, but she had been young. Sixteen, and so curious she almost jumped the preacher's son one day, but she wisely knew he would not even pull up her dress. He was too much like his father.

It had been on a church picnic though, about a month later. Six of the older kids went on a hike in the woods by the river and she and Johnny got lost. They dropped behind, then ran part way back to the picnic grounds and fell laughing on some grass behind some brush in a private little spot. They had been hitting each other and touching and she was getting hotter and wilder.

Johnny rolled over and kissed her. He leaned away but she reached out and pulled him down against her and kissed him hard. They kissed a dozen times and slowly he reached in and touched her breast.

"Go ahead, I want you to feel me," she said. He did, then slowly she unbuttoned the fasteners on her dress and his hand crept inside.

He took her hand and pushed it down to his crotch. They took off their clothes slowly, experimenting, drinking in their first sight of bare limbs, naked breasts, exposed crotches. At last, Johnny couldn't stand it any more. He rolled against her, pumping his hips, and he yelled as he shot his juice all over her bare thigh.

After that they made love three more times before they dressed and ran back to the picnic where the other kids had just come straggling in from the hike. The other boys on the hike grinned and the girls giggled, but nobody could prove a thing.

The next Saturday, Johnny came visiting at her

house and they got permission for a short bike ride. They rode down the street of the small town and then at the first patch of woods, they rode into the brush and had a wild time again.

Even now Wilma wondered what would have happened to them if Johnny's parents hadn't moved the next weekend all the way to Oregon.

Wilma wondered who she should try for next? She loved to target a man, or a lad of seventeen or eighteen, and pursue him and capture him in some hotel room. It was her only sport. She had grown to despise those damn charity committee meetings.

Who would be next? Wilma went to sleep with a smile on her face.

That same night, with Patricia at last asleep, Betsy Knox crept back into the master bedroom and the big bed but found the light still on and Philander sitting up in bed staring straight ahead.

"I want to tell you, Betsy. If Martin Jefferson urged Alexander to try to seduce Patricia, and that resulted in his assault and attempted rape of her, then I'm going to kill both Martin and Alexander."

"Oh, dear. I didn't think you'd take this quite so seriously." She slid into bed beside him and sat up to match his pose. "I mean it's serious, yes, and I'm sure now that Patricia will never marry Alexander. She said she never even will be in the same house with him ever again. I had thought perhaps of bringing some criminal assault and attempted rape charges against the boy, but killing him? No, no. That would never do."

"Are you thinking like Martin is, Betsy? He said

he couldn't afford to let anything like this interfere with our lucrative operation at the mint." He turned to her, his eyes still furious. "What good is the money if we lose our girls? It's for them that I agreed to do this in the first place. So we could make sure our children had more of a headstart in life than you and I did."

"I know, Philander, I know." She pushed close to him and put her arms around him. She pulled him down to cushion his head against her full breasts. "Denise is safely married to Victor. It was a love match, and that is secure. I know we had it all worked out. Redfield was supposed to marry Lucinda, and now both of them are gone, or might as well be.

"That left Patricia to take Alexander. I could tell that she has loved Redfield since she was a little girl. She doted on him. It hit her hard when he died."

Philander frowned. "I never knew that. Somehow I never noticed. She certainly didn't say anything about it."

"Of course not. All the time we were pushing her toward Alexander."

"Damn him! I think the boy is a little dense, not really loony like his sister, but definitely not normal. He's just a little bit crazy. I'm glad we don't have to worry about him being in our family. Especially not if he's dead."

"Philander, you just let that temper of yours cool off. It could get us all in real trouble."

"I think we're in real bad trouble already, Betsy."

"Whatever do you mean?"

"You remember what we talked about the other

night, about the letter? I'm more convinced of it now than ever. I don't see how they can help but send out an investigator from Washington D.C. and the Bureau of the Mint.

"You know I told you years ago that if the Bureau did a complete inventory and audit, there would be a small percentage of the gold missing. It would figure out something like one-half of one-percent, but over 10 years it has counted up to a huge sum.

"There would be no way to explain it. At the very least, we three would be fired and they would do their best to prove that we stole the gold. Our living standard would be checked, and they would find no rich uncle of mine in the East. Neither would they find any Old Money behind the Jeffersons or the Pickerings. On circumstantial evidence alone we could all three be convicted."

She lifted her head and frowned at him. "What does Edmund think about this letter theory?"

"We didn't tell Edmund. We still don't want him to find out about it. He would be crushed. You know how highly he thought of his son Redfield. He must never know. Please don't ask why, just trust me."

"Philander, that's what you told me 10 years ago when all of this first began. You said it would be a little extra money for us and that nobody would be hurt. You told me then to trust you and I did. Now, I'm afraid that I'm going to lose you. I don't want you to go to jail. I don't want you to do anything that would put us in any more danger. Promise me that you won't harm either Alexander or Martin."

Philander frowned and stared at her.

"Promise me that, Philander." She undid her

nightgown and let it fall around her waist. "Then, Philander, I want you to make love to me the way we did when we were first married, so gently and loving and soft. Please Philander, this time I want you to trust me. Promise me, my love."

He promised he wouldn't hurt Martin or Alexander, then they nestled together and it was like it had been 20 years before, soft and easy and gentle and unhurried.

· 8 ·

Saturday morning Spur sent a note to the Knox home for Patricia. Her mother got it and brought it for her unopened. Patricia had slept in that morning and was tousled and sleepy-eyed when her mother came into her room.

"You're getting notes from secret admirers now?" Betsy Knox said with a smile, as she handed her the plain white envelope. "Patricia, I hope you're feeling better this morning."

"Mother, he didn't rape me, he didn't hurt me, he just pawed me a little and grabbed me. Yes, he scared me and made me mad, but that's all. I'm fine." She took the envelope. "I saw Laura Grandifar a couple of days ago. This might be from her. She's back from college in Boston."

"That's nice. I've always liked Laura, not at all like her mother." Betsy waited a moment, decided Patricia wasn't going to open the note until she left, so she waved and went back into the hall.

When the door closed, Patricia opened the envelope and took out the plain white paper. On the bottom she saw the initial S. She read it.

"Patricia: Need to see you today. Those shrimp cocktails at noon or at three at the same place. I'll be there both times. It's important. S."

She stretched and looked down at her bosom. At least he hadn't scratched her or bruised her when he clawed off her chemise. She pushed out of bed and began her morning ritual of washing and combing and getting dressed.

Patricia decided at once to go at noon and meet Spur McCoy. He was an interesting, exciting man, and he was helping her with this terrible situation with her father. She looked at a clock on her dresser. It was nearly eleven o'clock. She put on a green dress that was one of her favorites, and a small off-green hat that went well with the dress. She had an orange for breakfast and found her mother in the solarium.

"I'm off shopping. I think I'll buy a new dress to replace the one that Alexander ruined last night. I'll be fine. I'll have James drive me downtown and then take a cab home."

"He could wait for you."

"No, Mother. I'm not sure where I'll be. I like to poke into little stores and places. I'll be fine, quit worrying about me."

"Who was the note from so early on a

Saturday?''

"Laura, she wanted to get together this next week for some gossiping.''

"That's nice.''

Patricia kissed her mother on the cheek and went out to call James to get the rig ready.

Twenty minutes later she got out in front of a large store on Columbus Avenue and told James to return with the rig to the house. He nodded and drove off. When she was sure he was out of sight, she turned and walked quickly to the area becoming known as Fisherman's Wharf. She found Spur waiting near the small shop that sold the fresh cooked shrimp cocktails in a tomato sauce.

"Good, I hoped that you would come.''

"Tell me what you've been doing,'' she said when they settled on the ends of the piling next to the bay water and nibbled at the shrimp.

"This morning I went down to the police headquarters and checked with Inspector Gale Daniel. He's the one who investigated Redfield's accident. He checked in their card files. They have worked out a system where they make out a 3 x 5 card on each conviction and sometimes each arrest they make and file it by name and cross reference the name by crime.

"He said there was no record of either Oakmarker or Sturgill in their files. He said nothing was new on the crash. I thought it was good to keep in touch with him.''

"What are you doing next?''

"Talking to you. What would they do with the gold scissel once they stole it? Take it out of the mint?''

"Yes, I'd think so, as soon as they could, perhaps the same day. Yes, the same day.''

"From which coins would it be best for them to take the scissel?"

She thought a moment, popped a shrimp and sauce into her mouth and ate it slowly, then frowned. "Probably from the double eagle. It's the thickest and would be easiest to gather up."

Spur nodded as he ate another wooden spoonful of the shrimp. "Good. Now the important part. What I want to do is follow these men after we think they might have stolen some gold. For that I'll need to know when they are scheduled to punch out the double eagles."

Patricia Knox flashed him one of her prettiest smiles, her red hair bouncing. "That is no problem at all. I know everyone at the mint, still have my pass. I often drop in for a visit. I'll go this morning and talk to Helen, the girl at the desk. She used to have a schedule out front."

"How many days a week would they do double eagles?"

"Sometimes once, sometimes none, depending on the supply. The mint produces almost on order from the big banks around the country and the treasury, of course."

They finished the little shrimp cups and stood. "I'll get a cab over to the mint, visit around a little and then come back here and see you."

"Be careful. I'm still a little worried about you doing all of this, but I don't have any other source of information."

"I don't have this red hair for nothing. I can fight with the best of them. In fact, last night I punched out Alexander when he ripped my dress half off me. I'll be fine."

"Alexander, he's the one they want you to marry?"

"He is, but I won't. The bas—" she looked at him quickly.

"The word is bastard, and he must be. I might take a poke at him myself one of these days. You're all right?"

"You sound like my mother. I'm fine. See you back here in an hour. Take a walk along the waterfront, half hour down and half hour back."

She reached over and kissed his cheek, turned and hurried out to the street.

He watched her go, small and bouncing, with that little twitch on her bottom that would always fascinate him even though he would never do anything about it. The lady had been jolted around enough with her true love being murdered, now finding out her parents are thieves and then this suitor trying to rape her.

She was bright and tough and would do all right for herself in the years to come . . . if he could help her get through the next two weeks.

He did take a walk, watching the big ships, both steam and sail, being unloaded. He saw flags of many different nations on the ships. By the time he made it back to the small shop that sold the shrimp snacks, he was late, but Patricia wasn't there either.

It was another half hour before she showed up, rushing along, out of breath and holding on to her small hat. She slumped down on the top of a piling and grinned as she was gasping for breath.

"I got trapped by some good friends who wanted to gossip. I loved it, but I made you wait. I'm sorry."

"I'm used to waiting. What did you find out?" He took her arm and they walked down the wharf.

"They will be punching double eagles Tuesday

and Thursday, so we have two chances. I don't understand how you can follow all three of them?"

"Been thinking about that. Who would be the one most likely to take the gold to someone to melt it down for them?"

"My father is the best metallurgist of the three. But I don't know who would do it."

"Pick two."

"My father and Mr. Jefferson."

"Done. Tuesday afternoon right after work, I'll follow your father, and you tail Mr. Jefferson. We both better have a horse and buggy because they both use them to drive home in, right?"

She nodded. "How will you follow my father?"

"Stay well back, but not lose sight of him. If he's doing nothing wrong he won't even check behind him. Why should he? Oh, what route does he usually take driving home, in case that's where he's going?"

"He always goes the same way, down Market Street to Van Ness, left on Van Ness to California Street and along it to Nob Hill. That's not quite two miles."

"I'll rent a hack and wait for him down from the mint on Market Street. After we've followed both of them, let's meet back at the corner of Market and Van Ness. If we both follow the ones who don't have any gold, or if they don't steal anything Tuesday, we'll try again on Thursday."

Her bright green eyes sparkled. "Yes, we have to find out where they melt down the gold and then sell it, right? This is exciting. I just hope that Daddy isn't the one who handles the gold."

"You sure you want to do this? It could put your father into a lot of trouble."

She blinked and took a long breath. She watched

the ships for a moment, then turned. "Spur McCoy, I know that he's already in more trouble than I can imagine. I just want him out of it and through with it before someone else gets hurt. My prayer now is that he knew nothing about what happened to Redfield. That I could never forgive."

"That we can't guarantee, Patricia. You have to understand that before we go any farther. Even so, I think you're doing the right thing. If this gold theft has been going on as long as we suspect, it's past time it was closed down."

"Yes, but it will be painful." She scrubbed the frown away and smiled at him. "Now come, my treat to you, a guided tour of the city as you have never seen it. I've lived here all my life and I know every nook and cranny. I have a buggy waiting."

The buggy took them up hill and down, through the jabbering thronged clutter and chatter of Chinatown; up the slope past Nob Hill where Patricia shielded her face so no one would recognize her; down the other side and around to the "back side" of San Francisco, out toward the Pacific Ocean that was well off to the west.

"We have people from everywhere on earth here," she said. "I can eat a dinner from a different country every night for almost a year . . . well, not quite, but for many, many days. This is the world's brightest city, except perhaps for Paris where I went once but I was too young to enjoy it."

They rode and looked and came back around the long waterfront with its many wharves and piers and ships, past where the local fishermen brought in their catch and bartered it with the wholesalers and the retailers and some buyers from fine restaurants.

At last the buggy pulled up in front of a small

building on Montgomery Street. She had already paid the hack. The driver tipped his hat and Patricia took Spur into a downstairs eatery and asked him to guess what kind of food they would have there.

"Is it European?"

"Hardly."

"From the Far East?"

She nodded.

"Indian?"

"Yes, East Indian, from Bombay. I've never been here before but my friends say the food is wonderful if you can get used to the seasoning."

There were ten courses, each more mystifying than the last. They did not order, the food and drink simply came and they ate. Rice and curry and meats, and soft deserts, then another kind of meat and more rice and soft breads and hard breads. At last a cold slice of melon. There had been dancers, and musicians played on strange instruments.

They came out after a two hour supper feeling satisfied but a little curious about what they had eaten.

"One of my friends said it is better not to know exactly what it is you eat here."

It was dark outside, the soft San Francisco fog had covered the city with a fuzzy blanket.

"I better get on home. Let's find a hack and I'll drop you off at your hotel, the Almont, isn't it?"

"Yes. So we're set for Tuesday."

"Yes, but no note. Mother was curious this morning."

They found a buggy for hire and headed back to the Almont.

"What will you do tomorrow?" she asked.

"Catch up on my sleep, take a walk, learn more about San Francisco, and try to figure out how they get rid of the second hand gold."

She dropped him off at the hotel, refused to take any money for the cab, and then the rig wheeled away toward Nob Hill.

Upstairs in his hotel, Spur opened the door to his room cautiously, but found it dark inside. He struck a match to light the lamp and saw that no one was there. He wouldn't have been surprised to find Laura Grandifar taking a nap on his bed, but he was just as glad she wasn't. He had some thinking to do on the case.

After an hour of drawing lines and circles and dots on a pad of paper he put it all away and went to bed. Nothing fit, nothing made much sense. Not until he could follow them taking the gold out of the mint and saw where it was processed, and then hopefully, who it was sold to.

What he needed now were witnesses, solid, un-contested, truthful witnesses who would build a strong case to convict the three men of embezzle-ment, and perhaps of murder . . . three murders.

At last he slept.

When he woke up the next morning someone was banging on his door. He came awake in-stantly, reached for his six-gun, then realized he was in San Francisco. He pulled on his pants and went to the door.

When he opened it, Laura Grandifar hurried into the room and closed the door. She wore a short, bright summer dress that came nearly halfway up her ankles and a large straw hat.

"Sleepyhead, time you woke up. I have a big day planned for us. First you get breakfast in your room." She went back to the hall and wheeled in a cart that had a cloth over it. She sat him on the bed, pushed the cart up and pulled off the cloth. There was breakfast for two, bacon and eggs, flapjacks, toast, coffee, fruit juice and a bowl of cut up fresh fruit.

"I knew you hadn't had breakfast yet, so I ordered a few things for us. Now don't worry about putting your shirt on, I've seen you with it off before. I like you that way. Now, we have about fifteen minutes to eat, then our carriage will be here. I have a tour planned. Oh, yes, bring along an extra pair of pants since the ones you wear just might get wet."

Spur laughed softly. "Laura, are you always this impetuous?"

She shook her head. "Heavens, no. Sometimes I get real wild. Just wait, you'll find out. Now let's eat."

Laura was only five-three and about a hundred pounds wet, but she ate more than half of the food on the little cart. They both reached for the last piece of bacon. She beat him to it, then bit it in half and fed him the other part.

"You mentioned a tour? Where?"

"You'll find out. Finish your coffee so we can go. I want you to keep up your strength. It could be a vigorous afternoon for you."

They finished the breakfast. He pulled on some town shoes rather than his boots, and a casual shirt.

"Bring your hat, we'll be in the sun lots, oh, and that spare pair of pants."

He folded a pair of trail pants into a knitted handbag she opened and looked at his six-gun.

"I promise that all of the natives we see today will be friendly. I suppose that you know how to drive a horse."

"That I can handle."

Five minutes later they walked out to the street where a fancy buggy sat. There were seats for two and a box packed full was tied on the small platform on the back. A fine looking black pawed the ground eager to be moving. Spur helped her inside the rig, then he stepped in and picked up the reins.

They drove due west on Greary Road and found little traffic, only an occasional buggy that seemed headed into town with everyone in his Sunday best.

"Now, where are we going?" Spur asked.

"We're going on a picnic to the ocean, to the beach. Just the two of us and the Pacific Ocean and a few trees and lots of sand and the sun is out, there's no fog, and it will be a perfect day."

"You'll probably get sunburned."

"Probably, but it goes away. I want today to be one for both of us to remember for a long time."

"That sounds like you're leaving."

"I am. Mother has arranged for a European tour, and I know she's just hoping she can match me up with a count or at least an earl or some tilted snob over there. We leave in two weeks. It will be dreary, but I will get to see Paris and Rome and London again. So, I might not have another day to myself because of all the dress fittings and material to pick out and all of those things to do before we leave on the train for New York and the boat."

"Such a bothersome fate you're suffering."

"Now you're making fun of me. That's not nice. You be on your best behavior or I won't give you any of the picnic lunch that I had fixed for us. You won't believe what cook prepared. I had her up at six getting things ready. I just prayed that you were still sleeping."

She slid over closer beside him on the buggy seat until her long leg touched his from calf to hip.

"Did you sleep well last night?"

"Yes."

"Alone?"

"Quite alone."

"Good, I wouldn't want to find that you were too worn out to be any fun today."

They drove along the road until they could see the point of land that extended toward Marin county to the north, then swung to the south along the coastline until they came to an expanse of sandy beach and behind it a grove of trees. They could see along the beach for a half mile and there wasn't another living soul to mar the landscape.

"My beach," Laura said. "I come here when I can. Isn't it primitive and wild and just the way God made it."

"Beautiful." He drove the rig off the track of a road and parked it at the very edge of the sand.

"First, we take off our shoes and roll up your pants legs. Then, we look for shells along the beach and wade in the surf. Come on, don't be a fraidy cat. It's fun."

For an hour they walked up and down the beach straying a mile in each direction before they came back with a small bucket filled with shells they had collected. There were sand dollars, nearly round shells with a star imprint on their undersides and no more than a quarter of an inch thick. They saved only the perfect ones.

They found half a dozen different kinds of shells and one small hermit crab with a large borrowed shell on his back as he struggled with it in a small tidal pool around some bare rocks. They left him to wobble along with the stolen shell that was too big for him. He might plan on growing into it.

They sat on the warm sand and watched the never ending waves roll in, saw the sun shining through the combers just before they broke revealing a thinly greenish section of the wave before it crashed down into the water or the sand.

"I've never spent much time at the ocean," Spur said. "In New York we went out to the beach, but the Atlantic is different somehow. It's angry, not gentle and peaceful like this. This roar of the surf could lull a man to sleep."

"Ah ha." Laura jumped up, pulled him with her and hurried back to the buggy. "Now we drive into the woods over there for our picnic in the shade. You're right, I'm getting too much sun. I'll be as red as a shrimp tomorrow."

The woods were a combination of three or four kinds of trees he didn't recognize and a few pines. But they made a cool shade and hid the rig from the road.

They put down two blankets on a spot of grass and then she supervised moving the big box of food to the edge of the blanket.

"Are you hungry yet?" Laura asked.

"Not really. We had a big breakfast."

"Good, it's nap time." Laura stretched out on the blanket on her back and looked at him. "You going to have a nap, too?"

"Wouldn't miss it for the world," Spur said dropping down beside her. He leaned over and kissed her lips. She put her hands on his face, then kissed him back.

"Oh, yes, sometimes a girl likes to be asked."

"I'm asking."

"Asking what, stranger?"

"If you'd like me to take off all of your clothes, or just pull up your skirt."

"Oh, Spur McCoy, you are wicked!"

"And you love it." He kissed her again, then put his hand over one of her breasts and caressed it gently.

"You do have a way about you, Mr. McCoy, but what if someone should see us?"

A man jumped from behind the buggy, a six-gun in his hand and it was pointed directly at Spur McCoy.

"Somebody does see you, pretty lady, and you're going to do exactly what I tell you to do or one of you gets shot!"

· 9 ·

Spur McCoy faced the man with the six-gun and in a second evaluated the situation. He was too far away yet for Spur to try to disarm him. The man was some low life who evidently saw them drive into the woods and figured on an easy robbery.

Spur sat up slowly.

"Hold it right there, mister. Don't move again or you're as good as dead."

He looked at Laura. "Missy, seems you was about to get your skirts lifted. No need to change any of that. Just sit up slow like and open the top of your dress. Go ahead, my trigger finger's getting itchy. You wouldn't want me to shoot this gent in the crotch, now would you?"

"No, no, don't do that," Laura said. She shivered

a moment, then pushed up to a sitting position.

"The buttons, Miss. Open them."

She sighed, looked at Spur again, then began slowly to unbutton the top of her light dress. Soon it was easy to see that she had on only a thin, expensive silk chemise under it.

Spur watched the gunman. The muzzle of the weapon began to drop a little. The man had on old boots, a pair of faded trousers and a patched shirt. His eyes stared at Laura's chest. The man had to move forward before Spur could do anything.

"That's the way, Miss Tits, let me see them. Damn, bet they are big ones."

The buttons were open now and the dress swayed open to show the chemise.

"Yeah, yeah! Gettin' interesting," the gunman said. "Push that dress off your shoulders. Come on."

Laura shrugged, and Spur got the idea she was enjoying this. Had she arranged the gunman as well? No, she would have no idea how to contact a man of this sort.

She pushed the dress off her shoulders and it fell to her waist. Her breasts peaked the soft chemise out dramatically. The material was so thin Spur could almost see through it.

"Now we're getting to it!" the gunman said.

He moved ahead eight or ten feet until he was only a dozen feet away from Spur and Laura. He dropped to his knees in the sandy soil under the trees.

"Now pretty girl, take that other thing off over your head, let's see what your pretty tits look like!"

She smiled fainly at Spur, then crossed her arms, grabbed the bottom of the chemise, pulled it upward and then quickly over her head. The movement made her breasts sway and jiggle delightfully.

A line of saliva ran down the corner of the gunman's mouth as he watched and the muzzle of the gun sagged more toward the ground.

"Oh, damn!" his left hand dropped to his crotch where he rubbed his full erection through his pants. "Yeah, yeah, love them titties. Lean forward, let them hang down. Come on, you got them, show them."

Laura leaned out so her breasts swung down.

"Son of a bitch! Look at them knockers! Beautiful."

The gunman glanced at Spur. "You, move over from her, six feet off the blanket. I'm gonna be using it."

As he said it the gunman waved with the gun, motioning Spur away from Laura to the left. That was when Spur saw that the six-gun was not cocked. He was almost sure that the weapon was an old single-action Colt. It had to be cocked by hand before it would fire. Even if it was a double-action, it would still take some fractions of a second for the man to see Spur move so that he could react, then to pull the trigger and to have the hammer moved back by the trigger action and fall to the ground firing it.

All of this flashed through Spur's mind in an instant. He shifted a little so he could move quickly. He decided either way, it was a gamble worth taking. He bent his legs and steadied his feet on the blanket.

He nodded his head away from the girl. "You want me to move over this way?"

"Yeah, yeah," the gunman said, glancing at him

a second, then moving his stare back at the delicious sight of the bare-breasted girl.

The moment the gunman looked back at Laura, Spur exploded from the near-crouch he was in. He lunged forward, covered half of the 12 feet, hit on his hands and knees and dove forward again at the surprised gunman who furiously tried to fire but the weapon wouldn't. It was single-action after all.

Spur clubbed the weapon from his right hand with his fist, smashing the wrist to one side with one blow. His motion continued and he jolted into the kneeling gunman with his shoulder driving him backward away from the weapon.

Spur landed on the man's chest as the guy lay on his back. Spur drove one fist, then a second into the man's jaw and he cried out in surrender.

"Stop, stop. I'm done. You've caught me."

"I should blow your head off!" Spur bellowed. He hit the man once more, then rolled him over on his stomach and sat on him. He looked at Laura. She sat calmly on the blanket, and one hand gently rubbed her breasts.

"You all right?" he asked.

"Almost. Get rid of him somehow and come over here and help me." She shivered. "All of this excitement has made me just wild and crazy to make love."

"You were about to get shot and raped and you weren't worried about it?"

"I knew you'd do something. Besides, there aren't any bullets in the gun, at least not in the cylinders that show. Chances are he wouldn't have just one round under the hammer."

Spur grabbed the six-gun and checked the cylinders. They were all empty.

The Secret Service agent whacked the attacker

on the side of the head with his palm. "You idiot. If I'd had a weapon of my own you'd be dead by now. Never carry an empty gun. And never point a weapon at someone unless you're ready to kill them." He stood.

"Get up, big bad gunman."

The man stood and Spur realized he was no more than 18 or 20 and half a head shorter than Spur. The big man lashed out with a right fist and hit the kid on the jaw and knocked him down.

"Stay there, bad man. Take off your boots, now."

The man shrugged and pulled them off.

"Now strip out of the rest of your clothes. Right now, right here."

"Don't make me do that."

"Right now, or I'll knock you down again," Spur roared.

The young man stripped, turned his back to them and waited.

"Pick up all of your clothes and walk ahead toward the beach.

Spur ran the man the last 50 yards, right down into the surf.

"Throw your clothes into the next wave and then take off running down the beach. If I ever see you again I'll run you into the police for robbery and attempted rape. You understand?"

"Yes sir."

He threw his boots far out in the surf, then his other clothes and turned and ran.

Laura had been watching from the fringes of the trees. When Spur got back she growled at him. "You are one mean man," she said softly. "I love it the way you made him take off his clothes. His whanger wasn't very big, was it!"

She pulled the dress off over her head and led him back to the blanket.

"Now we are alone and now I want to show you how much I appreciate your rescuing me from that crazy man." She was naked in a moment and sat on the blanket.

"You're next to get naked."

He sat down beside her. "This is too damn public for me. I'm not taking off my clothes."

She shrugged. "I could get the gun and threaten you, but you know that won't work. Hell, I don't care if you take off your clothes or not." She reached over and unbuttoned his fly and worked her hand inside until she found what she wanted and pulled out his erection.

"This is what I want. Fill me up the way you can do so well."

She lay down on the blanket on her back, spread her legs and pulled him over her.

"I like compromises."

He settled between her pure white thighs and drove forward. Buttons scraped sensitive skin but it seemed only to increase her pleasure.

Before he went any farther he reached between their bodies and found the small node of her clitoris and strummed it back and forth.

"Oh, no, don't do that, you shouldn't . . ."

"Why not?"

"Somebody told me it was bad, it could cause all sorts of problems and I'll get sick, and everything."

"Who told you that?"

"My mother, so it must be true."

"It's not true, I'll prove it to you."

He began to move in and out slowly and at the same time rub her clit. Gradually she began to react, her breath came in ragged gasps, then she wailed and at last her hips began to chatter against his and the first tremors darted through her. She screamed in delight. He kept rubbing and the full power of the climax drilled through her, shaking her like a rag doll in a dog's mouth, the spasms jolted her again and again until she at last collapsed in exhaustion.

"Enough!" she said and he stopped his ministrations and lay there listening to her cooling down from the first ever climax she had experienced in her life.

"Oh, damn," she said. "All that poking and never anything like this before. Why the hell didn't some-body tell me?"

"They were all probably so bowled over that they could get your thighs apart that they took what they could get and were totally knocked out by it."

"But I just kept going and going and going."

"The nature of the female animal, unlimited sexual pleasure."

"How about a little of the same for you?" She began to move against him then and tug at him with her internal muscles. Soon he was beyond saving and blasted his load into her willing vessel. He looked around carefully before he eased down on her in his own mini death.

"Not bad, not bad at all," she said, then they both rested, but Spur had his ears listening for any kind of return by the naked rapist, or anyone else. Nobody bothered them.

It was a half hour later that they sat up. She pulled on a pair of men's cut off trousers. She didn't bother with a top. She looked at him. "Come on, let's go get wet."

"You won't need those trousers. Nobody's around."

She kicked off the pants and grabbed his hand and began pulling off his clothes.

"If naked in the ocean is good enough for me, you get to join in," she said. Quickly she stripped him and then they ran for the surf.

They waded in up to their ankles and let a new wave roll up to them.

"Cold!" Spur yelped.

"It just takes a little getting used to." With that Laura dropped his hand and ran into the water, taking high steps. A four foot wave was just about to break on her when she dove neatly through it and came up laughing on the other side.

"Come on, coward!" she called.

Spur growled and ran forward, the icy water stabbing into his skin with every step. A wave rushed at him and he jumped as high as he could but it broke over his head and carried him 20 feet shoreward before he could get his feet on the sandy bottom again. Then he found himself in waist deep water and swam out to where Laura bobbed. He put down his feet but couldn't reach the bottom.

"Isn't this wonderful!" Laura screeched.

A wave roared in at them.

"Hold your breath and duck under it," Laura called just before the wall of water was upon them. At the last minute Spur did as she suggested and felt himself bob up to the surface only a few seconds later. The mighty wave had pushed him less than a foot toward the shore.

Laura swam effortlessly beside him.

"I love to come out here and jump and duck the waves," Laura called over the roar of the surf.

"You must love it, your lips are turning blue," Spur shouted.

"Yes, it's a little early in the summer. With the next wave, wait until just as it breaks, then push off and swim in with it."

He saw her swim up and then stroke for shore just before the wave broke. She went rushing along with the water. He waited for the next wave and tried it, but he had waited too long and thousands of gallons of water broke directly on his body, pushing him under the water into a maelstrom of foam, seaweed, and swirling sand. He felt his shoulder scrape painfully on the sandy bottom and then he aimed for the surface. It had taken him a moment to realize which way was up.

He came to the top of the water sputtering and wheezing. At least now he was in hip deep water. The next wave had crested well outside of his position so when it came to him he pushed off with the surge and swam strongly with overhand strokes until his fingers brushed the bottom and he found himself laying in the sand as the water swept back toward the sea away from him.

"Welcome to your first crash from a wave," Laura said when she ran up and stood beside him. "Did you take on some salt water?"

He looked up at her sleek, naked body with perfect breasts and hips not all that wide and grinned. "It was worth it just to see you looking like a sea sprite or at least a mermaid. Race you to the blanket."

She took off like a long legged sea bird racing along the beach after a sand crab. He clawed to his feet and churned along after her, letting her stay ahead so he could enjoy the sight of her tight little bottom bouncing along.

At the blanket she dug into the food box and came up with two big towels which they used to dry off, then shivered as they lay side by side in the sun. Soon the sun warmed them and she kissed his cheek.

"I'm starved, let's see if that food looks as good now as when cook fixed it."

It did. There was fried chicken, cold now but delicious. Sandwiches made of some kind of fish and chopped pickles and a chopped up egg were unusual, but he decided good. There was enough food for half a young army.

There was a gallon of lemonade, and fresh fruit and two more kind of sandwiches. It looked like the lady had fried a whole chicken that morning at the Grandifar mansion.

To eat, they had moved back to the blanket in the shade. Already Laura had a slight pink cast to her light skin.

"You'll be burned tomorrow," Spur said.

"It's the sun shining off the water." She looked at her breasts. "I'm going to be sunburned where I've never been sunburned before." They both laughed.

They put on their clothes at last, and Spur sat there watching her.

"It's like a ballet, a woman dressing. Did you ever realize that?"

"You must have had a lot of experience watching women dress to be able to say that."

"It's one of my favorite activities." Spur laughed. "Of course, I'd rather like to see a lady take off her clothes."

"Fine as long as the lady is me."

They finished eating what they wanted and walked the seashore hand in hand watching the sun brim the water, then sink slowly into the Pacific Ocean. With dusk, they returned to the buggy and started back to town.

"A perfect day at the beach," Laura said.

Spur reached over and patted one of her breasts gently. "How are you going to explain how you got sunburned on these two spots?"

"I won't. Who is going to see those spots?"

They laughed and set the horse at a faster pace.

At the hotel's side door, Spur stepped down and reached in the buggy to give her a goodbye kiss. It was dark enough by then so no one could recognize her.

"Watch out for those French men," Spur said. "They have some strange ways about them, I've heard."

"I'll watch out. I hope I'll have time to see you again before we go East. I'm going to try to."

He stepped back and she moved the buggy away from the hotel and toward Nob Hill.

At the desk of the Almont hotel, Spur found an envelope with his name on it.

"Came this afternoon," the clerk said.

Spur carried it up to his room, lit the lamp and then tore open the envelope and read the paper.

"Dear Mr. McCoy. We have a place for you on our staff at the U.S. Mint. It isn't a middle management position that I had hoped to find for you, but the committee felt that this job will take advantage of your experience and help fill a vacancy on our staff. We hope to see you promptly at nine, Monday morning, at the mint on Market Street.

"Our usual manner of dress is conservative dark suit, white shirt and tie. Your starting

129

salary will be $15 a week. We hope that is satisfactory. If you wish help in finding some permanent and less expensive living quarters, one of our personnel people will assist you."

The note was signed, "Philander Knox, Director, Management Committee, United States Mint, San Francisco."

Spur McCoy sat down on the bed and grinned. He had his job in the mint. He would have a new source of information, he could see the players at work on an every day basis. Perhaps he would pick up some details about the thefts that he didn't know about yet.

For a moment he wondered if they were worried about the letter that Redfield had written. From what Patricia said, her father certainly had been worried. Evidently he and Jefferson had ordered the young man killed. Certainly Pickering would not have a hand in murdering his own son.

Spur kept the option open that some time he might need to use Pickering to help convict the other two. There was a chance Pickering could be given immunity to prosecution if he would testify against his two partners. The district attorney might have a hard time accepting such an arrangement, but if it was the only way to break this case, Spur was more than willing to give it a try. He'd have to talk to the D.A. first, of course.

Spur found out what the bath arrangements were in the hotel. The second floor had a bathroom that could be reserved and hot water brought up from the basement. He got an eight o'clock time and appeared at that time with two big towels and a robe. The bath was a pleasure.

It had been an interesting day. Laura was a terrific woman. Tomorrow was going to be almost as exciting as today had been.

That night he went to sleep early and was up at six, eager and ready to report to work. He walked the eight blocks to the Mint to burn off a little of the excess energy he felt coursing through his body.

He pushed open the front door and walked up to the guard.

"Yes, Mr. McCoy, you're supposed to report to Mr. Knox's office, he'll give you your introduction and talk to you about your position here. Right this way."

· 10 ·

Philander Knox met Spur at the door of his office and held out his hand.

"Well, McCoy, good to meet you. Come in and sit down. We like to give every new man a small briefing about what we do here and how we do it. I'll tell you some of it and our foreman in the plant will handle the rest."

He launched into a summary of what the mint did, how it functioned, and then came to Spur's job.

"What we want you to do, McCoy, is to supervise the distribution department. One of our people there had to move back East. The job is simply a matter of good business practices. We have orders come in to send so many coins of a certain denomination to a certain place.

"All of our coins go out by registered railway express. I'm sure you won't have any trouble with it. The second man in the department has been there for more than ten years now."

An hour later Knox's tour was over and Spur was handed over to Fred Dexter, the man who should have had the promotion but didn't get it. Dexter was a man in his fifties who smiled a lot, did his work conscientiously, and was simply glad to have a job. Ambition was not one of his character traits.

It wasn't much of a job, and to Spur, it seemed to be one that could easily be eliminated with no loss of function. But he didn't tell them that. He digested what needed to be done there, went through the process with Dexter, and settled into his small office. There were six or eight elements of the job he had to learn and he memorized them quickly, then went to watch the six men in the department verify the count of others from the vaults, and sign off on the individual parts of the shipment.

A supervisor would then check on the number of packaged coins being shipped in the order, sign another voucher that the amount was correct. Just before the coins were nailed shut in small wooden boxes, the number and type of coins was again checked either by Dexter or Spur and again signed off on a declaration voucher in triplicate.

The last witness watched as the box was nailed shut and sealed with an official wax and seal and put in a cardboard box which was addressed.

From there that shipment, together with others slated to go out that day, would be sent by wagon to the dock where the boxes would be escorted on board the ferry boat to the railway express car at Oakland where again the signing off process would take place with the bonded express agent.

About three o'clock, Spur was asked by the young woman from the front desk, Helen, to come to Superintendent Jefferson's office. He wanted a word with Spur. Spur wondered what this was about but did not ask the young girl who still must remember how he blurted out Redfield's name that first day.

He knocked on the big oak door, then pushed it open and went into the superintendent's office.

Jefferson looked up from his desk, now scattered with papers.

"Yes, McCoy. How is it going, getting settled into your new position?"

"Yes, sir. It is interesting work, and I'm sure I'm going to like it just fine."

"Good, good. If you have any real problems, come straight to me. I know you usually report to Mr. Knox, but we don't stand that much on formal ceremony around here. Now, there was one more thing. I try to have each new management person to the house for supper. Would you be free for this evening? Our cook has prepared an especially nice repast for you."

"Yes, of course. I will be honored to take supper with you."

"Fine, about eight at my residence. Helen will tell you how to find it. We'll expect you then."

He went out and talked to Helen who told him the address. "It's the big white house with the dormer windows on the third floor. I'm sure you'll be able to find it."

She smiled and gave him the piece of paper with the address and he went back to his office. For a moment he wondered if it was a mistake getting a job here. Certainly it would make it easier for him in certain aspects, but what would happen when he needed to be gone for a whole day or when the case progressed. He shrugged. By that time he would simply quit and fade away from the mint itself. But he would be close around.

A short distance down the hall, Martin Jefferson watched the door close behind young McCoy and preened his moustache, then stroked his beard. He put down his eyeglasses on the desk and rubbed his eyes. There was something about McCoy that he didn't like, a feeling more than anything, as if the man couldn't be trusted. But he had the connection to the Secretary of the Treasury William A. Richardson. It was best not to cross that man. He had heard stories of his swift and certain retaliation of men he didn't like or who had hurt him as he climbed the political ladder in the East.

Jefferson shrugged it off. He would watch McCoy closely. He could always be let out due to personnel changes that would have no reflection on character, job performance or personality. Yes, that would keep the superintendent from any trouble with the Secretary of the Treasury.

He looked back at the sheet of paper on his desk he had covered when McCoy came in the room. He had one employee who was a master at reading material upside down and backward. He had once been a printer it turned out.

Jefferson gazed at the figures on the pad. It might be time. Lucinda was not a concern now. Alexander ruined his chances to marry Patricia. Wilma would always make out fine by herself.

Perhaps Mexico City was the answer. He looked down at the schedule again.

They were due to punch out double eagles Tuesday and Thursday. He could also tell Oakmarker and Sturgill that he wanted ten pounds a day from any of the scissel. That would be possible.

Ten pounds a day would net him about $15,000. He had about $20,000 in gold credits in the Banco de Mexico in Mexico City, and he could withdraw almost $50,000 from the First San Francisco Bank. That would be enough to live on comfortably for the rest of his life in Mexico, with Bonita.

He threw the pencil across the room. That damn Redfield! He had had a secure future here. He had lived off the Operation for the past ten years. Why did he get so high and mighty all of a sudden? They would never know. That damn letter could produce a disaster. The sooner the better if he was going to try to get away before this thing blew up in his face.

He checked his gold pocket watch. Nearly 11:00. He picked up his briefcase and hat and headed for the door.

"Helen, I have a meeting with the mayor for a light dinner. I should be back around three. Refer any emergencies to Mr. Pickering."

"Yes, Mr. Jefferson."

He went around the building to his buggy and drove down Market Street toward the city hall, then turned off through smaller streets and worked generally south to a street of neat, single family houses. Jefferson drove in the alley and stopped behind the sixth house down from the street. He tied the horse and hurried into the rear door of the house.

Standing in the kitchen waiting for him was Bonita. She had fixed her long black hair differently, and wore a white peasant blouse with a deep scoop neckline. She held out her arms.

Bonita was 22 years old, had never been married and had been his mistress since she was 17 and he had seen her walking down the street one sunny day. He talked with her, bought her supper, and then took her to a hotel that evening where they made passionate love until midnight.

He bought this house for her and had been with her twice a week ever since. Jefferson kissed her, then bent and kissed her full breasts straining against the soft cotton material. She wore no other garment beneath it.

Jefferson lifted up and kissed her soft lips again.

"Mexico City," he said softly. "In two weeks, we go to Mexico City."

Bonita squealed in delight.

"Truly? We are going? You are leaving the others here and just us are going?"

"Yes, just us, in Mexico City for the rest of our lives, where we will live like kings, and make love every day, and eat the best foods and have wines and music and dance and enjoy ourselves as only the very rich can."

Bonita laughed and kissed him passionately, then began a saucy, sexy little Mexican dance, pulling off clothes as she did and retreating step by step toward the bedroom. Jefferson followed, his eyes gleaming at the beauty of her, at her softly rounded body, slender and perfect with long lean legs that set his blood on fire.

By the time she got to the bedroom door, she wore only sandals. She kicked them off, turned and pushed her round bottom at him and laughed as she ran into the bedroom.

An hour later they lay in each other's arms, spent and glowing with satisfaction. Bonita lifted and leaned against one elbow.

"We will have children, many *niños*, yes?"

Jefferson reached out and fondled her saucy big breasts. He tweaked her nipple and nodded. "Three *niños*, no more. *Sí*?"

"*Sí*, you make Bonita so happy. Most happy girl in whole world!" She kissed him, then rolled on top of his naked body and humped her hips at him a dozen times. "Make love whenever you want to."

He laughed and pulled her back beside him. "It will be fine in Mexico City. No problems, plenty of money, and no federal agents looking for me down there. Two weeks."

Bonita's face broke into a frown. "What to take with me?"

"Nothing, just a small bag. We'll buy everything new in Mexico City. We'll get a boat going down the coast to Acapulco, then take a carriage over the mountains to the big town."

"*Es muy hermosa, Ciudad Mexico*, most beautiful city in the world. You will love Mexico City!"

"I sure as hell will, Bonita. Love mostly not having to look over my shoulder all the time to see if John Law is there. Sit up and make them tits dance for me."

Bonita giggled, sat up and twitched her shoulders just right that set her breasts in a little dance. He laughed, then bent and kissed them both, and slid out of the bed.

"Got to get back to work. Twice is enough for me these days, don't want to drag around at the mint or everyone will know I've been out messing around." He laughed, pulled on his clothes and checked his tie to be sure it was neat.

Bonita lay on the bed again, her legs spread wide, her pink slot winking at him.

"Bonita you are a sexy lady, but I got no more time right now. Damn party at home tonight and everything." He bent and sucked one of her breasts into his mouth, chewed a minute, then shook his head and went to he door. "Got to get out of here now, Bonita, pretty lady, or I'll be here all afternoon."

Twenty minutes later back at the mint, he asked Helen if there had been any problems. She shook her head. He continued to his office and went back to trying to figure out a way to get a larger number of coins cut out of the various thicknesses of rolls of gold for the gold coins.

Knox, his metal specialist, said it couldn't be done. If the coins went any closer together there would start to be force lines and stress lines inside the coins, and it could show through on the faces of the coins after striking. He would devise a new pattern and see what Knox thought of it. Eventually, they would have to strike some blanks and send them to Washington and see what the experts decided would be best.

But did he have to? Two weeks! Yes, he would function as normally as ever. He would make advance plans, lay out future projects, worry about promotions and personnel matters. All would be entirely normal. He would even write a letter asking the director to come for a visit.

But all the time he would be laying out detailed plans to leave the country . . . with Bonita. He actually cared nothing for his wife of nearly 25 years. They had grown apart. Alexander had been a great disappointment. He did regret Lucinda, but she had been on the borderline for so long. She was safe and well cared for now.

Wilma would take care of her. Wilma would have the house and all of her jewels and furs. She would not want. Her lifestyle might change a little, but knowing Wilma she would be hooked up with a new man supporting her within three months.

Now, back to work. He went through the routines that made up his job, even talked with Edmund Pickering a moment, but avoided Philander Knox. He was still furious about the confrontation with Alex and Patricia. That would pass. Perhaps not in two weeks. If not, then Philander and Edmund just might be left here holding down the mint and the record of theft. In that case, both of them would be looking at long prison terms.

When five o'clock came, Martin Jefferson checked his calender and schedule. Tuesday and Thursday were the double eagle days. He'd make it Tuesday, then the following week it would be every day! Yes, what a coup that would be!

He said good night to the night guard as he left, took his briefcase, and walked out the front door and waited until the guard locked it behind him. Now home and the small dinner party. He was sure that Wilma had invited someone else for this evening besides the new man, Spur McCoy. She never told him. He would put up with it. Only two more weeks.

Three hours later, Jefferson and three other men were enjoying chilled glasses of some local California wine in the drawing room. One of the men was a portly banker with a loud voice, the second one was a slender, tall industrialist and the third was Spur McCoy.

"This ship builder wanted to borrow $100,000 from the bank to build a fleet of fishing ships," the banker was saying. "He said fishing would be a big industry very soon and there was a need for such 60-foot fishing boats. But, he said he had no collateral other than his knowledge of boat building and fishing."

"So I bet that you didn't loan him the money," Jefferson said.

"Oh, I did. That was 10 years ago. Today he has a fishing fleet of over 40 boats, and he's worth more than three-million dollars. I still loan him money."

They all laughed.

A moment later a small Chinese man dressed as a butler came to the door.

"Dinner is served, gentlemen," he said in clear, unaccented English. The men put down their glasses and followed Jefferson into the dining room.

It was 40-feet long, with a 20-foot table in the center of the room and sleek cherrywood chairs matching the polished surface of the table. It was graced by a linen cloth and more than two dozen candles burning in elaborate silver candlesticks.

The four women at the near side of the room moved to their places at the table. Name tags were near the napkin at each place and the men found their spots. Spur realized he was not the odd man, but he had no idea who the fourth woman was. He found his name on the hostess's right and held her chair. The places were grouped in conversational distance at the near end of the long table.

Spur held Wilma Jefferson's chair and smiled at her. He had met her briefly when he arrived.

"Thank you so much for having me," Spur said. "It's always a little hard starting in a new town this way."

"Dear boy, that's no problem. If you ever need a nice girl to escort to some fuction, I have more than a dozen that I can recommend. Some, of course, I endorse more than others, I assure you." She laughed lightly.

Spur was aware that Mrs. Jefferson was watching him closely and seemed interested.

"I understand you're from Washington D.C.," the lady on his other side said to Spur. He turned to her and found Betsy Knox whom he had been introduced to earlier.

She smiled at him. "You might not remember, I'm Betsy Knox. I know how it is meeting a group of strangers all at once."

"Yes, Mrs. Knox. You're right, I spent two years in Washington where I was an aide to a U.S. Senator."

"How exciting. Did you get to meet the president and everything?"

"Not quite everything, but I have met President Grant. He's an interesting man, all general sometimes, and more like a local politician at others."

"What brings you West, Mr. McCoy?" the industrialist asked.

"Horace Greeley, I would guess," Spur said.

"Who?" Thelma Mae Pickering asked.

The banker nodded. "Yes, that journalist, the newspaper man who said, 'Go West, young man, go West.' I imagine that has brought a lot of people West, and we need a whole lot more out here. We've got a whole half the nation to populate, and sometimes it seems it's moving too slowly."

"Has the transcontinental train helped?" Spur

asked.

That led to a ten minutes speech by the Industrialist, who said he still had some of the original stock in the Central Pacific Railroad. It was going to make him rich beyond his dreams one of these days.

After the meal, Spur couldn't remember what they had eaten. It was good and well prepared but he had been almost constantly talking to Wilma Jefferson. Twice he had felt her stocking foot rub along his leg.

He looked up at her and she smiled. "Spur, may I call you that? You see, I for one believe that life is so short, that we have to take our pleasures where and when we can find them." She said it softly so only he could hear, and again she moved her foot along his leg.

Spur had mumbled something and saw a hint of a flush at the woman's throat.

After the meal, the men went to the den for cigars and brandy and the women vanished into another room. Spur was ready to go when Wilma Jefferson motioned to him and stepped into a small room off the entrance. He moved there and she closed the door and came up to him.

One lamp burned and Wilma stood so close she almost touched him.

"Spur McCoy, I meant that about taking our pleasures." She reached up and kissed his lips and washed them with her tongue. Her hand came up and rested on his crotch rubbing around gently. She held the kiss as she found his hand and brought it up between them to rest on the generous portion of her exposed breasts.

She ended the kiss and watched him.

"Does this shock you, Spur McCoy?"

"Surprise, but not shock." He slid his hand under her dress top until he cupped one of her breasts and squeezed it. "I appreciate a good woman who appreciates her body and knows what she wants."

"Good, tomorrow night in your hotel room #24 at the Almont. Leave the door unlocked. I'll be there about ten." She moved away from him, went out another door and motioned for him to go back to the hall.

He did, said goodnight to Martin Jefferson just as the banker was leaving, and walked with him out to the front of the house.

A young man hurried up to him. "Mr. McCoy. I'm to drive you back to your hotel or anywhere else you want to go. The rig is right over here."

That night, Spur lay in the darkness of his room considering the situation. Was Mrs. Jefferson simply a loose woman who enjoyed younger men, or was she testing him, trying to find out if he was more than he appeared to be? The Washington D.C. reference had made Martin look at him quickly again. He already knew whatever Spur had said this evening, but it may have been he was a bit sensitive about the nation's capital. Was it because of the letter that had been written?

He wasn't sure. Tomorrow, after work, he hoped to fill in a few holes such as finding out who took the gold to be remelted and sold. Once he knew that, he could move quickly. He considered that observation. Anyone who would deal in scissel would understand at once where it came from. It would be a criminal connection, and the ones involved might simply refuse to admit any knowledge of such an operation. If so, it would be harder, but not impossible.

That's when he would turn to Edmund Pickering.

An hour later, Spur was still mentally working on the case when he went to sleep.

· 11 ·

The next day at work in the mint, Spur made two trips through the cutting room where the big presses punched out the double eagle silver dollars.

He talked with Ben Oakmarker who worked near the big machine and picked up the scissel. He could detect no nervousness by the man. Spur wandered on through the receiving department, told Nance Sturgill who he was, and that he was becoming more familiar with the whole operation. Again he could see no sweating or worry on the worker's brow.

So much for short stopping any theft. He really didn't want to do that anyway.

The day dragged. It was afternoon before he

realized he hadn't rented a buggy to use to follow Philander Knox. He couldn't just trust to luck that there would be an empty one driving past exactly when he needed it. He was about to start worrying about it when Helen came in with a note in an envelope.

Inside he saw the message with relief.

"Hear you're working at the Mint now. Good. But that means you can't rent a hack for tonight. I'm ready. I will have a cab waiting for you a half block downtown from the mint on Market Street. Just tell the driver your name and you're set to go."

There was no signature. He folded the note twice and put it in his shirt pocket. Two hours to wait.

It was just after five that afternoon when Spur ran across Market Street and then walked slowly toward a buggy he saw parked about where Patricia said it would be. He looked at the driver.

"This cab waiting for McCoy?"

"Yes sir," the driver said waking up with a start.

Spur climbed in. "Hold it right here. We'll be following another rig, so I don't want you too close to it, understand?"

"Yes sir. I've done some following before, indeed I have. Stay close enough to keep the rig in sight and follow it, but not to lose it if it shoots up an alley."

"Right."

Spur sat there watching behind them. He saw two buggies come out of the lane beside the mint. They went in different directions. He prayed that the one coming downtown was Knox.

Spur scrunched down in the seat as the other

buggy rolled past 15 feet away. Philander Knox sat behind a sleek gray with the reins in his hands.

"That's the one, with the gray horse. Keep up with him."

The driver pulled out into the street where there were only an occasional buggy and a freight wagon here and there. They followed the rig easily from about 50 yards behind but nearer to the boardwalk.

When Knox turned down Van Ness Avenue, Spur's driver made the same turn and slowed a little. There was more traffic here and they came to within 25 yards of the other buggy. They went several blocks this time to California Street and turned to the right. A block and a half later, the buggy turned into a driveway in the Nob Hill section of town and vanished behind a three story fancy residence.

"Keep going straight ahead, driver, and go back to Van Ness and Market. We may have to do some more waiting."

"I'm gonna charge you for it, sir."

"Yes, I know. I'll need a written receipt for the charges."

"Sounds like you're a businessman," the driver said and reached in his pocket for a scrap of paper and a stub pencil.

They waited for a half hour on Market and then a buggy pulled up behind them and stopped. Spur was out of the rig in a moment and walked to the other cab. Patricia sat in the back with a large floppy hat covering her face. When he was sure who it was, he leaned in.

"So?"

"He must have had it in his briefcase. He took the case with him when he went in the back door. I have the address and name of the place where he went. It's in the light industrial section and the business looks like a metal shop of some kind."

"Good, this is the vital link. We don't really need to know who buys the gold. Once it's melted down we can't tie it to the mint, so we have what we need there."

He paid his cab and let him go.

"Show me where the place is, I want to know exactly. I might need to get down there in a rush one of these days."

They drove past the front of the establishment Patricia had determined was what they were looking for by watching Jefferson enter the alley entrance of the shop. It was called Halverson's Metal Shop. Spur burned the name and location into his memory, then they headed back toward his hotel.

"You've done good work tonight, Patricia. We're learning more about how they operate and who they deal with."

They worked back toward the Almont and Spur turned to her in the dusk of the summer evening. "What's Mrs. Jefferson like? You must know her pretty well."

"Oh, do I! Sometimes she is wild. She drinks too much. She is the social wheel of the three women in our little management group, dragging the other two along. She is dictatorial, loves to have her own way. She . . . she has a roving eye. I know for a fact that she had an affair with our driver. Our driver!"

"I was at her place for supper last night," Spur said. "Evidently, some new employees get this treatment. It was a small party. She seemed quite nice."

Patty scowled. "Don't let that fool you, she's a tiger."

Spur got out of the rig a half block from the hotel as was their usual method, thanked Patricia and walked up the street. He found a small shop where he could buy some spirits and picked out a bottle of whiskey and one of cherry brandy. He might as well be ready.

In the room, he knew there was a pitcher of water and he took the liberty of getting two water glasses from the dining room and taking them upstairs with him.

She wasn't due until 10 that evening, but with Wilma Jefferson he guessed that almost anything was possible.

He worked over some notes he'd taken on the case, but put all that away early and settled down with a magazine by nine o'clock.

A knock sounded on his door at 9:15 and he opened it to find Wilma Jefferson dressed in the latest fashion and with a fortune in diamonds gracing her ears, neck and fingers.

"I'm a little early," she said looking around at the room. "Good, no one else is here. I wasn't sure." She came in and he closed the door and locked it.

"You make sure of things, I like that." She saw the two bottles and the glasses on the small dresser and went over. "Oh, you haven't started yet. I'm afraid that I'm ahead of you. Make me a drink with some water and whiskey, I'm a little past the brandy stage."

She sat down on the bed and giggled. "I haven't been in a man's hotel room for . . . for years. It's so simple and stark."

She took the glass and sipped at it. "Good," she said and drained half of it.

"Last night, I was a little worked up. Know what I mean? I might have said some things. . . ." She shook her head. "Oh, hell, I even fondled your crotch and you grabbed my boobies."

Spur lifted his own drink and grinned. "A lady can always change her mind. You probably think that I'm too young, too inexperienced."

She shook her head. "Hell, no! I like young men. With your looks you can get any girl you want." She paused and frowned. "I had a girl. You could have got her easy but she's . . . she's away right now."

She tossed down the rest of the drink and held out her glass.

"You look better with your tie off. Let's take your shirt off too, right after you get me another drink."

He poured her another drink, a water glass almost full of whiskey with just a dash of water. She took it, drank some and nodded. "Now that is a real whiskey and water."

Spur sat down beside her on the bed, took the glass from her hand and put it on the dresser. Then he took off his shirt. She put her hands on his chest and laughed.

"Oh, yeah, a hairy chest. Love hairy chests. You hairy anywhere else?" She patted his crotch.

He patted her breasts and worked at the buttons and snaps. She helped him and a minute later her dress was open and her large breasts surged out. They were matronly, as were her hips and waist.

Wilma giggled. "Them slips of young girls don't have no tits at all these days. A man likes some tits he can get his teeth into, right, Spur? Hey, I bet you got a good spur in those pants of yours. You gonna show me your spur, Spur?"

"Soon." He gave her back her drink and she sipped at it, then finished it and he put the glass on the dresser.

She fell backwards on the bed and looked at him. "You in a hurry? You better be in a hurry if you want any help from me, 'cause I been drinking."

"You said your daughter had gone away. Will she be back soon?"

"Soon. She's in a private place, a hospital kind of place. I don't like to talk about it."

"Oh, I didn't know she was sick, I'm sorry."

"Not really sick, just not reliable. A little bit mixed up in the head. You know?"

Wilma sat up with effort and pulled her dress off over her head. She tried to put it on the chair but it fell to the floor.

"Hell, don't matter, I'll buy a new one. Got money. We got lots of money, now."

Her chemise flew off, and petticoats, and then a frilly kind of silk panties. She now lay there naked.

"Spur, let's see your spur," she said.

Spur kicked out of his pants and shorts and knelt before her. Her plump, naked body hadn't coaxed him into an erection yet, but her knowing hands did it quickly. She kissed his shaft's purple tip and then nodded.

"Goddamn, now there is a cock worth having. Do me Spur, quick, before I pass out."

Spur hadn't been with a cushiony woman for a long time. He had forgotten the differences. Soft and comfortable. No sharp bones, no hidden hard places, all soft and easy and smooth.

Almost before he knew it, he had climaxed and her arms closed around him like a cowpuncher's lariat binding him tightly.

"Why you get me talking about Lucinda? Love that little girl. Maybe next year we can take her out of that place. For her own good. It's for her own good, she knows that. Oh, damn, I don't want to talk about her."

She let go of him, pushed him away and rolled over and cried into his pillow. It was three or four minutes before she stopped crying and sat up, her huge breasts rolling and bouncing.

"You got anything to drink in here?"

He made her another drink, this one half-and-half, and she gulped at it without comment.

"You've always had money? Old family money from your parents?"

"Hell, no! Dirt poor, most of my life. Ten years we've had some money. More now. Money makes money. Society column in the papers, everything. Money makes friends, too. You're my friend. You poked me good. I felt you. Nice. Sweet and nice. I think I want another drink."

Spur realized if she passed out he'd never get her dressed and into a cab to go home. That could be a problem with the people at the mint. He made her a drink, but it was almost all water. She sipped it, shook her head.

"Don't even taste good anymore. "Did we connect?"

"Twice, don't you remember?"

"No."

"You were about ready to get dressed. Can you do that?"

"Damn right. I took 'em off, I can put 'em back on."

As it turned out he had to help her. It was nearly a half-hour later that he got her to the door. She insisted that she could get back to the lobby and to her rig.

He watched her weave down the hall, then held his breath as she went down the steps one at a time. She was halfway down when a large black man came to her aid. He said something about the rig was right outside the door, and Spur closed his own door gently and locked it.

Now what the hell had that been all about. He'd have to ask Patricia about Lucinda again. From what Patricia had said before, the girl was crazy. Maybe she wasn't quite that bad off after all.

He checked his pocket watch that lay on the dresser. A little after 11:00. He wasn't sure what he was going to do tomorrow. Was there anything else he could learn by being at the mint? Spur decided to stay there another day and see what happened.

Then it would be time to investigate the Halverson Metal shop. There was a chance he would learn nothing there. What he had to be certain about was that he didn't tip off this Halverson that somebody was asking questions about Martin Jefferson and his gold scissel.

A long way downtown toward the south, where the houses got smaller, Ben Oakmarker sat in his parlor with his wife and listened to music on one of the new fangled cylinder gramophones. He'd had four beers since supper and he was in a foul mood. Mostly he remembered the gold he had signed off on today. Sure, two percent of 100 pounds was only two pounds, but that two pounds of pure gold was worth more than $660. That was more than three times his salary for the whole year.

On a run of 500 pounds of scissel from them double eagles the boss took off 10 pounds, over $3,000 worth of gold. And the bastard did it once a week. Once, he did it twice in one week. Ben opened another beer and glared at his wife, then at the music box.

Hell, Jefferson could afford to have a whole orchestra come and sit in his big house and play live music for his guests. For taking the risk of going to jail, what did Ben Oakmarker get? He got an extra $10 a week. Big deal! Damn, he should tell them that he had to have $200 a month or he wouldn't play their games anymore.

"Without me they couldn't do it!" he said out loud. His wife looked over and shushed him. She loved that damn music box thing. He spent $20 buying it. That was damn near a whole month's pay for his regular job.

How did the three bastards get away with it? How? He let them, that's how. Look how rich all three of them were. He'd walked past their big houses, servants, a butler, a driver and three or four carriages, a summer place. Damn, he'd done it all for them.

What could they say if he walked into Mr. Jefferson's office? He paused in his alcoholic mental ramblings. No, make that he'd walk into *Jefferson's* office and just damn well tell the robber that there wasn't going to be any more gold for him. No more damn two percent. No more unless Ben Oakmarker got half of it.

He'd go right on signing off the two percent, but out of every ten pounds they sold, Ben would get his share. Half! That would be about $1,500. Yeah,

$1,500 a week. Then he could really do things. Hell, he'd buy a new house, and buy a carriage instead of just a damn little buggy, and he'd get great furniture, and buy Ceila all the pretty, fancy dresses and underthings she wanted.

"Yeah, I'd like that," Ben said out loud. Ceila looked at him and smiled.

Ben remembered back when it started. Christ, did he remember! He'd been about 19 at the time and this was his first really good job. He'd been working for two months when Mr. Jefferson stopped by in the cutting room one day and talked with him. That night after work they went to a saloon and sat at a back table and talked in low voices.

Mr. Jefferson said there was a way that Ben could earn five dollars more every week. That would almost double his pay. He had been alert at once, interested, but wondering if it could be honest. He listened.

The first thing Jefferson did was push a twenty-dollar gold piece across the small table.

"Take it, Ben, it's yours. Just for talking to me. If you decide you don't want to work with me on this, fine. You'll have to change jobs, but that won't affect your status here at the mint. I want to make sure you understand that.

"On the other hand, it's a way that you can do me a small favor probably once a week, and when your pay envelope comes, there will be an extra five dollars for you each week. Now that's a lot of money, Ben, more than $260 a year!

"Just think what you could do with money like that, Ben. Hell, you could marry that sweet little Ceila you been squiring around town."

"Mr. Jefferson . . . it sounds great . . . but just

what would I have to do? I don't want to do nothing wrong or anything."

Jefferson watched him carefully. "Ben, you come from a poor family. Nothing wrong with that, but it's a lot more fun and life is a lot easier if you have a little more money. I'm not saying you'll be rich, but it will be easier for Ceila. She can have a woman in once a week to clean and wash and do those things. She can have help with the children when they come.

"Ben, all I want you to do is watch Nance Sturgill weigh in the scissel you take him in the boxes. On certain batches, like the ones from the double eagles, you'll sign off that all of it's there when a small part will be missing. That part will come to me and from it you'll get your extra five dollars every week."

Ben thought about it for a minute then looked up over the beer he had been sipping at.

"Then we're . . . we're taking some of the gold from the mint. We're *actually stealing* gold from the United States Mint!"

He said the words softly, for all of his emphasis, and stared up in amazement.

"Just a little, Ben, they'll never miss it. The way we fix the weigh-in records nobody will ever know. It's foolproof, there is no way that anyone can find out about it."

Jefferson talked with Ben for another hour, and at last the young man nodded. He agreed to do what his boss wanted him to. And Nance was in on it, too. Hell, he'd take the chance. If anything happened, he could quit and run up north into the Oregon woods and nobody would ever find him.

Ben thought about the first night in the saloon and now shook his head. He should have charged more from the start. Hell, without him none of them would make a nickel from the gold. If he didn't sign the weigh slip . . . He grinned.

"Oh, damn," he said out loud.

The music had stopped and Ceila looked over and laughed at him, then went to see that the three kids were all sleeping.

"Yeah, damn right," he said softly.

He was going to challenge them. He was going to tell Jefferson that he was not going to sign off the weigh slips anymore, unless he got half of the gold. He rubbed his forehead to ease his stabbing headache for a moment. It hurt his head when he thought so much. Maybe half the gold was too much. Yes, he shouldn't push too hard. He'd tell them he wanted $200 a week. Yes, that was reasonable. With $200 he could do what he wanted to without running the risk of being caught.

Ben knew he wasn't as smart as the managers. He'd never been through much school. His parents had moved around a lot. But he did graduate from the eighth grade. He was near fifteen before he did it, but he stayed in school. They had just come to San Francisco then.

He got a job the next year in a fish house, packing fresh fish in ice they brought down from the mountains. It was cold, miserable work but he did it for a year and gave every penny he earned to his father.

After a year, he realized that he was working 10 hours a day, six days a week, but his father wasn't working at all. His old man sat around the house and drank cheap wine. That was all he did. The money Ben brought home bought his dad his wine and there was a little left over to buy food at the market.

The next day, Ben packed his few clothes in a box and left home. For two weeks he lived in an abandoned house, then the owners came and ran him out. He got a better job in the fish market, filleting out fish for the new restaurants that were opening in San Francisco.

He was making twice as much as when he started. He bought some clothes and got a spot at a boarding house so he wouldn't have to cook.

Then, when he was 17, he got a job driving a rig for a freight outfit and started earning a man's wages. It was about then that he met Ceila and began courting her. She was so pretty it made him hurt. He knew she was too good for him, but by some miracle she had liked him more than the four other young men who had courted her.

They had been courting a year and he wanted to get married. Ceila was only 16, but she said she was ready. Her father didn't think so. He ran a store but wouldn't give Ben a job. He said any man worth his salt could find his own job, and a better one than driving a damn wagon.

Six months later, Ben heard they were looking for help at the mint and he rushed out there and got the job. He'd been there ever since. But he wasn't going to let Jefferson and Pickering and Knox get any richer from his labors.

"Hell, they need me, and since they need me, they'll pay me more." He said it out loud.

Ceila came back in the room, her dark brown hair flying around her neck and shoulders, bright brown eyes sparkling. She caught his arm and urged him toward the bedroom.

He stopped and looked at her.

She opened the buttons on her dress front.

"Ben Oakmarker, you come with me. I've got

something you want and can't resist. Besides, you're just drunk enough that you'll slow down enough so a girl can get some pleasure as well. It won't be a wham bang, thank you Ceila. I declare, sometimes you shoot faster than a rabbit.

"I like it when you're nice and slow and really have to work to get it going." She took his hand and pushed it inside her dress top and under her cotton chemise on her breasts.

"Oh, goddamn!" Ben said.

He tried to kiss his wife, missed, and she giggled and led him into the bedroom. She knew he was just drunk enough, and would be so slow she could enjoy before he went all soft.

Ceila grinned. It was going to be one marvelous night for her. She didn't understand what Ben had been mumbling about, but probably something at work. She was secure, and happy, fulfilled and watching her babies grow up. Besides, right now she was going to get poked for half the night. Ceila laughed seductively and pulled Ben into the bedroom and closed the door.

· 12 ·

After she left Spur at the hotel, Patricia turned the buggy around and drove back toward her parents' big house on Nob Hill. She often drove the rig herself, it was much more interesting than sitting in back, and it gave her a lot more control of her movements. Tonight she didn't want the family driver knowing where she had been and who she had followed. It could get back to her father, and then to Jefferson.

She turned onto California Street a half block from her house in the Nob Hill section and heard a buggy coming up behind her. She paid no attention, but all at once it was beside her and crowding her horse against the curb to a stop. She looked at the other buggy but couldn't see the driver.

She sensed someone at her left. When she looked, someone grabbed her, put his hand over her mouth and hauled her out of the buggy. She tried to flail at him with her hands but a thin piece of rope was slipped around her and cinched tight, fastening her arms to her sides.

The man then hoisted her over his shoulder and hurried around her rig to the other one, dropped her in the back and quickly tied a soft cloth around her mouth so she couldn't scream, couldn't even talk! She was terrified. What was happening? Someone had abducted her. Why? The man in the dark clothes and mask over his face now tied her feet together with a piece of cloth and left her. He hadn't said a word.

Then he got into the front of the rig, slapped the reins on the back of the horse and the rig continued downhill, turning left to Bay Street, and continuing around the bay to the left.

She could see almost nothing. Carefully she pushed up until she could look out the side of the buggy. They were near the harbor and moving west. Where, for goodness sakes, were they going?

Five minutes later, the rig came to a stop. The same man came and bound a black cloth around her eyes, then lifted her from the rig and carried her over his shoulder down some steps. Soon she sensed that they were on some kind of a dock because it moved as the man walked.

There were some whispered words, then she was carried again as she felt the man step up and then down. Now she could feel the rocking of a small boat they must be on. The man carrying her stepped down again and at last lay her on a bunk or a small bed of some sort.

Her captor had not said a word. She struggled against the bonds but gentle hands stopped her. She tried to speak but the gag cut it off. A moment later the man left her and she heard a door or partition of some sort close, then she was alone.

She heard an engine start. It made considerable noise, and soon she sensed the small ship leave the dock and the engine speeded up as the craft moved out into the bay.

For several minutes she heard nothing new. Then the partition opened and someone came back in the place where she was.

"Don't be afraid, I won't hurt you," a voice whispered. She didn't recognize the sound of the man's voice. A man, yes, but that was all. Why was he whispering?

Now she could feel the pull of the bay waters and the tides on the boat. Where could they be going? Down the bay? No, they had turned left and moved north and west. Across the bay to Marin county, the wild beautiful section just north across the neck of the bay where it emptied into the ocean? Possible. But why? And who?

For just a moment she realized that no one would miss her at home for hours. She told her mother she wasn't sure when she would be back when she left with the buggy. Her mother had told her she should take the driver anytime at night, but she had said this time that was impossible.

"Don't worry, I'll be home as soon as I can. I'll be fine. Just don't worry about me."

Now those words seemed hollow and even dangerous. Tears threatened to come but the red-head beat them back under the blindfold. Why wouldn't he let her at least see where they were?

The sound of the engine picked up and the boat

seemed to struggle a little harder to overcome the tide. She had no idea if it was coming in or going out. She lay there, unable to move, only to think. Not even Spur McCoy would miss her. It would be her parents first. How long would it take for them to be alarmed and then worried enough to go to the police?

The sinking feeling she had experienced before now came back stronger. The San Francisco police couldn't do a thing in Marin county. She had no idea if there was a sheriff or anything up there. She did remember the family "cabin" that the three families had built together. It was a twelve room house they had put up on Hicks Mountain in a wonderful little valley with lots of trees and live oaks and some pine trees. But that was far up the stretch of land. Where in the world were they going?

After what seemed like an hour or more, she felt the boat touch against something, a dock, she hoped. The movement of the water had lessened, and now she heard men tying up the boat. They were at a dock. Probably in Marin county.

The panel opened again and someone picked her up, this time holding her in his arms in front of him, and carried her out of the cabin. She felt the refreshing breeze and knew she was outside. But where?

There were muted words and then he carried her across some more dock to solid land. Soon she was back in a buggy and the rig rolled away from the dock.

For the past hour she had been biting and chewing on the gag. It was a soft cloth and not thick nor wide. At last she bit off a piece of it and spit it out. She chewed again and pulled it in with her tongue and chewed more. At last another section came away and five minutes later she had chewed through the whole thing and called out sharply.

"Stop the carriage at once! I won't permit this. Stop it, I say, or I'll charge you with kidnapping and all sorts of other crimes."

The rig slowed and the man turned so he could touch her.

"You're all right. I won't hurt you." It was the same whispery voice as before.

"That's not good enough. You must know who I am. Who are you? Why do you hide behind the darkness and my blindfold? You're a coward, that's what you are. You're a sneaky, sniveling coward who is afraid to stand up and let me see who you are."

A growl came from the man and the rig stopped. She felt the buggy sway as he got out and evidently reached in. His hands untied the blindfold from her eyes and she blinked trying to get them to focus after being bound for all this time.

At last things came into focus and in the darkness she could see the buggy. She looked up at the side and there stood the man in black. She looked at him closely.

"Bend down so I can see who you are," she said sharply.

He bent over and a shaft of moonlight broke through and lit his face. She saw the scratches first, four of them down the side of his cheek, and the eye that was still sagging a little. Then she saw the rest of his face.

"My god, Alexander Jefferson! Why are you kidnapping me?"

"You know why," the whispery voice said. "You

know why very well. You're going to pay for hurting me so bad. Then after a few months, you'll learn to love me."

"Never! I'll kill you the first chance I get!"

"Then you won't get that chance. Thanks for the warning."

The whispering stopped. Alexander reached down and put a new gag through her mouth, this one so heavy she would never chew through it. He tied it tight.

"Now, go to sleep, we have a long ride ahead of us," Alex whispered, then he was gone.

At least he hadn't blindfolded her again. She saw no lights. There was a small town across the bay in Marin county, but she saw none of it. Perhaps they were already past it and into the wild country between the ocean and the hills.

Where in the world were they going? Then she knew. It was to the group family cabin on Hicks Mountain. Where else up in here would Alexander know about? The big mountain house was thirty miles north of town.

She did have a long ride, if she could figure no way to get loose. Again she tried to move her hands and her arms. Not a chance. The circulation was even bad in her hands. She tried again, then gave up. Exhausted, she at last went to sleep to the gentle sway and bouncing of the buggy on the trail road north along the California coastline.

Several hours later, Patricia awoke when the rig stopped. She had dozed on and off before, now she was fully awake. It was still dark.

Patricia felt Alexander get out of the rig, heard him give a small moan as he stretched, then he loomed over her in the darkness.

"I see you're awake," he whispered. His voice

sounded a little stronger now.

He took off her gag. She swallowed several times, then slowly got some moisture in her mouth so she could talk. The first words sounded a little strange, but evened out for her.

"So we're going to the Hicks Mountain house. I hope you warned the caretaker we were coming."

"They're gone this week. No one will be there but us."

"Oh?"

"You sound disappointed."

"How much farther?"

"Three or four miles. There will be no one you can call to. I'll leave the gag off."

"Don't expect me to thank you. You're nothing but a rapist and a kidnapper."

"Haven't raped you yet."

"You tried. You're too stupid even to do that right."

"I'll do it this time, right or wrong."

"I won't let you."

"I'll have you tied and spread eagled to the four corners of the bed. How will you stop me?"

"I'll find a way."

"Not a chance. Nobody knows where you are. The men at the boat were bribed not to tell. Not even the police will be able to find you."

"You'll be gone, and so will I. Someone will connect the two. And they'll figure out where a slow thinking man like you would run."

"Don't say that!"

He jumped away from her, kicked the buggy, then dropped in it and drove the horse up the road through the darkness and along the faint road, faster than it was safe.

"Alex, slow down!" Patricia called. "I'm sorry

I said that. I shouldn't have said that."

At once he slowed the horse to a fast walk and Patricia gave a sigh of relief.

Soon the trail began to climb and the horse tugged harder at the traces. She saw the first faint touches of light far to the east, then they were behind the slope of the mountain and she missed the sunrise.

By the time Alexander pulled the rig up in front of the big log built house, the sky was bright and the day had begun.

"Untie me, Alexander. My hands hurt, you shut off the circulation."

He came at once, untied the ropes around her stomach and her hands, but was careful not even to brush her breasts.

"Promise you won't try to run away," he said. "You know that it's three miles to the road, and then another ten miles to the closest house."

"I remember."

She looked at the big ranch style house. It had always been one of her favorites. As she stared at it she realized that this might be the last time she ever came here. When the charges came down against her father, they would take everything he owned to pay back what had been stolen. That would be the house in town, her mother's clothes and jewels, this place, everything.

The key was under the welcome mat at the front door.

He held the key. "I should carry you over the threshold," Alex said.

"You try it and I'll scratch the other side of your face and even up your scars."

He shrugged and went inside. The place usually had an older couple living there as caretakers.

They had been gone only two days and the place was immaculate. Always, there was a well stocked pantry with enough food to feed a field full of grape pickers.

"Now that we're here, what are we going to do?" Patricia asked.

"The first thing I do is rip your clothes off," he wheezed. His voice was stronger this morning. "Since you hurt me, you don't get to wear clothes up here. You'll be walking around naked all day."

"Try it!" Patricia shouted.

He chuckled. "You'll never know when I'm going to do it." He turned. "First some breakfast. I'm starved."

Patricia knew there were firearms at the house. She had seen her father with a six-gun he liked. He said it was easy to use because it had solid cartridges. You just pushed them in the cylinder, closed it, drew back the hammer to cock it and then pulled the trigger. It could shoot six times without reloading.

They went to the kitchen and when Alexander turned around he held the revolver she had remembered.

"In case you were going to look for this, don't. Old George kept it in the first drawer by the door in case of prowlers. It's the only firearm in the place."

"Your voice is better."

"It comes and goes."

He looked in the cupboards, then in the pantry and came back with half a dozen eggs and a slab of bacon which he sliced. He lay down the knife, then scowled at it. He took it and six other knives from the drawer and put them in a cupboard high against the ceiling. She wouldn't be able to reach it even if she stood on a chair.

"Right, all of the dangerous tools are out of reach. Now sit down and be good. I'll cook breakfast. I'm quite good in the kitchen. Eggs, bacon, toast, maybe some pan fried potatoes to go with them, and lots of coffee, yes, here we are."

An hour later the breakfast was over and Alex pointed to the dishes and a big dishpan.

"I put some water on the wood stove to heat while we ate. Now you get to wash the dishes. I don't know if you ever learned how to do that at your house. Here we share the labor."

Patricia did the dishes. She kept trying to figure a way out of there. He watched her every minute. He'd probably lock her in one of the third floor rooms, the attic rooms without windows used for overflow guests.

She had all day to figure out something. She remembered a friend of hers who said a man had grabbed her while she was downtown one day and pulled her into an alley. She got away from him when she hit him in the crotch with her fist. She hit him three times there and he fell over moaning and screaming in pain. The girl had asked her father about it, and he told her it was the scrotum that she had hit, the testicles were extremely sensitive. Maybe she could kick Alex there. She would watch for her chance.

But even so, what did she do then? How could she run away for thirteen miles? She kept wondering about it.

They went outside and sat on the swing and he pushed her. There was no chance she could simply outrun him. He was taller and stronger and would catch her quickly. What else? The horse! But the animal was unharnessed now and in the small pasture behind the barn. She wasn't sure she could catch the animal, let alone ride her bareback to escape.

"Let's go up by the spring and see if the dipper is still there?" Alexander said.

She watched him a moment. It seemed innocent enough. They walked side by side toward the spring. It was 50 yards above the house. The natural spring had been dug out and a big barrel sunk in the ground. A wooden V trough had been set back in the gentle flow of the spring so it came down the trough and ran into the barrel.

"Just the way it was last fall when we were here," Alex said.

He knelt beside the barrel, took a dipper that hung there and caught water in it as it fell from the trough. He drank and then gave the cup to Patricia.

As she held the cup he slipped behind her, caught her around the stomach and rolled her into the grass.

"Don't," she shrilled.

He held her, keeping her tightly against his stomach, avoiding her hands. His legs had caught hers in a vice grip.

"Why are you doing this, Alex? Why try to force me to make love to you? Why not be nice and sweet and thoughtful and then gently try to seduce me?"

"It wouldn't work, I tried that before."

"In that bedroom? You were lewd and vulgar."

One of his hands captured her right breast and held it firmly.

"That's not nice, Alexander."

"I don't care if it's nice or not. I want you. I want you all naked and spread out on your back. I want to poke you as hard as I can and watch your face."

His one hand held her around her waist and the other ripped at the bodice of her blue dress. Buttons popped and she saw the top flap open.

"Yes, yes!" he said.

"Alex, why are you ripping my clothes?"

"Why? I want to see your tits."

"Haven't you seen a woman's breasts before, Alex?"

"Not very well. Once my mother was dressing. . . ."

"Alex, you've never made love to a girl, have you?"

"Well, no. That's why I want to, right now."

"No, Alex, not now. Do you ever—you know— do it by yourself . . . with your hands?"

He looked away. "That's not nice."

"Doesn't hurt. I've known boys who did it. Didn't hurt them. You have, haven't you?"

"Once or twice."

"Show me! Alex, I've never seen a boy do it that way. Show me."

"Couldn't."

"You can, too. You showed me yourself the other night. Do that again and sit over there away from me and . . . you know, use your hand until you spurt."

Patricia wasn't exactly sure of what she was saying. Laura Grandifar had told her about one wild, crazy time she had with a boy when she was younger. She said it worked and he did it.

"Come on, Alex, you may as well do it. I know you want to."

"What will you do for me if I do?"

"Me . . . well, I could let you look at one of my breasts bare."

"Both of them!" He pounced on the idea.

Patricia sighed. Laura told her once a man pumped it off that way he was much less anxious about bothering the girl. It was worth a try. Slowly she nodded. "All right, but you get started first."

She looked away and he let go of her and crawled a few feet behind her.

"Look over here," Alexander said.

She turned. She remembered how thick the brush and woods were behind the spring. Maybe she could hide there. Maybe. She'd wait until he was started, and then he wouldn't want to stop, and. . . .

She looked at him. He had opened his pants and pulled out his erection. She was surprised at how big it was.

Alex grinned. "Ain't he a dandy? He's gonna feel so good!" He began pumping it with his hand. "Show me your bare tits," he said.

She let the sides of her dress gape open since the buttons were gone and lifted her chemise. She knew her breasts weren't as big as lots of women she had seen, but they had an effect on Alexander.

"Oh, god! Oh, damn. Look at them tits!" His hand pumped faster and he began to pant. His hips suddenly jerked in a spasm and fluid jolted out of the end of his penis.

Now! Patricia jumped up and darted toward the darkest, thickest part of the woods.

"No, no, come back. I'm not done yet. Come back."

But she was gone, charging into the woods, letting her dress flap now as she pumped her arms to go faster. She hurried through some black oak, then past a heavy growth of brush and brambles and deeper into the woods. She passed tall pine trees. Something scratched her, but she kept running.

That was all she could think of doing now, just keep running away from Alexander!

· 13 ·

Spur McCoy arrived at the mint 15 minutes early that morning and saw both Jefferson and Knox hurry in with worried looks on their faces. He went inside, checked with his department, and saw that everything was moving along well.

Then he heard the rumors. They were everywhere. One of the boss's kids was missing. The Knox girl had not come home last night. Mr. Knox had been up most of the night searching for her. None of her friends had seen her.

A moment later he heard that Alexander Jefferson was also missing. They suspected foul play with him.

"Somebody probably didn't like his high handed way of doing things," one of the workmen said.

"Probably knocked him down and threw him in the bay. Serve the peckerhead right."

Spur heard all the rumors and wondered what he should do. At first, he thought some of the people in on the gold heist must have grabbed her, but that didn't make sense. If someone thought she was onto their scheme, they would have taken her home. No, it had to be something else.

The streets of San Francisco were not the safest in the world, but last night she was in the buggy and had only a few blocks to go to her house on Nob Hill. What could have happened?

He sat in his small office thinking about it. She had been missing all night. She was not with Laura Grandifar or any of her other close friends. She had not been reported hurt at any of the hospitals, and the police had no reports of a found girl of her age. All this he heard from the other workers.

What did that leave? Murder most foul . . . not likely. An abduction for sexual purposes . . . more likely. An abudction by a friend or acquaintance . . . possible.

He thought it through again, and then jumped up. Alexander Jefferson was missing as well. Coincidence? Not hardly. Alexander had assaulted Patricia in a rape attempt. He would have the resources to try again, but this time in a carefully thought out plan.

Spur paced his office for five minutes, wondering if he should go see Mr. Knox. He could invent a story about how he had once worked for a year with the New York City Police. That might help. He would offer his services. He could ask about any other properties that were owned by the family.

The more he thought about it, the more certain

he was that Alexander had grabbed Patricia. The problem was, where would he take her? He wanted revenge, he wanted her body, two powerful motives for a kidnapping.

At last, Spur walked down the hall to Knox's office door and knocked. It opened at once.

Knox stared at him. "Oh, McCoy, it's you."

"Mr. Knox, I wondered if there was anything I could do. You must know the story is all over the plant by now. If there's anything I can do, chase down a lead, investigate some place, I have had some experience. I didn't tell you that I worked for a year with the New York City Police Department."

Knox started to shut the door but when he heard the last line he stopped. "You worked with the police? On what?"

"Mostly tracing lost persons, trying to find people who were reported missing. Most of them were drunk or lost, but now and then we did have something more serious."

"Come in, come in."

Spur stepped in the room and found the other two management men, Jefferson and Pickering walking around with long faces.

"You've contacted the local police, I would guess," Spur said.

"Of course," Jefferson said sharply. "All the usual, the hospitals, the morgue, the waterfront, all of that."

"Was Patricia upset about anything, worried? Was she angry? Could she have visited a relative?"

"We've been over all that," Knox said but in a more normal tone. "She told her mother she'd be home last night. She took the buggy out. We found it on the street a half block from our house. It looked like she was almost home."

Knox turned away and stared out the window.

"Frankly, McCoy, we're at the end of our string. We've been beating our heads against the wall here. We're about ready to give up. I'm convinced I'll be getting a ransom demand at any time now."

"No other ideas?"

"None."

"I'll see what I can do."

Spur left the room and went out to the woman at the front desk. He looked down at Helen and he could see tears in her eyes.

"You've heard," he said.

She nodded.

"Patricia is a wonderful person. So friendly and not uppity at all. She was nice to me."

"Helen, maybe you could help me. Did the Knoxes or Jeffersons have a vacation house out by the seashore anywhere?"

Helen frowned, rubbed her cheek a minute and then shook her head. "They did at one time, down south aways, but nobody went there so they sold it."

"Oh, well, it was just an idea."

Helen brightened. "But they do still have the place up north, the mountain cabin they call it. It's not a cabin, it's about fifteen rooms. All three families used to go up there on vacations and for weekends sometimes in the summer."

"All three families?" He asked.

"The Jeffersons, the Knoxes and the Pickerings. I heard they all went together and bought it or built it or something."

"So, do you know where this place is?"

She thought for a minute, then looked through her desk. "About a year ago they had a social up there, lots of society people. I sent out the invitations and Mr. Jefferson had maps printed. I think I still have one somewhere." She looked again, then took some things out of her desk drawer and piled them on her desk.

Spur felt like he was going to explode. He wanted to get out and kick somebody in the ass or shoot somebody. But there was nothing he could do. He gripped one hand into a fist and rubbed it on the other hand.

Then Helen looked up and grinned. "Found it!" She held up a pale blue piece of paper. "I'll loan it to you, but please bring it back."

"Thanks, Helen. I might have an idea. Oh, don't say anything to anybody about this, all right? I don't want to raise any false hopes. Right now it doesn't look too good." He folded the paper, thanked her again and hurried back to his office.

"Fred," Spur said coming up to his second-in-command. "I'm going to have to be gone for a while, maybe all day and tomorrow, I'm not sure. I've checked with Mr. Knox. You handle anything here that needs doing. Good luck."

Spur turned and hurried out the door. Once he was on Market Street he hailed an empty hack going downtown. He had the driver take him to the Almont hotel. He put on his trail clothes, including his leather vest, and strapped on his .45 six-gun. He put a box of extra rounds in his pocket and slid on his battered cowboy hat with the low crown and the string of Mexican silver pesos around the headband.

Then he went down and caught another cab. He looked at the map. It showed the mountain cabin well to the north of San Francisco, across the bay to the county on the north, and then another 25 or 30 miles.

A boat, they would need a boat to get across the bay. He called to the driver to take him to the waterfront.

"I want someone who can take me across to the other side, to Marin county, I think it's called. So take me to a boat."

A half hour later, Spur walked down the tenth dock looking for a boat he could hire for the run across to Marin. An old timer sitting on a piling whittling looked up as he came along.

"You got a boat?" Spur asked.

"Yep."

"It big enough to go across to Marin?"

"Yep."

"She for hire right now?"

"Nope."

"Thanks for all of the great conversation."

"That one is for hire, though," the man said pointing at a boat tied up on the other side of the pier.

"It know the way to Marin county."

"Should, it went over there last night."

"Did?"

"What they said."

"Where are they?"

"On board."

Spur went over to the boat and called. "Hey, anybody on board?"

A man wearing a black stocking cap and a pipe tipped upside down protruding from the corner of his mouth came out of a door from a small foredeck cabin.

"Hear you want to take a trip across to Marin," the sailor said with a grin.

It was an hour later when Spur hit land on the

far side of the bay and looked over at Marin county. Not a lot to see. Some trees, some cliffs, some marshy places to seaward.

He found a livery stable where he could rent a horse and rode away toward the north. A long look at the map showed where they had pointed out certain landmarks to follow for those society guests who had never been to the mountain. He hoped he could find it.

Thirty miles. Spur settled into the leather, patted the horse on the neck and headed north. If those society ladies could find the place, he damn well could.

Patricia Knox floundered through the thick underbrush, frantic, knowing that Alexander was bigger and stronger and faster than she was. She had to beat him some other way.

A thorn of a trailing vine slashed across her cheek and Patricia felt blood as she charged through the woods above the spring in back of the Hicks mountain cabin. She hadn't heard Alex behind her yet, but he had to be there somewhere.

She stopped for just a moment, remained totally still and listened. She heard a wailing cry, then the sound of brush crashing and she knew he was coming after her.

Her pause had let her gather her thoughts for a second. Perhaps she could circle back to the house, get the horse and ride away. No. She wasn't that good with horses. She might not even be able to catch the beast. She had not been a good student at her horse riding lessons.

What could she do? Where could she go? Climb a tree? In this dress? Impossible. He would look up there anyway. He always did when they were kids.

Patricia ran again, up the hill away from the house. Then she slowed. He might be listening. She stopped. From then on she moved cautiously a step at a time, trying not to break a branch, not let a pine tree bough swish back. Patricia tried not to make any noise at all. She found a spot where three pine trees grew in a clump, almost together. She wedged between them and by squatting she could be totally out of sight. She stood by the largest tree, watching the way she had come.

Mostly, she listened. For the longest times she heard nothing, then there came a wailing cry, a lost child yell full of anger and shame, running over with self pity and frustration. It sounded just like Alexander.

Patricia watched for what seemed a long time. She had heard him now and again, but then he seemed to be walking, not running. He couldn't follow her footprints in the woods, she was sure of that. Alex was a city boy.

Then she gasped and slid down the tree until she was out of sight. He had come from behind some brush not 50-feet down the hill. Alex seemed to be walking across the hill, not up the slope. If he continued, he would go past her in a minute or two.

Patricia waited as long as she could, then she lifted up just so she could see through the "V" where two of the trees crossed near the ground.

To her satisfaction, she watched him walking away from her. He stopped and looked around, then shrugged and moved slowly down the hill. He had given up!

But what did she do now? He had been right. She was 13 miles from any help at all. And if she went there, Alexander had the revolver and could follow her. She had to get the horse.

For the first time she realized she was sweating. The morning sun burned through the trees and turned patches of her into warm and then hot spots.

A drink. She would love to have a drink. The closest water was the spring. That was why they had built here, for the water supply. The spring would run more water than the family needed.

Did she dare try to go back to the spring? Would he figure that she would get thirsty and hungry and come looking for water? He might. Alex was not stupid, he was just dumb about some things, girls especially.

At last she decided she had no choice. She had to have some water. She moved back in the opposite way she had come, working over across the hill until she could see the tip of the third story of the cabin through the trees. Then she worked down the hill cautiously, watching ahead of her, looking critically for anywhere that Alex could be hiding, waiting for her.

She saw nothing. The spring lay now only 30 feet away. She saw the pipe that came out of the barrel and down the slope to the house where it supplied water in the kitchen and in a modern bathroom on the first floor.

Where was he?

She moved out quickly, used the dipper and took a long drink, then one more and walked rapidly into the woods on the other side of the well.

She dropped down out of sight and listened. Nothing. She looked down at her dress. The bodice was flapping where he had torn off the buttons. The pretty blue skirt of soft percaline and crinoline was now torn and tattered. One tear came almost to her hip. The dress was completely ruined.

She heard the horse nicker. She should try for the horse, it was her only bet. If she ran away down the road, Alex could use the horse and catch her. But if she had the horse, Alex would have no way to overtake her.

She worked around and through the brush toward the small pasture. She knew where it was, and found she remembered these woods from when they had played here as children.

Ten minutes later she was near the fence. She could see the horse through the thicket. From where she stood the animal seemed huge. How could she mount it? She had to try, there was no other way. Patricia spotted a cut-off stump in the middle of the small pasture. It was nearly three feet high. It would serve as a good step up if she could catch the animal.

Patricia looked across the pasture at the cabin for five minutes but saw no one move. She watched the well, but there was no one there. At last, she crept to the fence and pushed down one of the barbed wires, lifted the next one and stepped through. Her skirt caught on the barbs. She pulled it free and was through.

The horse saw her and walked toward her. It had no halter, just a bare necked animal. She stood and waited for it. The closer it came the bigger it seemed. She held out her hand as it came close, then it skittered away, only to stop and come back.

She held out her hand again, talking softly. The animal cocked its head to one side as she came closer. Patricia smoothed its long neck and up toward the ears.

Slowly she took a grip on the long black mane and turned the horse to move it toward the stump. The animal moved at her command, as if it always obeyed when held by the mane. At the stump she held the mane and lifted her skirt to her waist and took one giant step up to the sawed off top.

Once there she pushed one foot over the horse's back and sat bareback on the animal, leaned forward and grabbed her mane with both hands. She touched her heels gently to the animal's flanks.

The mare walked ahead slowly. Patricia pushed her head one way and she turned in that direction. They went straight toward the house where Patricia remembered the small gate. She leaned down and moved a bolt and the wood and wire fence swung open.

She left it swing wide and touched her heels to the horse again, twice this time, and the animal lifted to a canter bouncing her cruelly on the hard and bony back.

Patricia knew they were near the house. She saw it out of the corner of her eye and touched the mount again so that it began to gallop. She had all she could do to hang on as they rushed past the far porch.

A door slammed. She saw Alexander rush from the front door, the big six-gun in his hand.

"Noooooooooooooooo," he bellowed, then lifted the weapon and aimed it at her.

She and the horse flashed past him. He turned and kept aiming and then she heard the sound of the shot. It was a booming sound she had never heard before, but she realized she had never been shot at before.

The bullet cut through the air and burned a

groove across the rump of the big black. The animal screamed in pain, planted its front feet suddenly and bucked to try to rid the pain from her hindside.

Patricia had no way to stay in place. She clutched at the animal's mane, but at the same time she was propelled forward and tumbled over the horse's head, lost her grip and flipped head over heels toward the ground.

The black bucked again and took off down the trail toward the main road, not stopping as she rounded the bend and was lost from sight.

Patricia landed on her shoulders and back, skidded for three feet and ended in a crumpled ball. Her head banged against the hard ground and she wondered why it was getting dark so early before the lights all went out and she sagged into blessed unconsciousness.

When Patricia woke up less than ten minutes later, she lay on a big bed in one of the three master bedrooms. She looked up at the ceiling and knew at once where she was. Then she tried to move her hand. It was fast. She looked at her other hand then pulled on her legs.

She was spread eagled on her back on the bed and now she saw that her dress had been stripped off her and her chemise as well. All she wore were the new silk panties she had bought from that fancy French shop downtown.

Patricia looked around the room and bellowed in fury when she saw Alexander at a small tea table calmly eating a sandwich and some sliced peaches from a tin.

"You bastard!" Patricia screamed. "Untie me at once!"

Alexander laughed. "Not for a hundred-thousand dollars. I was hungry, so I waited. Oh, and I wanted you to be awake to enjoy it as well. I do believe it will be your first. At least I'm not a virgin any longer. I took care of that last week.

"The peaches are very good. You should have some, but then you're not eating or drinking. Not anything until I get all I want of you, and you beg me for more."

He smiled down at her. "Now, my feisty, little, redheaded wildcat, I've tamed you. I've pulled out your claws and put you on a leash and if you're not a good little girl, you won't get anything to eat or drink. I hope you realize that you are totally in my power. I can do anything I want to with you. Nobody knows we're here.

"Back in town they're probably frantically looking for you. I left a note they'll find, telling them I've gone to the current gold strike, wherever it is. They'll believe it, so there'll be no cause to think I might have grabbed your sweet little tits to be my own."

He paused and watched her. Then he walked over and petted her breasts where they lay flattened on her chest.

"My, my, not nearly so snotty today, are you? I never thought you'd try to run into the woods. The horse was a surprise. If I hadn't been such a good shot and just grazed the animal, you might have made it. But you didn't."

She tried to push away from his hand but he grabbed one breast and squeezed it until she yelped in pain.

"Remember, small titted woman. You remember who is in charge here. It sure as hell ain't you. I am the master of this house. Alexander Jefferson will tell you what to do, and within a few days, you'll do exactly what I tell you to do and love doing it."

He laughed softly. "Now, pretty girl, the peaches and the sandwich are all gone. I've had a bottle of cold beer while I was waiting for you, so I'd say now is the time we get started with the unveiling of the treasure, the soft little pussy that Patricia has been protecting so hard for so long."

He watched her.

"Come now, girl, this is a big day for you. Women tell me they never forget their first sexual experience, or the man who makes them into a woman."

He reached for her crotch and Patricia screamed.

· 14 ·

Spur McCoy pushed the big bay horse, moving her along at five to ten miles an hour and then walking her for spells. He figured he had to average over five miles an hour. Even so it would be well after noon when he got to the mountain house.

For a while, he galloped the bay for a quarter-of-a-mile and then walked her for a half, then galloped for another quarter. She held up well and he pushed the mount, sure now that he was making better time than before.

The landmarks were easy to find and he was sure he was on the right route as shown on the map. This trail wasn't much used. From time to time he could make out the tracks of a buggy. He didn't know if it was the one Alex might have used but it encouraged him.

It could also be a false lead, but the more he figured it, the more he was sure this had to be where Alex would have gone. It was logical, reasonable. If not, he had only wasted one day and made a good try. The small girl's safety was well worth the effort.

Another hour passed and he kept pushing the horse. He soon realized that he had to take care of the mount. If she broke down he'd be on foot the rest of the way because there were no towns and even settlers' cabins were spaced far apart.

He watched the horse closely as he pushed forward. By noon he knew he was getting close.

An hour later, he turned up a small lane toward the hill that he had seen for some time. He was a mile up the lane when he could see the big house through the trees. Just than a black horse thundered around a curve at him with no halter, eyes wild, and a blood streak showing down its back.

The mount could have been shot.

Spur kicked the bay in the flanks and hurried forward. The big log house was still over a mile ahead. He rode to within a quarter-of-a-mile of the place still in heavy cover, then saw that the lane came into the small valley and went on to the big house. The rest of the way had no possible cover for him. Smoke came from the chimney. It could be caretakers. But why then a horse stampeding away from the place?

Spur turned into the woods and brush and worked his way forward until he was only 50 yards from the house. Then he tied his mount and moved cautiously on foot forward.

He had cover all the way to a side door. Now he saw a buggy with two seats sitting near a small barn. They were here!

He tried the door. It was locked. He moved under a window toward the front door and slipped up the steps silently. The big front door was partly open. Spur edged inside without touching it and listened.

Off to the left and up some stairs he heard a high, wild laugh.

"About damn time!"

The voice came through whispery and strained.

Spur ran in that direction, making no noise on the carpet. He moved up the steps three at a time silently and paused at the top. Which way down the hall?

He heard the laugh again, strained, wheezing, like a man might make who had his windpipe damaged or his voice box injured.

Spur drew his six-gun and moved that way watching the doors, alert and ready.

Then, in an instant, a form leaned out of a door two down and fired a six-gun before Spur could react. He had been lifting his weapon when the bullet hit him. He slammed backwards, but somehow held on to his Colt. He was on the floor, and his head hurt like a million stallions were stampeding through it. He saw the man grinning down the hall. Spur lifted his Colt and fired once but knew his aim wasn't even close.

Alex jumped back in the master bedroom where Patricia still lay on the bed. He had taken off his shirt and had cut the last shreds of the fancy panties off Patricia so she was naked. Then he thought he saw a horseman far down the road and watched and listened until he was sure. So he waited for him.

"Oh, God, I killed him!" Alex exploded. "I don't know who he was but he had a gun and I shot him in the head and I killed him. Now I'm in real trouble. What can I do now? Patricia, you always helped me, what can I do now?"

"Yes, Alex, I'll help you. I'll tell you what you must do. First untie me so I can help. Quickly now, untie me."

Alex moved like a man in a fog, but he untied her hands and she loosened her feet. She found the dress and pulled it back on so she was mostly covered. Some pins would fix the bodice when she had time.

"Now, Alex, give me the gun. You don't want to keep it. It just hurt someone."

Alex shook his head. "No, got to keep the shooter. Let's look at him."

They went into the hall and Patricia rushed down to the man who lay on the floor. Blood gushed from a wound on his head and she knelt down quickly so she wouldn't faint. She couldn't faint now. NO!

She held on and her head cleared. She looked at the man. She wiped some of the blood away and saw his face. Spur McCoy! He had found her. Was he dead?

Blood kept flowing from the wound on his head. If he was bleeding, he wasn't dead. Now she saw that the wound was a crease, a wound that bled a lot but the bullet had cut only a quarter-inch furrow along the side of his head. He couldn't be dead.

She rushed into the nearest bedroom, pulled the sheet off the bed, ripped it into squares and strips and went back to the hall. She put a large compress of the folded sheet over the wound and held it in place with many wraps of the long strips of sheet around his head. She pushed with her hand on the compress and soon the bleeding stopped. Then she changed the bandage and put a clean one on.

"Now, Alex, help me get this man to the bed. You didn't kill him. He'll hurt for a while, but he'll be fine. You didn't kill him."

"But now they'll come and get me, the police. They'll say I tried to kill him and shot him and I'll have to go to prison."

"No, Alex. It won't be like that. I'll say it was an accident. You two were out hunting with your pistols and the gun was dropped and it went off. Now help me get him to the bed."

At last Alex pushed the revolver into his belt and helped her lift Spur. They half carried, half dragged him to the bed in the closest bedroom.

Spur was unconscious but not dead. She didn't know how much damage had been done. She had heard that head wounds bleed a lot but sometimes they weren't as bad as they looked. She hoped it was true this time.

Patricia went into the hall and found Alex.

"I think he's going to live," Patricia said. "What we have to do now is go find the black horse so we can take Spur back to town and to a doctor. Can you help me do that, Alex? Walk down the lane until you find the horse. I'm sure she's standing down there somewhere still frightened and tired of running."

"No. No. I can't help him any more. I've got to get some food and then go up in the woods where nobody can find me. The sheriff and his men and tracking dogs will come and chase me. I've got to run right now!"

"No, Alex. No! I told you the sheriff won't blame you for the head wound. I'll tell them it was an accident."

He brushed her aside and for the first time she realized how strong Alex really was. He stormed to the kitchen, found a flour sack and threw canned goods and potatoes and a lot of other food into it. Then he took some matches, a hatchet, his pistol and a rifle from the closet.

Patricia couldn't stop him. He ignored her, pushed her aside like she was a child and ran out of the house and up to the well. He filled a large canteen and then vanished into the woods, climbing directly up the hill.

Patricia called to him to come back, but he paid no attention and kept going. She frowned and hurried back to the second floor bedroom where Spur McCoy lay and she didn't know for sure if he would live or die.

When she got to the room, Spur sat on the edge of the bed feeling his head.

"He shot me," Spur said, not quite believing it. "Another half-inch and I'd be a corpse."

"Lie down, you shouldn't be sitting up."

Spur fought down a headache and looked at her. He blinked. "I see two of you, Patricia, two of everything. Let me lay back down for a few minutes. Tell me what happened."

She told him the whole story from the way Alex had grabbed her off the street, the boat ride, then the buggy. She told him how she got away into the brush and then got on the horse, but Alex had shot the horse and it threw her.

"That's why that black came racing past me on the way up here. Did Alex hurt you?"

"No, he was going to, but he didn't have time. You came and stopped it."

"Good. Let me rest a minute. Is there any food around? I'm starved."

"That's a good sign."

She fed him a heated up tin of ham, some slabs of bread and jam, two cups of coffee and some tinned applesauce. At the end of his meal he sat up slowly and looked at her.

"Your dress is a mess, Miss Knox, but you're safe and that's the important part. Also, I just see one of you now." He stood up, wavered a little, then walked to the window and back. He touched his holster.

"Where's my Colt?"

Patricia ran to the hall and found it against the wall where it had fallen. She brought it back. He examined it, spun the cylinder, then took the fired round and put in a new one. He slid it into the holster.

"You know I won't let you go anywhere, don't you? I'm your nurse and nurse says stay in bed for at least a day."

He bent and kissed her cheek. Dark shadows fluttered against his eyes for a moment as he bent his head, but they cleared.

"Pretty lady, I came all the way up here to find you and to save your pretty little neck from Alex. I figured it was him. I don't know why his parents didn't. I'm not about to let that maniac go free. I'm a lawman. I have a responsibility. I have to go bring him back with you."

"I was afraid of that. I know why his parents didn't make the connection. He told me he left a note telling them he was off for the gold fields, wherever they are digging now. So they figured he just took off again. He's done it four or five times before."

"Now I see. Glad I didn't know about his note." He bent down in a squatting position, then stood. He blinked a couple of times, then turned his head around in a circle twice. "Yep, I guess the body can take it. Now, which way did you say he went?"

Ten minutes later, Spur McCoy was back in his element. He could read the footprints in the soft forest floor like a roadmap. A scuffed leaf here, a trampled young plant, a blade of grass just starting to straighten after being bent down by a boot.

McCoy moved slowly, used the cover he found, and didn't blunder into the open. He knew Alex had the rifle from the cabin. What he didn't know was if the young man was a good shot or if the six-gun shot had been a lucky fluke. He was betting his life if he decided that Alex couldn't shoot well.

The trail did not move in a straight line. Alex seemed confused about where he wanted to go. For a while he headed up the hill from the well. Then he seemed to have spent some time in one area, sitting down, digging in the dirt, maybe even laying down for a time. Then he went up the hill again, and moved around to the side as if he were searching for something.

What could it be? A childhood memory of a small cave? A hidden place where brush and trees were too thick to see through? A fort of some kind?

From what Patricia said, Alex had been irrational when he left. He had been frightened and acting a little crazy. Maybe he had dropped over the edge into the crazy place. If so, it would make it all the harder. A normal man is enough afraid of death to at least look at the alternatives.

With crazies you couldn't be sure what they would do.

Spur had just found new tracks aiming upward again when he had to cross a small open area. There were enough trees and brush 20 feet away for him to circle the spot and find the tracks on the far side.

He shrugged, decided not to take the extra time, bent low and rushed across the 30 feet of open space. A rifle shot whined off a rock two feet to one side of him and Spur raced to the closest cover. He dove in just as another shot splintered a branch six-inches over his head.

He rolled away, then looked for the blue smoke that would give away the gunman's position. It was almost at the top of the mountain, which wasn't all that high as mountains go. More like a hill.

The range was at least 300 yards. The man could shoot a rifle.

Spur changed his tactics. Instead of following the prints, he charged for the top of the hill. He worked through the best cover but moved directly upward. He was a little out of shape and was puffing by the time he got to a point where he was about the same height as the spot where Alex had fired. There was a group of rocks there and some scrub brush, but little else. Alex had moved.

Sound. That could be his best lead now. Spur concentrated on his hearing and tried to tune in various parts of the top of the mountain. It wasn't a peak, more like a dome with a few scrub trees, grass and a pine or two, but no good cover. The best protection would come in the ring of brush and trees down 20 yards from the top. It was on these areas that he concentrated for any sound of movement.

He sectioned the areas that he could see from his vantage point, taking a small square of the target and watching it intently, scanning it side to side and up and down and then watching it overall for any slow movement.

He'd almost been killed once by two Apaches who'd moved across a barren desert landscape 100 yards in front of him. They had moved so slowly he missed them until it was almost too late. The two Apaches were in the open, but crawled along an inch at a time and the human eye had trouble recognizing the change in landscape of that small a move. After three hours they were almost at a safe place where they would have attacked him.

The first four areas he checked here on the mountain produced nothing. Then on the fifth spot he thought he saw movement. He scanned the area again, looked away and looked back. Yes. Beside a rock, a leg had extended with brown pants. It adjusted again as if the man were lying down getting into a firing position.

Sixty yards away. There was no safe approach route. If he had a rifle he could shoot Alex's leg off before he could recover. Now that Spur knew where the target was, he began improvising ways to reach him. Forty feet. He had to get within six-gun range at 40 feet. How?

He saw a thin line of brush with two pine trees in that direction. He started his trek. He had to crawl on his belly for the first 20 yards. He did so with his Colt in his right hand and out front in case he was surprised.

He made it. He stood up behind the two-foot thick pine and looked at the spot where he had last seen Alex. He lay in the same spot, only now Spur could see most of his torso and both legs. Only his head and shoulders were screened.

The route? From there he had 10 yards of open ground, but he was on the target's flank, so Alex would not be looking at the open spot of ground. Alex was concentrating on the area in front of him and downhill, along the route he had taken going up the hill. Good.

Spur took the 10 yards in a crouch with the six gun ready. He made it to the jumble of rocks and slid behind them, then peered over the top at Alex. He had sat up, looked to his right and left and Spur could see a frown. This wasn't going right for Alex. He must have no idea where Spur was.

Alex moved a dozen feet to the right which put him slightly closer to Spur, but still not close enough to risk a confrontation.

The route from here would be tougher. Spur had 20 yards of rocks he could work along, staying behind them and out of sight. But the rocks presented a noise factor. Cautiously, slowly, he traversed the rocks and came to his end point, a foot-thick pine that had been torn and twisted by the coastal winds that did not seem to be blowing today.

Spur peered around the trunk of the tree and saw Alex looking directly at him. He lifted the rifle. Spur snapped a shot, then aimed the next, and the round slammed into the receiver of the weapon, jolting it out of Alex's hands.

"Don't move, Alex. It's all over. You didn't kill me. There's no reason you shouldn't go back to San Francisco with us and explain it all."

"No, they'll kill me."

"Nobody is going to be killed. Your rifle is ruined now. You can't shoot your six-gun worth beans or I'd be dead by now. Just lay down the revolver and stand up.''

"No, then you'll kill me for what I wanted to do to Patricia.''

"Not true, Alex. She said you didn't rape her. No worry there. I won't charge you with shooting me. No problem there. We can talk to Patricia. I think she'll tell everyone that you both decided to come on a short holiday up here so there won't be any police involvement at all.''

"Not true. You're tricking me.''

He fired the six-gun from where he held it in his lap. Spur hadn't been able to see it clearly. The unaimed shot brought a reflective response from Spur. His round ripped into Alex's shoulder and slammed him against the rock. He screamed and lifted the six-gun again, but he didn't aim it at Spur.

Alex kept moving it until he put the barrel of the weapon in his mouth pointing at the top of his head. Before Spur could even shout, there was a report of the six-gun going off.

A big patch of Alex's skull and hair flew off as blood and brains sprayed the surrounding shrubs and rocks. Alex lifted upward a few inches from the blast of the round, then fell over backwards.

"Goddamn,'' Spur McCoy said.

It took him almost an hour to lug the big body, the rifle and the pistol back down the mountain. When he was close enough he called to Patricia. She had been at the well waiting for them. When she ran up to where she could see Spur coming down, carrying the limp form, she dropped to her knees crying and wailing in torment.

He put down the body and sat beside her.

"I didn't want this to happen. I know that Alex

has been near the edge of sanity for a year or so. I tried to talk with his father about it, but he simply brushed me off, saying it was all made up, that Alex was as sane as he was. I couldn't make him understand."

She cried again and leaned against Spur who put his arms around her. She stopped and dried her tears and looked up at him. "It seems that I do a lot of crying when I'm around you, Spur McCoy. Usually, I don't cry this much."

"You've had good cause. We better get started back to San Francisco before your parents loose their minds worrying about you."

They hitched up Spur's riding horse to the buggy. She pawed the ground and protested a little, but Spur had a man-to-horse talk with her and she settled down.

They stowed Alex in the back of the rig which Spur saw was a cabriolet with two seats. He and Patricia sat in front and they moved down toward the road. It was about three o'clock and the coastal fog was starting to roll in.

"It'll be dark by the time we get to the bay," Spur said. "I just hope we can find someone to take us across."

They did. They hired a boat, found a cab on the other side and hurried up to Nob Hill. Spur carried the body to the side door and into a hall. Then he told Patricia he would see her in the morning. He wanted to let the three conspirators decide what to do and say about Alex after Patricia told them what happened.

It was still Wednesday. It had been a long day. He wasn't sure what he was going to do tomorrow, but decided that he would report to work and quietly resign, then he would be free to work all day on the small problem of some $600,000 to $700,000 in embezzled gold from the San Francisco U.S. Mint.

· 15 ·

When Patricia burst into her parents' living room, Betsy Knox went into hysterics. Her father rushed over and hugged her, then suggested she have a bath and some clean clothes.

"No, father, we have to talk. Send for Mr. Jefferson. He needs to be here as well. I want to be sure that he sees me exactly the way I am now."

"I don't understand, how does this affect him?"

"Because of Alex. Please send someone to bring Mr. Jefferson here as quickly as possible."

Betsy at last calmed down enough to hug Patricia, then she went to have a cool bath to settle her nerves. Her baby was home, all was right with the world.

After a servant had been sent four doors down

to bring Mr. Jefferson, Patricia's father looked at her sharply. "Now tell me what this is all about."

"Soon, father, soon. I want both you and Martin Jefferson to understand exactly what happened since last night at about eight o'clock, and this is the best way to do it."

"You look like you've been through a lot."

"Yes, father, I have been, but I wasn't raped. I'm sure that's what you're most concerned about."

"Thank God."

"No, father, you'll have to thank Spur McCoy. He found me and saved me and with not a lot of time to spare."

"McCoy? How in the world could he know where. . . ."

The front door bell sounded and then the door opened and Martin Jefferson barged into the living room. He wore a smoking jacket and slippers and his hair was mussed and his beard looking a little askew.

"What in the hell is this all about? Oh, Patricia. Thank God."

"No, Mr. Jefferson, as I just told father, you can thank Spur McCoy, he found me. I'd like to tell you both together what happened. Would you mind sitting down?"

They sat and waited.

"I was coming home last night driving the light rig and was almost here when a heavier buggy cut me off and forced me to stop. Then someone grabbed me, gagged me, bound me hand and foot and put me in the back of a buggy and drove to the docks. There I was blindfolded and lugged onboard a boat and taken across the bay to Marin county where I was hauled into a buggy and driven north.

"It wasn't until then that I got the gag chewed through and screamed at the driver. He stopped and let me see who he was. My kidnapper was Alexander Jefferson."

"No!" Martin thundered. "I have his note that he was going to the gold fields."

"That was part of his plan, Mr. Jefferson, and you swallowed it completely, as he figured you would. Now please let me finish." She told the rest of the story, muting the sexual parts but making it obvious he had captured her for his sexual pleasures. Patricia told the rest of the story right up to but not including the part about the final shot.

"So where is Alex now?" Jefferson asked. "Did he run off again?"

"When Spur shot his rifle out of his hands and had him captured, Spur told Alex that there would be no charges. He told him that I would agree that Alex and I had gone away together voluntarily and that Spur got creased in the head when a gun fell and accidentally discharged. There was no rape, so he had no worry there. But Spur said that Alex simply wouldn't believe him.

"Then Alex put the six-gun from the cabin in his mouth and killed himself."

She looked at the two men. Her father relaxed visibly, then glanced at Martin. Jefferson went rigid, he shivered and balled his fists trying with all his might to control himself.

"No!" Jefferson said at last, his voice small and tightly rigid and contained. "I don't believe it."

"You better believe it, Mr. Jefferson. Otherwise, I'm going to charge Alex with kidnapping, assault, attempted rape, and mental anguish. Then I'll sue you in civil court for two-million dollars for not controlling your son and for mental anguish and physical pain and suffering. And I'll collect. You know I'll win such a suit. I have witnesses. We can find the men who took us across the bay and who rented the buggy to Alex on the Marin side."

"She's giving us all a chance to let this die down without a big scandal, Martin," Philander Knox said gently. "Think about it. As you said recently, we can't afford not to keep this as quiet as we can. You know that. I know it's a shock losing a son, I thought I'd lost my daugher. *I know how you feel.*"

"Like hell you do! Where's my son?"

Patricia took them to the hallway near the side door where Spur had put Alex. His hands were on his chest and his body quite rigid by now. The whole top of his head was a bloody mass.

Martin went to his knees beside his son, and Philander caught Patricia's arm and hurried out of the hall with her.

"Let the man be alone with his son to say goodbye," Philander Knox said.

Ten minutes later, Martin Jefferson spoke to them briefly. "I'll handle it. I'll tell the police he went north to our place up there and shot himself. That friends brought the body back here not realizing it shouldn't be moved. There won't be any problems. But I'm warning you two that I don't believe the story. Not a word of it."

"He went crazy, Mr. Jefferson. Exactly the way I told you. I tried to stop him from running off. We told him there would be no charges. He wouldn't believe us. Just the way you aren't believing us now. I hope you don't go crazy, too."

Martin Jefferson gasped in disbelief at the girls' words.

She turned and marched away down the hall and up the stairs.

Philander put his hand on his partner's shoulder. "Forgive her, Martin. She's been through a terrible experience. But the story does sound true to me. You must admit that Alexander has never been the most stable young man."

Martin ignored his words. "I won't be to work tomorrow. Cover for me. I'll be burying my son. Your family is not invited." Martin Jefferson turned and helped two men carry the body of his son out the side door and up the street to his own mansion.

Patricia waited for her father at the landing on the second floor.

"Father, I'm sorry this happened, but it was not my doing. Alexander shot himself. Now it looks like the three families are tearing themselves apart. Edmund Pickering is not sure how his son died and he almost won't speak to Martin Jefferson. Now Martin is furious at you and me. Where is it all going to end?"

"I don't know, daughter, I don't know."

"Daddy, will you tell me why Redfield died? I don't believe the story about the accident. Redfield told me he would never drive down that street."

"He died in the buggy accident, Patricia. That's all I know."

"Father, I simply don't believe that," Patricia said. She turned abruptly and marched away to her room down the hall.

The next afternoon, a small item appeared in the newspaper that Alexander Jefferson had taken his own life with a pistol shot. Private services for the family only were held earlier in the day.

* * *

When Spur went into the U.S. Mint the following morning, he walked directly to Philander Knox's office. The third in charge of the mint looked at Spur with a frown.

"Tell me, Mr. McCoy. How did Alexander Jefferson die? I want you to tell me your story."

"My story is the same as you heard last night, I'm sure, from Patricia. He kidnapped her. I found out about the country place and knew that Alex was missing as well. It seemed to fit together. He had the motive for revenge. I followed them to the cabin, got there in time to prevent the rape and then Alex shot me, a crease the doctor looked at this morning. Your daughter is an excellent nurse.

"Then while I was unconscious, Alex ran up the mountain with a rifle, a pistol and a sack of food. Patricia said he went a little crazy. I slipped up on him in the woods. I've had some experience doing that sort of thing. When he realized he was about to be captured, he shot himself through the top of his mouth and blew off the top of his head. You saw the body."

Knox got up and paced the floor.

"Mr. Knox, I'm turning in my resignation. I know I could never work for Mr. Jefferson now. He probably thinks I killed Alex because he wounded me. I won't expect any compensation. Tell Patricia I hope she's feeling better."

Knox stopped and turned to Spur. "Had you met my daughter before yesterday, Mr. McCoy?"

"Matter of fact, I met her here the first day I arrived. I asked for Redfield Jefferson through some oversight on my part, and Helen burst into tears and fled, and that's when your daughter explained to me why the girl was so upset. I understand Helen had a crush on Redfield for years."

"I see. Patricia spoke highly of you."

"I think she's a remarkable young lady, but if you're asking if I have any romantic interest in her, the answer is no. She'll find some man her own age, or all the young men in San Francisco are idiots."

Knox smiled at that. "Thank you, Mr. McCoy. I'll tell her you said that."

Spur turned and walked out of the mint. As he left, he turned into the guard the small identification card they had issued him. The guard looked at him curiously but said nothing.

Spur caught a cab to the Almont Hotel where he had a short talk with the room clerk and moved from his room on the third floor to room 416 on the fourth floor.

"There's a man in town who is looking to spill my blood. I'd prefer that he didn't. You keep me on the books at my old room, but put any messages for me into box 416. Got that?"

"Yes sir, Mr. McCoy."

Spur slid a ten-dollar gold piece into his hand and nodded. "This is just between us. You keep me alive, I'll make it worth your while."

He went up and moved his gear to the new room, kept the old one locked, and changed clothes. He shed the tie and black coat, put on a less formal coat and a string tie, his cowboy hat and slid the two shot .45 derringer into the special pocket at the side of the jacket. It didn't show at all.

He went downstairs and caught a cab to the Halverson Metal Shop and went in. There was no one in the small front office. He rang the bell but got no response, so he pushed through a door into the back. A customer stood waiting for some molding to be done.

When the five-foot tall man with absolutely no hair on his head came forward, Spur knew he had to be the metal man. He had forearms and shoulders like a bull.

Spur motioned the man farther from the other person and spoke low. "I recently came into the possession of some gold bullion—with the mine imprint in it. Makes it hard to sell, know what I mean? How much would you charge me to melt it down and recast it in two pound chunks?"

"How much gold?"

"Twenty pounds. I've heard that you're honest and reliable and ultimately discreet."

"I don't blab, if that is what you mean. Cost you $20, take about two hours, mostly for cooling off. You'll be here and watch the whole process so you got no complaints about my stealing any of the gold."

"Sounds good. Do you work at night?"

"On special occasions."

"I'll be in touch with you to set up a definite time we can do business."

Spur left. He had seen what he wanted to. Halverson was about as crooked as a witch's cane. He probably had been a thief or robber in his younger days, now worked the next step in the criminal chain, helping the robbers to disguise raw gold so they could sell it on the used gold market.

Outside, he walked down two blocks before he caught an empty hack. He had the man drive him through Portsmouth Square where he looked at the huge gambling halls. He might not have a lot of time to investigate them. He read their names as he rolled by: El Dorado, Bella Union, Parker House, Mazourka, Arcade, Varsouvienne, Dennison's Exchange, Veranda, Empire, Fontine House and the Meade.

Instead of stopping, Spur had his driver take him back to the Almont Hotel where he went up the back way, claimed his six-gun from his 416 room and went back to the third floor. Room 316 two doors down the hall was unoccupied. He used his skeleton key and opened it, went inside and closed the door except for a crack.

It was just past noon time, but there could be a surprise visitor anytime. He expected that a man like Martin Jefferson would waste no time in his own style of revenge.

Spur pulled the room's only chair up to the door and sat down so he could see out the crack and watch his old room. About an hour later, Spur saw two men come into the hall and up to room 310. One looked each way, then the shorter bent and turned a key in the lock of 310. He pushed the door open and must have seen the dummy form Spur had left in the rumpled bed.

There were four shots, and the man who had stepped into the room came out.

Spur leaned around the door with his six-gun out. "Looking for me, gentlemen?" he asked. The lookout lifted his weapon to fire but Spur's bullet nailed him to the wall exposing the shorter man who lifted his weapon and fired his one remaining round that missed.

Spur put a .45 slug in his thigh, then rushed down the hall, grabbed the man and threw him into room 316 and closed the door. The man on the floor fumbled to reload his weapon when Spur kicked his gun hand, spinning the Colt out of his fingers. He looked at the gun, then up at Spur.

"Four bullets into my sleeping body? You're not a nice man."

The man skittered backward toward the window.

"Who hired you to kill me?" Spur asked.

The man refused to speak. Spur kicked him in the side aiming at his kidney. He hit it. The man bellowed in pain and drew his legs up to his stomach to lessen the drilling, numbing pain. He turned and threw up.

Spur waited. When the would-be killer had wiped off his mouth, Spur asked the same question again. The man failed to answer, so Spur pulled back his boot to kick the man's other side.

"No, god no. Some guy on the street. Didn't give me a name. Paid me $50. Said get a partner. I did. The guy gave me your room number. Said do it anytime you were here."

"Describe him."

"Tall, six feet, maybe 210 pounds. Pot belly. Full beard that he kept stroking. Put on specs to read your room number off a piece of paper."

"Yeah, that's enough," Spur said. It was a perfect description of Martin Jefferson. Spur motioned with his gun. "You're free to go."

"Yeah, thanks. No hard feelings?"

"None at all," Spur said.

The man stood and moved toward the door.

Spur shook his head. "Not the door, killer, the window. Three stories won't kill you but it'll bust you up some. Next time you think twice before you take on a killing job."

Spur caught the man as he bolted for the door, picked him up and wrapped his arms tight against his body and carried him to the window.

With one throw, Spur propelled the man head first at the window. His head broke the glass, and one knee banged at the window frame, then the man was through and screaming the three floors to the alley below.

Spur stepped into the hall. Two men stood looking at the body on the floor.

"What's the trouble here?" Spur demanded.

The taller man shook his head. "Looks like somebody got shot to death," he said. "We heard the shots."

"Take care of it," Spur said, walked the other way to the stairs and went up to room 416.

When he came down an hour later to slip out of the hotel, the body, the gawkers and the San Francisco police were all gone. All that remained of the shoot out were some blood stains on the hall's carpet runner. You start trying to kill folks, you must be ready to die yourself. Spur had no regrets.

Spur thought of watching the Halverson Metal Shop tonight but decided not to. Martin Jefferson didn't work today, so he would have no chance to pick up any gold scissel. Tomorrow night, Friday, might be a different matter.

Spur checked with the room clerk when he went out for supper. There was a note in his box.

"Spur, must see you tonight. Meet me at the Bandbox Restaurant at 6:30 for supper. Urgent." It was signed with a P.

Spur went back to his room and packed half of his clothes and goods in the small carpetbag. At the desk he explained to the man that he was still paying for both rooms at the Almont.

Ten minutes later, halfway across town, Spur checked in at The California Hotel under the name of James Redfield. He was sure that Martin Jefferson would try for his hide again.

Then he found the restaurant and waited for

Patricia to come. When she came in she didn't look at him, but went through to the private dining rooms. A moment later a waiter came out and showed him the way to a small cove off the main dining room that was screened and shaded from the main room. Patricia smiled when he came in. He noticed then that they could see out but no one could see in.

Patricia reached up and kissed his cheek. She grinned like a teenage girl. "Father told me what you said about not having any romantic interest in me. What a shame, we would make an ideal couple. Now to important things. I want to tell you that I applied today and was accepted as a teacher for the fifth grade at a school here in town. Isn't that terrific? I know we're going to be without funds shortly, and I figure either me or mother must have a job, so it's me."

"Congratulations."

She said she'd already ordered for both of them. "We might as well enjoy the stolen money while we can. I guess it put me through college. I'd never thought much about that. How much do you think they stole in the past 10 years?"

"No way of knowing. We may never know, unless your father keeps good records. My guess would be, maybe $750,000."

"Oh, my." I was thinking I would pay it back if I could." She laughed and he laughed with her.

Their food came, some fancy French dish that Spur never was quite sure what it was, but it tasted good to a hungry man.

He told her about the two men in the hotel.

"My goodness, you think Mr. Jefferson actually hired them?"

"The one described Jefferson right down to his

specs to read the room number. It was him and he'll try again."

He looked at her. "Don't worry about it, happens to me all the time. Part of the job. Now, what was so urgent?"

"I just didn't want you to slip away and I'd never see you again. Urgent to me, but not to you."

"I'm not going anywhere until I blow this thing apart. Oh, a question. Is Lucinda really crazy? I get the idea she's being held somewhere so she won't shout to the world that her father is an embezzler."

"I'm not sure. She did some weird things, but nobody thought of them as being crazy. Then one day she did do something crazy. She told me once that she thought there was something funny going on with our three families, but she never said what. That was three or four years ago. She's only been locked away for about a year. The more I think about it, the more I think you might be right. She always was a talker. If she knew what I know now, she'd blab it to everyone in town."

"Maybe before we blow this thing apart, we should go visit Lucinda. Would that be possible?"

"She isn't allowed visitors."

"A few dollars can often bend the no visitor rule at most places. Twenty dollars will buy a lot of looking the other way.

"Let's try it."

After the supper, Spur asked her what she wanted to do and she said walk. They walked down the block and around the gambling halls.

"I went in once with $100 and lost it in exactly 12 minutes," Patricia said. "I've never been back."

She looked up at him as they walked, her arm through his. "You really don't have any romantic intentions regarding me?" she asked.

"No, not romance as in courting and getting married. I'm a traveling man, remember? And I've spent too much blood and struggle to help you keep your virginity for your husband to take it away from you now."

"Oh. I see. I guess." She reached up and kissed his cheek. "I think it's time I went home. I haven't caught up on my sleep yet."

He took her home in a carriage, watched her go up the steps and safely in the door, then he rode back to the California Hotel and went to sleep. Nobody in San Francisco knew he was there, not even Patricia.

· 16 ·

Martin Jefferson reported to work Friday as usual at five minutes to nine and made his normal Friday morning walk-around inspection. He paused at the Receiving Department and talked briefly with Nance Sturgill, the weightmaster. Their voices were soft, guarded and low.

"I'm terribly sorry about your son, Mr. Jefferson."

"Yes, a tragedy, but life goes on. Today, Mr. Sturgill, I want two percent of the scissel on any gold coins made. I need up to 20 pounds if you work that many coins. The same on Monday. I've had some problems and need some quick money."

"Yes sir. I understand."

That morning they were punching out blanks for

the gold eagle, the ten dollar coin. When Sturgill told Ben Oakmarker, the man who brought the scissel to the weigh room, Ben slammed his hand down on the top of the counter.

"Why the hell should we? Let's demand more money. I'm going to tell him I want $200 a week or I won't sign off on the two percent shortage anymore. Hell, let him squirm for a while."

"Now ain't a good time, Ben. The man just lost his son."

"So what, you and I could be heading for prison, too. I'm not taking the risk no more for no lousy $10 a week. I'll tell him Monday."

"Go easy. This morning he was in no mood to have anybody tell him anything."

"Too bad. That's the kind of mood I'm in, too."

By ten o'clock Friday morning, Spur McCoy had checked his key box at the Almont Hotel. He had two messages, one from Laura Grandifar asking him to send her a note so they could get together for dinner or an evening on the town. The second note was from Patricia.

"Found out for sure where Lucinda is. Suggest we meet at noon and try to see her. The more I think of it, the more certain I am that Lucinda isn't crazy, just a little strange, and I think the family is frightened of what she might say. Noon at our shrimp place."

Spur went down to headquarters and checked with his friend on the San Francisco police force. Gale Daniel leaned back in his chair and shook his head.

"Sorry, no developments at all on the Redfield death. With the witness dead and two homicides in the same location, it makes me want to ask a lot of questions. But I don't know who to ask." The cop looked at Spur with squinty eyes. "McCoy, you know more about this than you're telling me? I thought we were working together on this."

"Sorry, Daniel, there is more involved here than I've told you. It's concerning the mint, government business, and I can't tell you a lot more until I'm authorized to tell you. There will be some surprises for you in a week or so, I can assure you that."

"Then the kid was murdered?"

"Absolutely. Exactly by whom, I'm not sure, but I'd guess it was the second man you found with Stoop Lackwalter. The big problem is to prove who hired the killer as we talked about before."

"Then you still suspect Martin Jefferson but can't prove it. Damn shame. I don't know if this would help," Daniel said checking through a file on his desk. "But we did have some inquiries about Lackwalter and the second man. Oh, we finally got a name on the man with the scar on his face who died near Lackwalter. He went by the name of Downer, usually. Downer Felling. Also known as Scar Felling and Downing French. He was a hired killer who was good at his work. His last boss must also have been good at it."

"So who asked about Stoop and Felling?"

"Gent named Edmund Pickering, who said he was the young Pickering's father. We had a good talk, and he seemed to think that his son had not died in an accident."

"So he's digging into it. Good, can't hurt our cause any. I have some more spade work to do."

"If you need any help, arrest warrants, anything like that, or a few good men, I can do it for you."

"Thanks, I just might want some assistance like

that." Spur shook Daniel's hand and left the police station. He took a thinking walk, trying to sort everything out. The pieces were starting to drop into place. The only problem was that he needed a lot more pieces, and hope that some of them would turn into solid convicting kind of evidence.

By the time he worked his way through the streets and to the fisherman's long wharf, it was nearly noon. He saw Patricia under her big hat near the shrimp cocktail place.

He bought three of the tasty snacks and they sat well down on the wharf watching the small boat owners unloading their catch.

"You know where she's staying?" Spur asked.

"Yes. It's called the Cromwell Clinic, a private place that's about half hospital and mostly for sick people who don't have much of a chance of getting well. It's all very secret, and used mainly by well-to-do clients. Like the Jeffersons."

"Patricia, was Lucinda ever violent? Did she break up things and hurt people, or use a knife, say, to stab someone?"

Patricia laughed. "Not Lucinda. She was full of fun and gentle and soft spoken. Sometimes she'd pretend to be somebody else and get loud and wild, but she never even scratched anyone. I don't remember her ever hurting a soul."

"Good, Patricia. Let's finish our shrimp and go find her."

On the buggy ride, he asked Patricia about her sister Denise and her husband Victor Pickering.

"Do you think they know where the family fortune is coming from?"

"Denise, I don't think so. She's fairly realistic but not inquisitive. However, if she did know, I don't think she'd allow Victor to be part of it. He's older than I am, and I never knew him well. I'm just not sure."

She watched Spur for a moment. "If this all comes out, all three families will have to give up everything we own, right? What about the seconds, we second generation kids?"

"If the court can show that anything you have came from your parents and the stolen money, the court will take it. Did the Pickerings help Victor buy the house he lives in?"

"Oh, yes, a wedding present."

"It's gone to auction for sure."

"Oh, dear." She shrugged. "Well, our parents brought it down on our heads. Nothing we can do now but salvage what we can. At least I have a job for this fall."

The hired cab rolled up to an iron gate in one of the better sections of Telegraph Hill and stopped.

"We have to ring and wait for someone to come talk to us," Patricia said.

"I've got a lot of good arguments right here." He clinked six double gold eagles back and forth in his hand. Spur told the driver to wait for them.

They rang a bell at the gate and soon a tall man with broad shoulders and a surly expression came to the locked iron barricade.

"Yes?"

"We're here to see Lucinda Jefferson, bringing her some new clothes and some candy she loves," Patricia said flashing her best smile. "The manager said it would be all right."

"Our patients are not allowed visitors," the unsmiling man said.

Spur clinked the coins in his hand so the man could see them.

"I understand there are exceptions," Spur said. He took one of the $20 gold pieces and stepped close to the gate and held it out at his waist where no one could see it.

The man took it and frowned. "It might be arranged. The physician in charge is gone today. Still, it's a risk for me."

Spur held out another coin. It vanished and the man put down his hand once more. Spur pushed another double eagle into it and the man grinned and unlocked the gate.

"Follow me and be quiet. This could cost me my job."

They followed him along a gravel path behind a screen of trees to a side door. He unlocked it with a key from a ring full. They went along a narrow corridor. The place didn't look like a medical facility, more like a prison. Each door had two locks on it, not the usual door kind, but fancy ones with round brass fittings. They went up a flight of stairs and along another hall. From the front, the building didn't look nearly this large to Spur.

At last the guard stopped at a door and used keys that were slender and flat and opened the door. He knocked, then pushed it in a little.

"Lucinda, we have some visitors for you," the man said in a kinder voice than they had heard him use before.

The door swung open slowly. A woman sat on a bed in a thin, cheap cotton nightgown. When she looked up her face was haggard, her eyes sunken, her long brown hair was snarled, dirty and in ropes from lack of care.

She looked at Spur, then down at Patricia and her face lit up with a sad smile.

"Patty!" she struggled off the bed and waddled toward Patricia. That was when Spur realized that Lucinda was at least eight months pregnant.

Lucinda threw her arms around Patricia and they hugged and patted her extended belly under the gown. Then Lucinda touched her hair and looked away.

"I'm sorry . . . sorry I don't look better. I haven't worried about my hair. . . ."

"Lucinda, you look just fine, and a baby! That's wonderful."

"Daddy didn't think so. First he told me I had a serious illness. The doctor probed and growled and nodded and then went out to talk to Daddy. The next thing I knew I was in here. That's been over a year ago. I wasn't sick at all. Daddy was afraid that I would say the wrong thing. I've always talked a lot, as maybe you can tell, but he shouldn't have put me in this jail house. Then after I became pregnant, Daddy never came to see me again."

"We know about the three families stealing the gold, Lucinda," Spur said.

"Oh, Lucinda, this is Spur McCoy, my best friend in the whole world, the man who saved me when I was kidnapped but I'll tell you about that later. Spur, this is Lucinda Jefferson."

They said hello and her handshake was firm, she looked him straight in the eye.

"No, I'm not ashamed to be pregnant and not married."

"How. . . ." Patricia began.

"It happened in here. I'd been here about five

months, and they wouldn't let anyone see me. Then one night three of the men came in and took turns holding me and raping me. They made it a game. It went on for almost two weeks. And then I was pregnant."

"Lucinda, would you like to get out of here?" Spur asked.

She looked at him with pleading eyes. "With all my heart, but Daddy knows I'm pregnant and he said maybe after I have the baby and we got rid of it, I could come home."

"I think right now would be a much better time, Lucinda," Patricia said. "We are not without certain persuasion."

"Goodness . . . I've been here so long . . . with no hope . . . absolutely no hope. . . ." She began to cry. Patricia held her and Lucinda sobbed.

As she cried, Spur stepped silently to the door and tried it. Locked, as he was sure it would be. The guard must be just outside. Spur pressed against the derringer in his pocket. He had six more .45 rounds for it in his pants pocket if he needed them.

Lucinda stopped crying and pointed under the bed. "Everything I own in the whole world is under there. I don't know what mama did with my room at home."

"We'll *damn* well find out," Lucinda," Patricia said. They looked at each other and smiled. The small box under the bed had a much thumbed Bible, two combs, a small gold pin and two cheap earrings. That was all.

"We'll leave this here or they'll suspect something," Patricia said.

"Yes, I like that about finding out where all of my things are," Lucinda said. "We *damn* well will." The women grinned at each other and hugged each other again.

They found her shoes, and Spur looked the other way as they got Lucinda squeezed into a dress from the closet. Then they took a long coat she had brought with her and put it on. She showed to be pregnant, but only if you looked carefully.

"Now, we practice walking. Walking is supposed to be good for pregnant women," Patricia said. They walked the length of the room and Lucinda lost some of her waddle.

Spur talked with the women quietly. "This might get a little rough. About the only way to get out of here is to pretend you're a visitor leaving. We should be able to get out the same way we came in." He took out the derringer.

"Lucinda, I've got this little gun I probably won't have to use, but I want you to know I have it. We're going to reason with the guard who brought us in, to help us get out."

"Most of the guards are mean and I don't like them," Lucinda said.

They were ready at the side of the door. Spur knocked firmly on the panel and a moment later it opened. The guard leaned in with the door and Spur grabbed his arm and yanked him into the room. By the time the guard caught himself, the muzzle of the derringer was under his chin pushing upward.

"Little friend," Spur said softly. "If you want to see the sun come up while you're still alive tomorrow, you better do exactly what I say, make no indications anything is wrong, or make any signals to any other guards or employees here. Are you clear about my meaning."

The guard's wide eyes stared at him. "Yes," he

mumbled.

"I'm a United States government lawman on official duty, and I can kill you without a second thought. No one will even question it. Do you understand that?"

The guard swallowed. "Don't never do nothing to interfere with a law officer. No sir. What you want me to do?"

"We're going to walk out of here the same way the two of us came in, only there will be three of us and you. Lucinda is going out of here. If she doesn't, you die. It's that simple. If we get out and no alarm is sounded, you live. If we don't get out, you'll die on the spot or near the gate. Is that completely understood?"

"Yes sir. Not many people on duty right now. No trouble, no problem, I swear." Sweat began to run down his forehead. The guard wiped it away, more came surging down and dripped off his nose.

"Any other guards out there, roving patrols, dogs, anything like that?"

"No sir. Just me and Charlie who is at lunch right now. He starts late."

"Let's go."

Spur opened the door after the guard unlocked it from the inside with a key, then they walked down the hallway. Spur held Lucinda's arm supporting her, helping her move. They walked slower than they had coming in.

A door slammed ahead of them. No one came out. Spur watched behind them, saw one door open a crack, but someone was only watching, not coming out.

They went down the steps. That was the hardest part for Lucinda. She groaned and yelped once or twice, then grinned. She was so happy to at least be making a try to get free.

They got to the side door and Spur looked out. A man walked by slapping a night stick in his hand. He vanished around the corner of the building.

"Man out there with a stick," Spur whispered to the guard. "Who's he?"

"Charlie, new man. I can get us by him if he comes back. He's on his way to the kitchen."

They went out the door and Spur helped Lucinda to walk faster. It seemed to take a year to walk down the gravel path. They were a dozen feet from the gate when Charlie came up a path from the other way. He froze for a moment when he saw the four of them.

The guard with Spur stepped forward.

"Charlie, how was lunch?"

Charlie pointed at the three people.

"Some folks leaving after bringing us a new patient."

Spur saw a signal go between the two men. The secret agent nodded at the other guard, then jumped forward and swept the side of the derringer down across the side of Charlie's head. He sagged but didn't go down. Spur's hard right fist slammed into Charlie's jaw, dumping him unconscious beyond a small hedge.

The guard with them started to run away.

"Not another step," Spur spat and the guard stopped and looked at the little gun not three feet from his belly.

"No sir, this way to the gate."

Spur had paid the hack to wait for them. Now he was out of his seat, helping the ladies into the back. Spur stayed with the guard. When the women were in the hack, Spur sent them away and motioned with the derringer to the guard.

"Stay outside with me and close and lock the gate. You and I are going for a little walk."

"Look, I helped. . . ."

"Up to a point. That's why you aren't dead right now. Don't push my good nature. Move it."

They walked three blocks away from the clinic. Then Spur let go of the guard and told him to keep on walking away from the clinic. Spur watched the rigs along the street and a moment later saw the hack with Patricia and Lucinda in it making another circle of the block. He stepped into the buggy's front seat beside the driver.

Patricia gave the driver an address and they wheeled away. Less than ten minutes later they stopped in front of a small residence hotel.

Spur helped the ladies down from the cab and then saw the sign: "Women Only." He moved back and let Patricia and Lucinda into the place. Ten minutes later, Patricia was outside again with a big smile.

"Lucinda is simply thrilled that she's free, and that I'm here to help. She's all set in a room. Now for some shopping. We need clothes for Lucinda, some pretty things, and I'll come back and wash and fix her hair. The poor dear. She said her father threatened to put her away if she didn't keep quiet about the gold. Then she said just the wrong thing and he sent her to the clinic. Isn't that barbaric?"

Spur went along as she shopped and carried the load of boxes and packages. It was nearly five o'clock when they got back to the women's hotel, and he carried the packages into the lobby, then Patricia waved at him.

"Spur McCoy, we've done a good thing today. I've taken a room here as well so I can be with Lucinda for the rest of her term. We both thank you so much. I never really knew Lucinda well, just the brave outside that made her sassy and a little wild. Now I'm getting to know her."

She paused. "Whatever happens with Daddy and the other two and to our families, I know it has to be done. I've helped. If there's anything more I can do, let me know here or at home." She kissed him on the cheek and then ran down the hall carrying a stack of boxes.

Spur hurried out to the cab and had him drive to the mint, but Spur looked down the alley and saw that the three management men's buggies were already gone. Missed them. They could have heisted some more gold today.

That idea gave Spur a thought. Just before the final arrest on Jefferson, he should catch him in the act of having the scissel melted down. Catch him with it in his briefcase just as he was going in the smeltering shop. Spur would need at least two other men with him to confirm it for unshakable courtroom evidence. That might be a good job for Inspector Daniel and another of his policemen. Yes.

Now, what next? He had been told by someone at the mint that the boss was a fanatical record keeper. He had records of everyone who worked there including days off, times they were sick, and how many children they had.

A nagging concern for Spur wouldn't go away. If Jefferson was such a good record keeper, would he also keep records of how much gold he had stolen from the mint and how much he sold it for?

It sounded logical. So where would he keep the records? The safest place would be inside the U.S. Mint. Who was going to find it there? In his desk, behind a loose board, under the floor or even in the vault—any such record book might be easily hidden anywhere. Spur decided he would have to put that problem on the shelf for the moment.

Pickering had been asking the police questions about his son's death. Was this the time to approach the man about making a deal? Pickering would find out the details about how his son had been murdered by Martin Jefferson, if Pickering would agree to testify against Jefferson and Knox at the trial. Immunity from prosecution for Pickering would be hoped for but not promised. Was now the time?

Spur wasn't sure. He went back to his new hotel, the California, and up to his room where he scribbled down what he knew and what he wanted to know about this thievery.

He worked until midnight and rubbed his eyes and put away his twice re-sharpened pencils. The more he worked it and thought it through, the more he decided he had a real lever that he could use to pry Pickering loose from the group and turn him against them. He would try it, tomorrow if he got a chance. But how could he meet Pickering? Why not just go to the mint and ask to see him. What better way?

Spur turned out the light and hoped for sleep. It had been a good day. Lucinda was out of bondage. That was another one he owed Martin Jefferson if it came to any kind of a physical standoff. Spur grinned just thinking how it would feel to slam his fist into Jefferson's face!

· 17 ·

The next morning, Spur tried to decide whether to take his six-shooter Colt along with him. At last he left it in his room at the California Hotel. Not many people wore guns in San Francisco these days, at least not in the business world. He made sure that his derringer hideout was completely hidden, put four extra rounds in his pocket, and took a cab to the mint.

The guard seemed surprised to see him, and went back to give Mr. Pickering the message that Spur McCoy wanted to talk to him. The guard came back and motioned to Spur.

"Mr. Pickering was not pleased. Said he didn't think we'd see you again after what happened to Alex Jefferson. I thought you should know before you go in there."

"What was it that happened to Alex Jefferson?"

"You shot him and they covered it up with a suicide story. That's what everybody is saying."

Spur laughed softly. "So that's the story. The boy blew the top of his head off after he went crazy and tried to rape Patricia Knox. That's what really happened."

The guard lifted his brows and knocked on Pickering's door, then opened it and stepped back.

When Spur walked into the room Edmund Pickering was standing beside his desk with a cocked six-gun in his hand.

"Close the door and sit down," he ordered.

Spur did as instructed.

"Young man, you've got one hell of a nerve coming in here after what you did."

"What did Martin Jefferson tell you I did, Mr. Pickering?"

"That you drove his son into insanity, then shot him and made out like he killed himself."

"Then why isn't the law after me? Mr. Pickering, do you believe that story Jefferson is telling?"

"Did. Not so sure now. If it's true, why would you walk in here?"

"Because it isn't true. Did you ask Patricia what happened? She was there. Alex was the one who kidnapped her and tried to rape her, again. What does she say happened up at the mountain house?"

"Don't know. Alex kidnapped her?"

"Ask her. Mr. Pickering, maybe it's time you start asking a lot of questions about what Martin Jefferson does and says. I know you've been talking to the police about the death of your son. I can't even imagine the anger and torment you must be going through. By now, I'd imagine that you have decided that Redfield was not killed in an accident in his buggy."

"The police said that was a possibility. They had a witness."

"But now that witness, Stoop Lackwalter, is dead, along with another man they think killed Stoop. Who do you think killed the man with the scar, Scar Felling?"

"How do you know all this?"

"It's my job to know all of this. So answer my question. Who do you think killed the man who probably killed Redfield before he caused the terrible buggy wreck down the hill?"

"I don't know."

"Mr. Pickering, you must have known about the letter Redfield wrote to Washington about some problem at the Mint. You knew about that, didn't you?"

"Yes, but I never knew what it said the problem was. Evidently Knox saw it, or a copy of it, and told Martin."

"Do you want to know what the letter said, Mr. Pickering? It might help you figure out what's going on around here."

Pickering lowered the six-gun and went behind the desk. He sat down. "I'm not sure if I want to know or not."

"But you suspect what it might have said. Something that could ruin the lives of at least five families who have men working at the mint."

Pickering looked up quickly. "Who told you that? Who are you anyway?" The six-gun came up again.

"May I answer those questions, Mr. Pickering? Are you sure that you want to hear the answers."

Pickering lowered the gun and looked out the

window. "Yes. Yes, I guess it's about time. Ten years is a hell of a long time to look over your shoulder."

"Your son told the Bureau of the Mint in Washington that someone in the San Francisco mint was embezzling gold. That letter is what got him killed."

Pickering lifted the gun again. "Are you guessing, Mr. McCoy?"

"No. I have a lot of facts, just not quite enough yet."

"You'll never live to use them. Now we have to kill you. Why did you come here this way!" The last was a cry, a wail, a wish that Spur had never said the words.

"Because it's my job. Mr. Pickering, my name really is Spur McCoy and I work for the Treasury Deparment in the Secret Service. One of my jobs is to protect the currency, that means the gold it's made of as well."

"Oh, damn. The Secret Service! Now you are dead." He lifted the weapon and aimed it at Spur's heart."

"I don't think you're going to shoot, Mr. Pickering. You still want to know how Redfield died, and who ordered him killed."

The gun wavered. "You're right about that. But if I let you live, the five of us wind up in jail. They'll just throw away the keys and leave us in there until we rot."

"Probably. I think you all deserve it. But there's more to it, isn't there? Who ordered Redfield Pickering, your youngest son, cut down before he had a chance to become a man?"

Pickering put the gun on the desk. "Yes, damn-it! I'll give up everything else just to nail the bastard who killed my little boy who hadn't quite grown up yet."

"I can tell you, but it will be costly to you."

"I have plenty of money, stolen money of course, as you know."

"I don't want money. I want facts, figures, and most of all, I want your testimony about how the thefts of the scissel began, whose idea it was, and exactly how much gold scissel has been stolen with the two percent system."

"My god! You know everything." He stood and walked around the room. "You're telling me if I give you this information, and testify in court, you'll tell me now who killed my son?"

"That's about it. I can't guarantee you immunity from prosecution, only the United States attorney in this area can do that. But I'll recommend that to him."

Pickering stared at him. "Better I take off for Oregon or Alaska or somewhere. Hell, I can guess who told somebody to snuff out the life of my son. I can guess." He shook his head, picked up the weapon and motioned Spur to go ahead of him out a back door in the office. It opened into a narrow hallway that ended in some steps that went down. Along the sides were small window slits with glass in them that could be used for observing the people below in the mint.

"Spy holes?" Spur asked.

"In this business we don't trust anyone," Pickering said.

"Takes a thief to know a thief," Spur said.

Pickering flared and lifted the gun, but then he sighed. "Yeah, you're right, but I'm not letting you go now. We should have a few more days. If we kill you now, the Feds will just send somebody else. Looks like the beginning of the end."

"Starting to look that way. Why don't you take a chance on getting out clean by testifying for the prosecution?"

"Can't do that. My family will go down, my kids, the whole thing will unravel."

"It's already coming apart. You don't think I'm the only one who knows about it, do you?"

They came to the bottom of the steps and turned to the left into a room with no windows. Spur figured it was a basement.

"Yes, I think you did come here alone and that no one else from Washington knows about it. So we do have some time. There's no way out of this room. Only one way in and only three men have a key to get into this observation walkway. Not even your screams can be heard topside."

Spur seemed to give up. His shoulders slumped. His hands fidgeted with the buttons of his jacket.

"Hell, I should have known better than to appeal to your fatherly instincts. *You don't care who killed Redfield in cold blood.*"

Pickering shivered. The gun wavered. He looked up at the ceiling in fury. That's when Spur pulled the hide-out derringer from his jacket and jumped against Pickering. Now the six-gun pressed against Spur's chest, but Spur's hide-out .45 pushed against Pickering throat.

Pickering gasped. "You bastard! How did you do that so fast?"

"Practice, old man, reflexes and practice. I'm used to dealing with guns, you're not. Now, we have a standoff. You shoot me and I shoot you. Is that what you want? That way you don't have even a one-in-a-hundred chance to live and get out of this mess without going to prison."

"Bastard!"

"Yes, I know, we're two of a kind. Only I didn't steal $800,000 from the U.S. Mint."

"Eight hundred. . . ." Pickering stopped. "My god, I guess it could be that much over 10 years. Eighty-thousand a year would be that much. Oh, damn."

"Take your time. You've got a fifty-fifty chance of getting immunity from prosecution. If so that means they can't charge you with a thing or send you to jail. You'll have to turn in all of your bank accounts, property, stocks and bonds, horses and carriages, anything that can be auctioned off for cash to help repay the government.

"So what? You'll still be alive. Think about living another 30 or 40 years, instead of dying in 20 seconds. Think about that—living for 40 more years or dying in a few seconds with your brains blown all over this room."

"Immunity? A chance?"

"A damned good one. I've done it before."

"Are you really with the Secret Service?"

"True."

"I'll put down my gun if you will," Pickering said.

"Fine with me. I don't want to die either."

They watched each other and both slowly lowered their weapons.

"Is it Jefferson who killed my boy?"

"He's the one who must have hired the deed done. He probably hired Felling who killed Redfield probably with some blows to the head, then staged the wreck. Felling dug up the witness. Then Felling knifed Stoop on orders from Jefferson after I started asking Stoop too many questions. Jefferson watched from 100 yards away, and once

Stoop was dead, Jefferson shot down Felling. It's the only story that makes any sense."

"It's good enough for me. Yes, I'll testify for you. I'll tell you the whole stinking, thieving story. But first, I want my time with Jefferson. I don't care if he never lives to stand trail or not."

Spur grabbed his wrist. "Pickering, you can't deal with Jefferson first. I'll set up the deposition for this afternoon. I'll have to get a court, talk with the U.S. Attorney, and get a stenographer to take down word for word what you say."

Pickering was fingering the six-gun. Spur reached down and took it gently from his hands.

"Mr. Pickering, did you hear me? You can't even talk to Jefferson about that today."

"I heard you. I won't. I've had suspicions before."

"You know there's a chance you still could go to jail."

"I realize that." He sighed, his shoulders slumped and he shook his head. "How in the world did I ever get myself and my family mixed up in all of this?"

"It happened a long time ago, Mr. Pickering, and then just grew."

They walked up the steps from the basement and to the first floor but still in the observation run.

"Is there a back way I can get out of here? I'd rather not have Jefferson or Knox see us together."

"Yes, I'll show you a way."

"Can I count on you being at the courthouse at one o'clock?" Spur frowned as soon as he said it. "No, I don't know where to tell you to go. I'll pick you up here and we can go down together. I have some arranging to do before that time."

"Don't worry, I'll tell you everything I know because I want the first shot at Martin Jefferson."

Spur hoped the man would contain himself. He caught a cab down to the courthouse and at last found the United States Attorney. They had a long talk as Spur told him there was a crime in the city that he wanted one of the principals to make a deposition on before he was arraigned.

"What kind of charges, Mr. McCoy?"

"Embezzlement from the United States Mint."

"Wow. How much?"

"As much as $800,000. There are three of them, no five actually. I have one who will testify for the prosecution if he gets immunity to any prosecution."

"Possible, on a case like this. Lay it out for me."

At the end of an hour the top U.S. attorney in San Francisco was grinning. "He's got immunity. We better keep him under lock and key after we get his deposition."

"We can't do that or we'll tip our hand. The three of them are about ready to tear each other's throats out as it is or maybe take off for China."

"We'll give it a try."

At five minutes past one o'clock, Spur picked up Edmund Pickering from in front of the mint. He was there with his hat and cane waiting.

"All set?" Pickering asked.

"Ready to go at one-thirty." Spur watched him as they rode in the buggy. "Any regrets about this deposition?"

"Not a one. My big regret is ever agreeing to the dastardly embezzlement plan in the first place, ten years ago."

At the courthouse, a bored judge swore in

Pickering, then left the bench and Edmund Pickering began telling his story of the great embezzlement. It had been Martin Jefferson's idea. He had been promoted to superintendent of the San Francisco mint, and at once began to scheme to defraud the government.

Pickering talked on and on, with an occasional question from the U.S. Attorney. He told exactly how the gold was stolen, how the coverup was made, and what would have to be done to determine the actual shortage over the 10 years.

"Did anyone keep a record of the gold taken?" Spur asked.

"Oh, Martin did, in a little single edge ledger bound in red leather. He kept it in his desk somewhere. I've seen it from time to time but not for the past couple of years. It didn't interest me any more."

Pickering told them where the scissel was melted down, who the current buyer was and that they paid a 3 percent discount because of the copper in the gold, and a commission for the buyer.

"Did the gold buyer know that it was stolen gold?" The United States Attorney asked.

"Oh, absolutely. There is no chance that he did not know. Who else would have that much pure gold each week? He knew. He's partly to blame then, right?"

After an hour and a half, and two different court stenographers working in shifts, the deposition was completed.

"I want that sealed until we bring charges," Spur said. The U.S. Attorney agreed. The lawyer looked at Pickering.

"I understand there is another reason you

dislike Mr. Jefferson?"

"Yes sir. He killed my son."

"Murdered him?"

"Hired someone to do it. The police put it down as an accident. Wasn't any accident. The letter I mentioned, my boy Redfield wrote it to Mr. Spur here, and Knox and Martin found out about it. Martin had him killed. I aim to have a word or two now with Martin about that."

"No violence, Mr. Pickering. Then I'd have to charge you with a killing. Promise that you'll stay away from him for the next day or two until we can get our charges all straight?"

"Promise."

Outside, Pickering took a deep breath of the afternoon sea breeze that was bringing traces of fog from the ocean.

"You've done the right thing, Mr. Pickering," Spur said touching the man's shoulder.

"I hope so. Mostly I hope that Thelma Mae and Victor think so. Family has always been important to me."

Pickering turned and walked away down the street, mingling with the people on the sidewalk.

Spur leaned against the side of a building. The wheels of justice were grinding. Already the U.S. Attorney would be writing up charges against the five men, arranging for the warrants for their arrest. That might take a day or two. Spur wondered what he could be doing.

He stopped by the police station headquarters and talked to Inspector Daniel and brought him up to date on the key witness.

"I'd say you've about wrapped it up. No jury in this town could go against a witness like Pickering."

"Maybe. I'd be happier with Martin Jefferson safely locked away in a cell in your jail."

"This is Saturday. Probably won't get the warrants until Monday. You best go back to your hotel and have a good supper, then wager a dollar or two at one of our big gambling halls. I never use them, but I hear they are the best in the West."

"Might do that."

Spur went past the Almont Hotel and checked both his boxes. There were two messages. He read them at the side of the lobby.

One was from Patricia.

"Thank you again for rescuing Lucinda from that terrible place. The two of us took a walk this morning. Lucinda had on a new dress that allowed for her condition and a hat that covered most of her pretty face. Oh, I washed and combed out her hair, trimmed off the ends and did some waving on it. She looks a thousand times better now than yesterday.

"Just wanted to thank you for your help. I could never have done it by myself. Hope the case is coming along well. I stayed here last night, sent a note to mother so she wouldn't worry.

"Let me know if you want some expert detective help.

"Love, Patricia."

Spur took a long breath and smiled. A fine young lady. He wished her well.

The other note was from Laura Grandifar.

"I must have missed you. I tried your room

twice yesterday and today but you don't seem to be here. I want to see you. Don't be naughty and say no to Laura. Write me a note at my house. You have my address."

He folded both notes and went back to the California Hotel where he had an old fashioned beef stew supper and two pieces of cherry pie. He looked forward to a long night's sleep, and then tomorrow a Sunday stroll along the bay and perhaps a little fishing, if he could talk some ragamuffin out of his pole and can of worms. Not much he could do on the case now but pray and hope that the U.S. Attorney didn't mess things up.

· 18 ·

B en Oakmarker steamed and boiled and silently raged most of Saturday afternoon. They were punching out gold coins and Mr. Jefferson had demanded at least ten pounds of scissel. Hell, it was no skin off his nose. Martin Jefferson was doing the stealing. But he and Nance were helping him.

He knew he was breaking the law, had known it from the first. But just recently he realized he wasn't getting enough pay for the risk. He should have seen that years ago.

Ben wheeled the last load of gold scissel from the half eagle stampings into the weigh room and hoisted the box on the scales.

"We still doing it?" Ben asked.

"He's the boss. He told me to pull two percent so I'm doing it and I'm signing."

Ben grinned. "Hell, I'm not signing! That's the club I've been trying to find. I'll sign when he gives me my $200 every time he takes gold out in his briefcase. I'm going to go see him tomorrow, or tonight. Hell, he ain't getting away with this no more."

Ben sweated. The sudden realization that he was starting to protest shook him. He was short and stocky and dark, but right then he felt 10-feet tall.

"By damn, yes! I'm going to see that bastard tonight at his house. Or maybe at the metal shop. Yeah, that sounds better. First, I'll go home and get my persuader."

Nance Sturgill weighed out the gold, deducted 2 percent and marked down the short figure. Then he carefully picked out 2 percent of the gold scissel in the weigh box.

"Don't go and ruin the whole thing, Ben. We've had it pretty good."

"Not like the three sons-of-bitches who got rich! Without us they couldn't do it. No more. Not me." He threw down his apron and headed for the door.

"Not quitting time yet, Ben," Nance said.

"It is for me. Don't matter. Either I win with Jefferson tonight and it won't matter my leaving early, or this whole thing blows up in all of our faces and we go to jail. One or the other. There's no middle ground for me no more."

He slammed the door, walked to the side entrance, went through inspection in the special room and hurried outside. It took him over a half hour to find the little metal shop where Jefferson took the scissel. He'd followed the boss one night to find out for sure who was doing the melting down.

Ben slid down behind some old boxes in the alley and watched the door he knew led to the Halverson Metal Shop. It was only 5:15 by his pocket watch when a buggy pulled into the alley and Martin Jefferson got out with his briefcase and went into the open back door.

Ben followed him and rushed up while Jefferson still held the briefcase. He slammed his fist into Jefferson's wrist and he dropped the case. Ben grabbed it and stepped back, the case in one hand and a six-shot revolver in the other.

"What the hell . . . Oakmarker?"

"Damn right, Jefferson! I've got a message for you. I don't work for $10 a week no more. Everytime I sign that register for light weight, it's costing you $200."

"Shut up, you fool!" Jefferson snarled. "Other people can hear you."

"I don't give a shit. I want more money. You take out scissel once a day, I get $200 a day. Right now you took yesterday and today. You owe me $400, right now."

"And what if I say I won't give you that much?"

"Hell, then I send a letter to the San Francisco Police and to the Director of the Bureau of the Mint. Won't take them a week to have a man out here roasting your balls over Halverson's forge fire there."

Halverson stayed in the background. It was none of his business.

"You're crazy," Jefferson said trying to be more rational now. "If you did that, you'd go to jail right along with me."

"Not me. I'll know they're coming and be in Mexico or Canada. I got some money saved. And I've got about $3,000 worth of gold right here. You see, I'm holding the gun, and I ain't afraid to use it. That includes you too, Halverson, so don't go sneaking off."

The metal man nodded and sat down on a cold anvil.

"Smart idea," Ben said. He looked back at Jefferson. "You sit your ass down, too. First lace your fingers together and put them on top of your head. Want to see if you got a weapon."

Ben searched him and found a hideout derringer, a small .22 caliber that could get lost in a man's hand.

Ben swung the briefcase of gold to Halverson. "Melt it down, and cast it in four chunks. I'm taking some of my back pay."

The metal man nodded, lifted the case and began his usual melting and recasting ritual.

"You'll never get away with this," Jefferson said.

"Why not, you going to tell the Director of the Bureau on me? Not likely. Or go to the local lawmen? Not a chance. I've got you on the rail, Jefferson. No more are you going to treat me like dirt. You pay up, or the game is over."

Jefferson let his hands down slowly from his head. "Look here, Oakmarker, there's no reason we can't work out something. The $200 a batch sounds fair, make that $200 for Nance Sturgill as well. We can be most accommodating. There's no reason to change our procedure."

Ben stared at Jefferson. "Damn, I don't know why I've been afraid of you all these years. You're nothing but a common thief." Ben walked around the little shop, keeping them all well in range. At last he stopped near Jefferson.

"Hell, I've decided. I don't want to worry about lawmen coming for me no more. I'm changing the plan. I want enough to get away, right now, tonight. I want $20,000. You can say I quit and put on a new man at my job Monday. Yeah, you get me $20,000 and the game is all yours again."

"Twenty thousand . . . that's a lot of money."

"Not to you, it ain't. You steal that much in a couple of months."

Jefferson saw the iron bar. It was a chance. He put one hand to his chin thinking. "Maybe I could do it. You'd want it tonight, but the banks are closed until Monday. I'm not sure what is in my safe. We could take a look."

Ben laughed and for a moment looked over at Halverson who was heating up the forge.

In that half a second, Jefferson struck. He scooped up the half-inch thick iron bar three feet long and swung it hard directly at Ben who stood only six-feet away. He lunged forward as he swung.

Ben looked back in time to see the attack. His gun came up and fired all in one motion. The steel bar hit him on the left arm, numbing it, but the bullet had taken some of the force from the blow.

Ben's .45 round slammed into Jefferson in the right shoulder, driving him back against a large metal punch press. He leaned there, dropped the iron bar and his hand covered the wound trying to hold the blood inside.

The roaring blast of the exploding .45 round sent shock waves of sound through the small metal shop. Halverson put his hands over his ears. Jefferson screamed in pain. Ben Oakmarker calmly thumbed back the hammer on the six-gun and aimed at Jefferson's face.

"You bastard! I should kill you right now. Don't doubt it, I've killed men before. Most of them a hell of a lot better men than you are." He glanced at the metal man. "Halverson, get over here and find some bandages or some cloth and tie up his damn shoulder. I don't want him bleeding to death before I get my money. Move!"

Twenty minutes later the gold was melted and poured in four different molds of two-and-a-half pounds each. There was no imprint from the molds on the metal. They let it cool.

"Next we go to your place, Jefferson. If your safe doesn't have enough cash and gold, we move on to the Knox house and then Pickering. The three of you must have enough to keep my mouth shut. You're not talking much, Jefferson. Don't you like taking orders for a change instead of giving them?"

Jefferson glared at him.

"What's $20,000 to you, as against rotting in a federal prison for 50 years. That's what you'd get. How much have you stolen all together? I bet you kept track."

Jefferson turned away from him. Ben stepped up and slapped Jefferson's cheek. His head twisted to one side from the blow.

"When I ask you a question, you answer me, you big pile of shit. How much?"

"I'm not sure."

"About how much?"

"Over . . . over a half-million dollars."

"Damn, I guess you're good for something. You think big. But now I'm the one thinking big. Christ, I don't know why I didn't do this five years ago.

I've got your nuts in a vise, you move and I'll squash you like a bug.''

When the gold was cool enough to move, Halverson wrapped the four bars in newspaper and put it back in the briefcase. Ben saw that there was nothing else in the case. It must be a duplicate of Jefferson's real one that he only used to carry the gold.

- "Outside, Jefferson."

Ben turned to Halverson. "Melter, you keep your mouth shut about this and I'll let you live. I should put a hole in your skull right now. But you're enough of a crook to know I'm giving you a break. No talk, you keep on living."

Ben pushed Jefferson out the door and waited as he struggled to get up the step into the buggy. He put the briefcase beside his feet and drove. He knew the way to Nob Hill. Often he had driven by slowly, staring at the big house where Jefferson lived.

Now he was going inside and helping himself to the goodies of the house. Too bad Jefferson didn't have a daughter or two. At the house he swung in the drive and behind the house.

"How many servants in the place now?" Ben asked.

"Two."

"Where's the safe?"

"In my study."

"Say nothing to anyone. Go straight to the safe and open it."

"If I see my wife?"

"Tell her to come with us."

"No!"

"Why not, she knows how much you steal. She has to know. Now inside and no trouble or you're one dead mint superintendent.''

They went in the back door, saw no one and walked down the hall. A young woman dressed in a maid's black and white looked out of a room, nodded and went back to work cleaning the room.

Two more doors down, they turned into the den. Ben closed the door and locked it, never letting his glance off Jefferson.

"The safe, quickly."

"Twenty thousand and you'll be gone and forget you ever heard of us?" Jefferson asked.

"Absolutely. I'm a man of my word."

Jefferson moved a picture on the wall, twirled the knobs and unlocked the safe. He reached for the handle to open it, but Ben was there. He pushed the muzzle of the revolver into Jefferson's side, and pulled open the safe door himself. Just inside lay a derringer.

Ben took it and slid it inside his shirt, saw there were no more weapons and waved for Jefferson to proceed.

The superintendent took out a wrapper of twenty-dollar greenbacks. "Much easier to carry than gold," Jefferson said. "The discount is down to about ten percent now. I'd suggest that you take half of it in greenbacks."

He held up an inch thick stack of twenties that had a rubber band around them and a small piece of white paper that said $2,000.

"There's a hundred bills in each stack. Two of the twenties makes $4,000, and one of fifties makes another $5,000."

"Martin, are you in there?" a muffled voice came through the heavy door.

"Yes, Wilma, some business. You go ahead with supper. I'll be out presently."

"All right."

Jefferson frowned, then looked in the safe again. He took out a heavy leather sack. When he opened it, he showed Ben brand new mint perfect $20 gold coins.

"Two hundred double eagles there. Another $4,000. You have $3,000 worth of scissel in the briefcase, that makes $16,000. That's all the cash I have."

"Damn, that's close. Put it all in the briefcase."

"So now you'll leave, get your wife and go to Mexico?"

"Not before I get my other $4,000. Let's you and me go see Mr. Knox. He always seemed like an agreeable man to deal with."

"Why not have him come to you?" Jefferson said. "You're the boss now."

"Yes, good idea. Call one of your servants to go tell Knox to get his bones over here, fast. Tell him to bring $5,000 in gold or paper. You've had a small problem."

Jefferson nodded. "Yes, that should do it. Why don't we make the $5,000 in paper. Knox likes the convenience of paper money."

"Fine, just do it. Your shoulder is starting to bleed again. I wouldn't want you to bleed to death right here in your den."

Jefferson unlocked the door and bellowed down the hallway.

"Peter! Peter! Get in here, I want you."

A few moments later a short man in a white coat and black tie hurried up. He took a note that Jefferson scribbled. Ben grabbed the note from the man's hand and read it:

"Knox. Bring $5,000 in greenbacks at once. A small emergency. Now, please. Jefferson."

Ben gave it back to the man.

"Now run, man, get this over to the Knox residence as quickly as possible."

The servant turned and ran out the door.

"We wait," Ben said. He watched Jefferson sit down in one of the straight chairs well away from the desk or other furniture.

Ben had the weapon ready as he eased down on the edge of the desk. "You really thought Nance and I were happy getting a pittance for signing our lives away every week?"

"You said nothing about it. It seemed like a good procedure for 10 years."

"What about the boy, Redfield? Was that just another procedure for you, too? Most of the people at the mint figured you had him killed. They don't know why, but that's the way they figure it. Some kind of a loyalty problem. Nobody knows about the stealing. You kept that quiet for a long time."

"You helped there, Ben. I wish you well in your new home, wherever it might be." He looked at the door. "You'll be leaving tonight, I'd think. Feel free to take the buggy we came home in. I'll have Peter keep it ready for you."

"So you want me to leave so you can send the police down on me? Not a chance. I'm taking you with me. If any of your people want to see you alive again, they better just shut up about all this. Especially Mr. Knox."

"I'm sure he won't say a word. He has as much to lose here as I do. You can appreciate that."

Ben snorted. "I only appreciate that $20,000 I'll have in my hands, and thinking about all of the things that money can buy me."

The door knob turned, then someone knocked.

Ben had the gun up covering the door and Jefferson.

"Come," Jefferson said.

Philander Knox barged into the room, a canvas bag in one hand. He stopped and stared at Ben and the gun, then at Jefferson.

"Martin, what's going on here?"

"Close the door, Knox," Jefferson scolded. Knox closed it.

"Mr. Oakmarker has the upper hand, I'm afraid. "Just give him the $5,000 and he'll be on his way. He quit his job and has promised not to say a word to anyone about what went on at the mint. He could get in as much trouble as we could."

Without a word, Knox reached in the bag.

"Easy, Mr. Knox," Ben growled. "If a gun comes out of there, you're going to be dead."

Knox slowly drew out a stack of bills, then one more. Twenties, two stacks.

"Satisfied?" Knox asked.

"Very good," Ben said. "Now, Mr. Knox, if you would come over to this door, a closet, I believe."

It was. He opened it and pushed Knox inside, slammed the door and turned a key in the lock.

"You're next, Jefferson," Ben said. He put the $5,000 in the briefcase, hefted it and grinned, then pointed at the hall door. "You and I are going to go on a nice drive in the evening. Whether you come back or not depends on how helpful to me you are. Understood?"

Ten minutes after the buggy left the Jefferson residence, Mrs. Jefferson came in the den looking for her husband and heard Knox banging on the closet door with his shoe.

It took another 15 minutes for Knox to explain

to Edmund Pickering what had just happened.

"The whole thing is falling apart," Knox said.

"Maybe more than you know. Right now what we have to do is find Jefferson and Ben Oakmarker. My guess is that they went to Oakmarker's house so he could pack a traveling bag."

"With $21,000 he could buy whatever he needed anywhere he went," Knox said.

"We're dealing with a frugal man. Even with lots of money, he's going to act like a frugal man. Let's go."

Knox knew where Oakmarker lived. From time to time it had been his job to check to see that the two workers were not living too far beyond their means.

They got to the house 10 minutes after Oakmarker and Jefferson had left. His wife was in hysterics. All they could understand from what she said in her crying and screaming was that Oakmarker said he had to go on an important business trip and wouldn't be back for a month.

They sat in the buggy outside the Oakmarker house staring at each other.

"Where would you go if you were running from everyone?" Knox asked.

"To Oakland and the train east."

"That means the ferry. It won't leave from the dock until ten in the morning heading for Oakland."

"Too long a wait. He might be seen. The police might be looking for him. We might find them."

"So what else?" Knox looked into the darkness.

"With that much money he could hire a boat to go over to Oakland. He'd be there in an hour and ready to take the morning train east."

"Let's check the waterfront."

By then it was about 7 o'clock. Along the dock area there were two places where a wide variety of small boats docked. Many of them were fishing craft that worked the bay and the shoals as well as the deeper waters off shore. Here and there was a small steamer for hire.

They found three, but none of them reported hearing of anyone going across the dark bay.

"Not a lot of fun in the dark," one captain said. "I wouldn't make the run for less than $50."

Knox nodded. He understood that. Fifty dollars was two months pay for most working men.

After an hour of canvassing the docks, they found no one who had heard of anyone looking for a boat for a trip across the bay to Oakland.

"They could rent horses and ride around the south end of the bay and then up to Oakland."

"Too far, take them too long, even if they didn't get lost. Ben sounds like a tough character."

"That was one of the reasons I put Ben in the position as second signer on the weighmaster, because he'd had some problems with the law."

Pickering looked surprised. "How could you trust a man like that?"

"Easy. He needed the job and he'd be crooked for us for a price. Now I remember why he had served time. He killed a man in Utah."

The co-conspirators stared at each other.

"Now it's not so much a matter of finding both of them," Pickering said, "it might be a matter of finding Martin's body wherever that madman chooses to dump it."

· 19 ·

They drove up and down the streets for an hour, then sat in the soft glow of the light from a gambling hall and stared at each other.

"We're getting nowhere, this is hopeless," Knox said.

"I agree," Pickering echoed. "What I think we should do is get Spur McCoy to help us. He found Patricia when none of us could."

Knox frowned. "That was an entirely different matter. There's a secrecy element here."

"He wouldn't have to know anything about the why, just that Martin's been taken away by an angry man from the mint."

Knox sighed, at last he nodded. "McCoy was staying at the Almont Hotel. Not an elegant one, but adequate."

Five minutes later they discovered that Spur McCoy was not in his room.

"Hasn't been in all day," the desk clerk told them. "A message for him is in his box. If you gents will give me your names, I'll see that he gets your message at the earliest opportunity."

"If you can do that, we'll make it worth your while," Pickering said. "This is important; no, it's urgent!"

Pickering wrote out a message and asked for an envelope. He put the paper inside, sealed it, wrote Spur's name on the outside and handed the envelope to the room clerk along with a quarter eagle gold piece.

The desk clerk beamed. "Yes, sir! I'll see if I can locate Mr. McCoy for you gentlemen. It may take an hour or so."

"We'll be back here in an hour," Pickering said and walked out the front door to their buggy.

When the two men were gone, the room clerk called his brother and told him exactly what to do. The 12 year old ran out of the hotel and caught a cab. Ten minutes later he would be at another hotel. The clerk watched him go smiling. This Spur McCoy must be an important man. He had told the clerk that if anything urgent happened there was a way he could be contacted: the Hotel California.

It was a little less than an hour later that Spur McCoy waited at the Almont's darkened exterior and saw two men drive up. He recognized the small size and thin ascetic form of Philander Knox. He met them at the street.

"McCoy, we need you to help us. We can pay you." Knox said it quickly before Pickering could get in a word.

"Let's get in the rig and talk as we're moving," Pickering said.

Once they were driving, Pickering outlined the problem. He said simply that one of the employees, a Mr. Oakmarker, had kidnapped Mr. Jefferson and they were extremely worried about his safety.

Spur picked up at once that something had gone wrong in the five man theft ring.

"So all we have to do is find Mr. Jefferson at night in a town of 100,000 people," Spur said. "Sounds easy."

He watched them in the darkness. Both were angry, confused.

"You've checked the obvious places you think this Oakmarker might have gone."

"Yes, all of them we know about," Pickering said. "We figure he might be heading for the railroad over at Oakland across the bay."

"Didn't he work closely with the man who weighed the materials as they came in, what was his name?"

"Sturgill, Nance Sturgill," Knox said. "They did work together. He might have gone there."

They turned the rig around and drove for 20 minutes. At the house, Knox went up to the door and talked for two minutes, then came back.

"Nance says he hasn't seen the man since he left work early this afternoon."

Spur rubbed his chin. "Let's try to put ourselves in his boots. You kidnapped your boss, maybe took some money, then left with the boss and his buggy. What would you do? Where would you go?"

There was silence in the dark buggy.

"You said you tried the boats." Spur said. "That would have been my first choice of the best way to get to Oakland and the train. The quickest. Next would be to wait for the first Transbay Ferry in the morning. It's Sunday, so it should start about eleven? It must be 70 miles around the south part of the bay to drive or ride to Oakland, that's out of the question."

They drove along for a while, all three men thinking.

"When does the first eastbound train leave Oakland in the morning?" Spur asked.

"I'd say it's still the same, six-forty-five A.M. Daily." Knox gave the information.

"Three, four miles across the bay," Spur said at last. "If he was desperate he could do that in a row boat."

"He's smart," Knox said. "I found out he killed a man in Utah before he came to work for us. He knows something of the outlaw way of living."

"So he wouldn't want to attract attention," Spur said. "He wouldn't hire a boat. He'd wait for the first ferry and then dump Jefferson either alive or dead. That means he'd hole up somewhere out of sight, probably gag Jefferson and tie him up. So that's what we have to look for. Jefferson's buggy backed into an alley somewhere near where the ferry docks. Let's take a look."

Systematically they prowled eight different streets near the ferry landing. Once Spur got off to look at a parked rig, but there was no one in it. Knox said it wasn't Jefferson's buggy.

They worked out another block from the ferry and went down the alley. Halfway down they saw a horse hitched to a rig that had been backed between two buildings.

"Looks like Martin's black mare," Pickering said.

"Sure as hell is!" Knox whispered. Spur lifted the Colt from his holster. When he got the message at his hotel he knew he should come well armed. He took two steps toward the buggy, but was still 50 feet away when someone yelled and slapped the reins on the back of the black horse.

The animal leaped forward with a trained reaction, then raced out the far end of the alley.

Knox wheeled his rig up quickly, and Spur jumped in.

"That's Jefferson's horse and buggy," Pickering shouted. "Chase him down, that has to be Ben Oak-marker driving!"

They raced down the alley, followed the heavier buggy to the left and then across town until it was racing west toward the ocean.

"What's he trying to do out here?" Pickering asked over the noise of the wheels and the jangling of the harness.

"No idea," Knox said. "He can't outrun us. My gray is as fast as that black, but we're loaded heavier. Still, we're keeping up with him."

They had swung out along the road to the ocean, then turned south along the surf. There were trees and some salt marsh, but the rig plowed right through the soft spots and headed deeper into the grove of oak and brush and a few scrub pines of some sort.

"What the hell's he trying to do?" Knox shouted.

"If he has $20,000 in cash with him, I'd say he's trying to get away," Spur said.

"He won't get far this way," Pickering said.

"This road runs into a marsh and dead ends in another half mile."

A short time later the front buggy slowed and a pistol shot sounded. The round came close enough so the three in the back buggy could hear it whiz past them. They slowed.

"No sense getting killed chasing him," Knox said. They watched the other rig make a wide arc and come back to the road retracing the tracks back toward town.

Spur took out his Colt and motioned to Knox. "Pull us up another 20 feet on him. He won't be watching back here now."

When the rig was closer, Spur leveled in and fired three quick shots. When the sound echoed away, they heard a long wail of pain.

"Guess I hit somebody," Spur said. "I just hope it was this Ben guy."

They raced back the way they had come in the soft moonlight. There was enough light to see the road and the rigs careened along sometimes half out of control, but neither driver gave any indication of backing off.

Then Knox's horse began to fall behind.

"Damn, she's getting tired," Knox said. "She doesn't get enough exercise, just to work and back."

They watched as the black buggy ahead pulled farther away. It was 50 yards ahead of them now.

"Goddamnit, no!" Knox shouted. He laid the lines on his horses back half a dozen times. The startled animal reacted and began making up the distance.

They were back on the San Francisco streets.

"Where the hell is he going now?" Pickering

demanded.

They made two more turns and the street slanted up abruptly.

"He's going up Telegraph Hill," Knox shouted. "Only one way down, we can block off the son of a bitch!"

Ben Oakmarker swirled the buggy around at the very peak of the hill where lovers often came to look out over the faint lights of the city or to watch a sunset.

Oakmarker headed back toward the route down but Knox pulled his rig across the trail. Rocks rose on one side and the land sloped down on the other. Oakmarker was blocked.

Spur came out of the rig and put a shot across the top of the black buggy as it came to a stop.

"Get out of there, Ben," Spur called.

Ben fired a shot that grazed the gray and it screamed and stamped in the traces.

"You've got nowhere to go, Ben. Might as well give it up."

"Hell, no. Jefferson'll kill me. You must be with Knox and Pickering. If Jefferson don't finish me off, they damn sure will."

"Why, Ben?"

"They know why. What was your name? You that guy who worked a day or two . . . Spur?"

"Right."

"Hey, you and me, just common folks. We got to stick together. We're not uppity society folks."

"It won't work, Ben," Knox shouted. "Give us the money and we'll let you go."

"Like hell you will." Ben fired again, missed, and Spur and the other two ducked down.

"You hurt Martin any?" Pickering called.

"Tied him up so he wouldn't go nowhere. We was waiting for the ferry. No reason to hurt him."

"Untie him, let him bring the gold over here and we'll let you walk away from here alive," Pickering said. "We won't come after you."

"Oh, hell yes. You won't even start to do that."

"You've got a gun," Pickering said.

They heard a roar, a shout behind the other buggy and then a scream and a shot. Spur lifted up ready to run forward.

"It's safe over here now," a new voice said. "The bad man has lost his gun and is flat on the ground."

"Jefferson? That you?" Knox called.

"Damn right, it's me. If I had to wait for you guys to rescue me, I'd be dead. Get over here!"

The three ran to the back of the other carriage where they saw a form on the ground.

"He dead?" Knox asked.

Jefferson ignored him. "Who the hell is this? McCoy? What the hell you doing here?"

"I asked him to help us find you," Pickering said. "He did."

"You got back the money?" Knox asked.

"It's in my briefcase." Jefferson looked at McCoy. "You've done your job now, McCoy. We'll give you $500 and you take that other buggy and drive back downtown and leave it in front of the Almont Hotel."

"I don't see why you'd want me to do that, Mr. Jefferson. As a concerned citizen, I will be glad to accompany you to police headquarters with this kidnapper and to testify against him. It seems to me, as an honorable man, that's the least that I can do. I, of course, will accept no gratuity from you."

"I expected that you would say something like that."

As they talked, Ben Oakmarker came back to consciousness after the blow dealt him by Jefferson. He lay there quietly for a moment, then sprang up and raced off in the darkness.

"After him!" Spur shouted.

Jefferson touched his arm. "No, not if he's going in that direction."

A moment later there was a scream, and then another and another that came fainter and fainter.

"He went over the edge?" Knox asked.

"Sounds like it," Pickering said. "He probably had never been up here before. It's at least 100 feet down there to the rocks."

Spur watched them with a pretended concern. "Don't you think we should go down and see if he's injured?"

"He's injured all right," Jefferson said. "They used to call this suicide leap. He's injured nigh unto dead."

"Then we need to report it," Spur said.

"Not me," Jefferson said. "Sometimes it's better just to accept the poetic justice of it. He tried to steal from us, he kidnapped me, then he fell to his death. Yes, pure poetic justice, I'd call it. Now, if you gentlemen would remove your vehicle from the roadway, I'll be returning to my home."

Pickering walked to Spur. "Let's let it be, Mr. McCoy. I'll give you a ride back to town."

They got in the buggy, turned it out of the roadway and made a circle as Jefferson worked his rig slowly down the hilly trail to the more normal street.

"It was poetic justice at that, wasn't it?" Knox

said. "Oakmarker trying to rob us, then falling to his death. He got what he deserved all right."

"Then you're sure that he's dead?" Spur asked.

"Almost no one lives who falls or jumps over there," Pickering said. "Happened several times now."

There was little conversation as they drove back to the Almont Hotel.

Knox touched Spur's shoulder. "That's twice you've been of tremendous service to me, Mr. McCoy. I insist on doing something for you. Let me take you out to supper Monday evening. The best restaurant in town."

"I always eat, yes, Mr. Knox, that would be most welcome."

Pickering stepped out of the buggy so Spur could exit and as they stood on the sidewalk he whispered. "I nearly shot Jefferson tonight. I don't know how much longer I can hold out."

"Monday is our magic day. Wait for Monday." Spur shook hands with Pickering. "Yes, it was an interesting evening, Mr. Pickering. Thank you."

Spur stood on the sidewalk watching the rig drive away. He went inside to the Almont to check on his box and felt someone watching him. He glanced around the small lobby and saw Laura Grandifar rising from one of the big chairs.

He went to the clerk, found no messages and walked toward the outside door. The woman followed him. On the sidewalk, she caught his arm.

"Thank you for not rushing up and kissing me in there," she said. "That clerk was getting suspicious."

"So was I," Spur said. He hailed a cab and gave him directions.

Laura smiled in the darkness of the buggy, reached over and kissed his cheek, then turned his head so she could kiss his mouth. She leaned against him and made the kiss a long one. When their lips parted, she laughed softly.

"That, Mr. McCoy, is how much you can trust me. With all of my heart and soul, to say nothing of a long, leisurely night in your room at the hotel, wherever it is."

They stopped at a late night store and bought apples, three kinds of cheese, crackers and two bottles of California wine.

"Now that's the kind of a man I like," Laura said. "One who plans ahead. I always get so damn hungry."

She went up to the room first. He caught her on the last flight of steps and carried her the rest of the way. Laura giggled and kissed his cheek.

"I just love to get carried around."

He put her down to open the door, then she ran inside and found the bed from the faint light that came in from the hall lamp before he lit the lamp in his room. She jumped on the bed and watched him.

"Hurry up," Laura rumbled deep in her throat. "I've been wanting you all day!"

He lit the wick, slid the glass chimney in place and turned up the flame a little. Then Spur closed the door, locked it and slid the back of the straight chair under the door handle. Even if the door were unlocked it wouldn't open until the chair broke into pieces. By then Spur would be ready.

He sat on the bed and pulled the cork out of one of the bottles of wine and sipped it out of the bottle.

"Me next," Laura said. She drank some, then put the wine on the dresser and pulled Spur down beside her. She reached and found his crotch then whispered in his ear.

"Spur McCoy, I want you to stick me fast and hard, and don't you dare take off any of our clothes. Just lift up my skirts, I'm not wearing a thing under them."

She wasn't.

She opened the buttons on the fly and helped him, then turned on her back and motioned to him. Spur grinned and went between her white thighs. She moaned as he poked into her, then her legs went up around his sides and locked over his back. She squealed for as long as he pumped into her. When he erupted and dropped on her, she locked her arms around his back and wallowed in the glory of it.

Soon she nudged him, caught his hand and pushed it down between their bodies. "The other one, you know."

He found her clit and strummed it a dozen times, then that many times again and suddenly the pent up explosion came, shaking her like a leaf in a tornado, slamming her from side to side, rattling her with a series of hard spasms as she climaxed a half dozen times.

When she at last tapered off, she smiled at him, then closed her eyes and he wondered if she had gone to sleep.

He changed the position of his arm and she opened one eye. "McCoy, you move another muscle and I'll kill you. I love it just the way we are. I'm not moving for the rest of the century." Her eyes closed and she giggled, then relaxed again.

It was twenty minutes later before they sampled the wine again, cut the apples and had the cheese and crackers.

Laura finished half an apple. She now sat on the bed naked, with her legs crossed. Her breasts were full and pink tipped and Spur thought never more beautiful.

Suddenly she held up her small hands doubled into fists like a bare knuckled prize fighter.

"Round Two," she said and grabbed him. They fell onto the bed laughing.

· 20 ·

Martin Jefferson watched the other buggy moving along behind him. He was furious. He had given Knox back the $5,000 in paper money, and checked to see that the rest of the money was still in the briefcase. His shot shoulder hurt like fire.

Oakmarker hadn't had any time to spend the money since he took it. Martin had been with him the whole time. Now the idiot was dead. How did he think he could go up against the three of them and win? Martin himself was twice the man that slime Oakmarker was.

He drove slowly and turned off the normal route to Nob Hill. He had to think it through. Yes, he would be gone Monday. He would make all the arrangements tomorrow. Monday morning he would go to the bank as soon as it opened, draw out the money he had there, have the rest of his gold reserves in hand, and be ready to catch the coastwise steamer for San Diego and Mexico Monday afternoon. It would sail with high tide.

Martin Jefferson drove on home. Spur McCoy popping up again bothered him. He was too interested in the mint and the managers to be coincidential. Yes, he would send a man to eliminate the man. He must be here in response to that damn letter Redfield had written. When McCoy came to the mint, he at first asked to see Redfield Pickering. It fit together now tighter than ever.

He took a detour on his way home. Martin stopped in a back street and went up to an unlighted door. He knocked three times and waited. After several minutes the door unlocked and cracked open an inch. There was no light inside.

"Yeah?" The voice was a growl.

"Have some work for you. Worth $200, gold."

"Tell me who and when."

"Tonight, tomorrow at the latest. His name is Spur McCoy. Used to stay at the Almont Hotel. The room clerk there can be bought. He might know where McCoy moved to. He's slippery and good with a gun."

Martin took two gold double eagles from his pocket and pushed them at the crack in the door. A hand with black hair on the back of the fingers took the coins.

"Yeah. I can do it. Tonight or in the morning. Now get out of here." The door closed.

Martin smiled as he walked away. This man was

the best in San Francisco. The job would be done.

He made another turn and drove to Bonita's house. As usual, he parked in the alley and went in the back door. She was already in bed. He lit a lamp and watched her uncoil from her bed. She slept nude, he had taught her that. She sat up slowly like a tabby cat, uncurled and reached out for him, her breasts dancing the way she knew he liked, her lean legs parting and moving toward him in a demanding dance.

"Woman, I've been shot. Get some cloth and some alcohol and help me stop this bleeding."

For just a moment Bonita's eyes went wide with fear. Then she nodded and scurried into another room. He sat down in a chair and when she came back had his jacket off and shirt off. The bullet had sliced a half inch through his shoulder's outer muscle. Gently she stopped the bleeding with a white cloth pressed firmly against the wound.

"Alcohol?" she asked.

He took the bottle and sloshed it over the wound. Jefferson screamed with the pain, and shook his head. The pain had been more than he had expected.

"Finish it," he said through clenched teeth. Bind it up tight so it won't bleed."

She put on a compress and bound it tightly with strips of white cloth. When she was done the bleeding had stopped. He put his shirt back on and then his jacket.

He shook his head again to scatter the pain. At last he looked up. "Yes, it hurts, but now it feels better. Thanks." He kissed her.

"Now, get your things ready that you want to take with you, Bonita, sweetheart."

She stood up on her knees, her pretty face

beaming.

"We leave Monday afternoon. Just two more days."

"Oh, *bueno, bueno!* I am so happy!" She kissed him and hugged him. "You have time now for one or two, no?"

"Can't tonight. There are a lot of things I have to get done before Monday. But I promise you on that boat going down the coast, I'll keep your little pussy so hot it'll be steaming."

She kissed him again and reached for his crotch, but he slipped away. "Not tonight, Bonita. You can always get me worked up when I don't have time and now's one of those times. One small bag, that's all you can take. Your jewelry and combs, personal things. Clothes we'll buy down there, in Mexico City!"

He kissed her again and slipped out the back door. His mind raced as he figured everything he had to do. The second safe in the basement. He'd have to get in there. The stocks and bearer bonds would be good in Mexico City, as would the rest of his paper money. He'd convert another $30,000 in gold to paper so it would be easier to carry.

He would take the last gold bullion with him and the jewels. Yes, he'd take most of those he had bought for Wilma. She wouldn't be able to keep them anyway when the crash came. As soon as he left, there would be an examination of the books. Pickering and Knox would take the anger of the law. Good enough. They must know things were coming apart. That damn letter from Redfield. At least he got paid back for it . . . in blood.

Martin drove into his small stable and was met by a sleepy stableman who took the horse and rig. Martin carried the heavy briefcase into the house.

It was a little after midnight. Wilma slept in her bedroom down the hall. He wouldn't tell her he was going. She would just throw a fit. He couldn't put up with that.

Inside the house, he went at once to his secret place in the basement. Not even Wilma knew about it. He had it installed one summer when she had gone back to Chicago to visit her sister. He moved a workbench he had puttered around on years ago, lifted a trap door in the floor and opened a heavy wooden box. Inside lay two leather pouches.

In one were cut and polished diamonds, unset. He had picked them up three years ago when a friend of his needed $300 to set up the robbery of a jewelry store. The robber had bought off a guard and hired a second man and wiped out the jewelry store of more than $50,000 worth of stones.

Martin had his pick of $25,000 worth of the diamonds. The robber tried to cash in his stones and a month later was arrested and sent to prison.

Now, three years later and in Mexico City, the stones would be worth full value. He took out the pouch and looked at the other pouch. It held ten brand new $1,000 bills. He had forgotten about them. He had bought them from the bank one day on a lark. Martin picked them out and fanned them in front of him. Beautiful! He loved what money could buy and do for a man.

He put the hideaway back the way it had been and went up to his den. He sat in his big chair, lit two lamps and looked around. He had enjoyed it here. A hunting trophy or two, some fine memories, and all the money he wanted to spend. It would be the same in Mexico City where his dollars were as good as gold and would go about ten times as far as they did in San Francisco.

Bonita said the prices were that much lower. They would live and love and enjoy themselves. He had worked long enough. Now was the time to play!

He went to the wall safe and took out a packet of stocks and bearer bonds. He wasn't sure how much they were worth now, but they would be negotiable from Mexico City at a discount, of course. He could stand it.

For a moment he wondered how it would be for Wilma. The government would take the house and everything it could find he owned to sell for compensation. All of Wilma's jewels and dresses and the buggies and horses. It wouldn't be pretty, but at least he wouldn't be here to witness it.

The same thing would happen to Pickering and Knox, only they would be sitting in jail or a federal prison somewhere, rotting away for 30 to 50 years! He had seen the government prosecute men from the mint before. No mercy, and the maximum sentence.

Wilma? Hell, she would be all right. She was only 42, had a woman's body that men still liked. She wouldn't be able to buy her men any more, but she'd still get poked her share. She'd leave town as soon as it broke, he knew that. He knew Wilma. What people thought of her was more important than what she actually was or what she thought of herself. He snorted, turned out the light and went up to his bedroom.

To his surprise, Wilma lay on his bed waiting for him. She looked at him, sat up and he saw that she was naked. Her breasts sagged only a little, not as much as he would have expected by now. She held out her arms.

"Martin, I'm afraid. I have this premonition that something terrible is going to happen. Come and make love to me the way we used to, and tell me that everyng is going to be all right."

He looked at her. One more lie, what would it hurt? He stripped and sat down beside her. She didn't mention his bandaged shoulder. For an hour or two it would be like it had been, Wilma would be satisfied and her intuitive fears smothered and pushed back—for two days. Monday, she would know those fears were justified.

The man had talked with the clerk at the Almont for only a minute or two before the clerk realized that he meant business. One or two people had tried to get Spur McCoy's new address, but he had been able to resist. This time he couldn't.

The two of them were in a small room off the lobby, and the man had just made an inch long slice down the clerk's cheek. He had brayed in pain and conceded.

"All right! Don't cut me again. McCoy's at the California Hotel."

The broad shouldered man with a patch over one eye that had been gouged out in a saloon fight, grunted in pleasure.

"You sure he's at the California Hotel?" the man asked, his voice cultured, educated.

"Yes sir. I wouldn't lie to you. You might cut me again. The California. I know he's still there. Leastwise, he was earlier tonight."

"Good," the one-eyed man said.

The knife came up again and this time moved swiftly, cutting the clerk's throat from side to side, slicing through both carotid arteries. Blood spurted out each side shooting 10 feet across the small room, staining the walls.

The killer held the clerk's head by the hair to keep the blood off him. When the spurting stopped, even though the heart pumped frantically to keep up the pressure, the killer threw the clerk to the floor. He stepped over the body, wiped his blade on the corpse's white shirt and cracked the door looking into the lobby. No one was there. He slipped out that door, then the side door of the Almont Hotel, and walked down the street to find a cab.

It was slightly after two in the morning when the one-eyed man tested the door of Spur's room at the California. It was locked. He used a set of simple skeleton keys and opened the lock without the smallest sound. Then he turned the knob and tried to edge the door inward. Stuck. He tried again exerting enough pressure to move any small item. Solid.

A chair. The only thing he knew that would give that kind of pressure was an upright chair back under the knob. He'd have to break the chair to get in. By then, a man with a gun would blow him to hell.

The broad-shouldered man with one eye moved away from the door, found the steps up to the roof and went up them. A lock on the door became a quick victim to a pair of bolt cutters the big man took out of a small carpetbag he carried. On the roof he counted over to be sure he had the window to the right room, then took a coil of half-inch rope from his carpetbag.

He tied one end to the berm around the top of the roof that made a three-foot false front, tested the knot and then put a sawed off shotgun on a cord around his neck. It had both barrels loaded.

He sat on the edge of the berm in the darkness and supporting his weight with the rope, worked soundlessly down the front of the hotel between the windows. The half-inch rope was belayed around his two strong hands.

He made sure he had the right room by counting the windows again. He was now even with the window of the room and he could see a lamp burning low inside. Now he ran the rope around his shoulders and around his waist, tieing it off so he could use both his hands.

Then the one-eyed man bent his legs with his feet against the wall. He eased his body in toward the wall, and with a mighty shove with his bent legs, pushed himself away from the wall and at a slight angle. He swung out six-feet, and swung back a moment later.

He had judged it right. His feet hit the window of the room and crashed through. He ducked his face to avoid the flying glass, then was in the room. His hands on the shotgun brought it up and toward the bed.

He never got off a shot. Spur McCoy had heard the feet on the wall outside the window. He had been attacked this way before. Laura lay on the floor under the bed. He was at the far side of it with the mattress shielding him and Laura. The moment he heard the feet break the window he came up with his .45 held in both hands.

As soon as the man crashed through the window and lifted his head after the glass fell, Spur had a shot. He fired twice. Both rounds blasted into the attacker's face. One hit his nose and roared through the nasal cavity directly into his brain, decimating vital body function nerve centers. The second round tore through the man's good eye, slanted off bones and came out the side of his head ripping away a sizeable chunk of skull and brain tissue with it. The body sagged on the rope and swung back toward the window. His legs caught below the sill, holding him there inside the window, a hung corpse.

When the roar of the two shots in the closed room faded, Spur reached down and pulled up Laura. "Finish dressing fast. We have about a minute to get moved to another room."

Spur pulled on a shirt to go with the pants he had already gotten into when he had heard the sounds. He moved the chair from the door and in the hall checked two rooms. The second one was unlocked and vacant. He hurried Laura into the room, went back and grabbed all of his gear and rushed it across the hall just as a door down the way opened.

A sleepy-eyed man stuck out his head.

"Christsakes, keep it quiet out here. Man's trying to sleep down here." The head vanished.

Spur went on into the new room and saw that Laura had finished dressing. Shock still showed in her eyes. "He's . . . the man is dead?"

"If he isn't, it's a damn miracle." Spur tucked in his shirt and put on his socks and shoes. "We both better get out of her before the law comes. They're getting too damn good at their job in this town."

It was five minutes before they were well enough put together and had everything gathered up and stuffed in Spur's carpetbag. They went down the back stairs and into the alley.

"What a way to end a fine night," Laura said.

"Sorry. It kind of goes with the job. You asked me where all those scars on my body came from.

Little visitors like that one one make up part of it. He had a sawed off shotgun, did you see it? He'd have blasted us both into jelly."

Laura shivered. "You're not making me feel much better."

They went down the alley to the street and two blocks to another hotel, the Pacific. Spur registered them as Mr. and Mrs. Martin Anderson. The sleepy night clerk said they'd have to find their own room. They did.

The room wasn't as good as the last one. They undressed and lay on the covers. At last Laura curled against him and shuddered a few times as she cried silently. When it was over, she kissed his cheek.

"I think I'd like to try to get some sleep now. I'm not used to getting attacked and seeing a man die right in front of my eyes. If . . . if it wasn't for you knowing what those sounds meant, right now both of us would be dead, right?"

He kissed her cheek and put his arm around her protectively. "Could be. I've never been dead so I'm not sure what it feels like."

"Don't joke."

"Sorry. Yes, he would have killed both of us if he'd had the chance. Somebody paid him for the job. He was a specialist."

"Doesn't it . . . doesn't it bother you that you killed that man tonight?"

"Not as much as if it had been the other way around."

He felt her shiver. "Laura, I'm a professional. When someone tries to kill me, that gives me total license to try to kill him. The winner lives, the loser usually dies. Yes, I admit I'd rather have shot the weapon out of his hand. But when I have a hundredth of a second to decide where to aim, it's a lot more automatic than that. I simply have to aim at the best way to stop the person. In this case, I couldn't gamble that I could hit his right hand or the shotgun, when I had his head and his torso to aim at. I wouldn't take that chance missing and let him kill you."

"Oh." It was a small sound. She looked at him, then pushed up and kissed his cheek. "You are truly a good man, Spur McCoy. I'm proud to know you."

She sighed. "But I'm not going to sleep another wink the rest of the night. What time is it?"

He struck a match and looked at his watch. "A little after three A.M. Two hours to the beginnings of daylight. Then we can get up and dress and go for a long walk before breakfast. It's Sunday."

"Yes, I know." She watched him in the shadows. "The reason you're in town . . . your work at the mint . . . and your knowing Patricia. Does all this mean that there's a problem at the mint? Are some of the managers in trouble?"

"Yes. Deeply in trouble. I think one of them hired that man to try to kill me tonight."

"Dear Lord! Which one?"

"Martin Jefferson."

"Oh! That's going to make shock waves through the social calendar of San Francisco. Suddenly there will be four or five prime party nights wide open."

"Probably more than that. Did you know Redfield Pickering?"

"Pic? Sure. I really hated it when he died. Such a nice guy. Not at all like his father. I mean, all of us kids liked Pic. Why did he have to die in that accident?"

"It wasn't an accident."

She pushed away from him and sat up staring at him.

"Not an accident? Then . . . then somebody murdered him and made it look like. . . . Oh, dear Lord!"

"That's about the size of it. This is a real mess. Don't tell anyone, but I know that all three of the top management families are tied up in this unholy alliance."

"Poor Patricia!"

"She's the one who has helped me untangle it. She's a tough little nut. Did you know she's got a job to start teaching school here in town next fall."

"Why, for goodness sakes?"

"Because she'll have to be earning a living by that time."

"You mean the money, the wealth of her family. . . ."

"It'll be gone, all of it, and more, a whole lot more."

"Don't tell me any more. No wonder Mr. Jefferson is trying to stop you."

She lay down and snuggled against him. "Now, I think I can go to sleep. I don't have any problems, not a single one, compared to those of some of my friends. As soon as it happens I'm going to have Patricia come and stay with me. I'll have to do something honest and helpful."

When he looked down at her, Laura had fallen asleep.

· 21 ·

Emund Pickering had been up half the night pacing the floor. Damnit, he knew for certain that Martin had ordered his son murdered. Edmund knew he couldn't stand by any longer without confronting the man.

Martin seemingly had snapped back quickly from the death of his son, Alexander. But there was a big difference. Edmund often had the idea that Martin couldn't love anyone. He seemed barely to tolerate his children, especially Lucinda who he had put away in a private mental ward. Martin thought only of Martin.

Edmund watched the dawn come and still he paced. He had to confront Martin and be ready to kill him. That was his only recourse. Yes, it might not be Christian, but he had to. Still, the Bible talked about an eye for an eye. What could be more clear and simple? An eye for an eye, a life for a life.

Yes, by God! He would do it.

Edmund took out the small five shot .44 revolver he had bought years ago for target practice. He had never become an expert with it but he could use it and hit what he aimed at within six or eight yards. Close enough.

He walked into the master bedroom and saw that Thelma Mae was sleeping soundly. He wouldn't bother her. Not now. This was Sunday. He would beg off church. Martin never went. After the women went to church, he'd go see Martin. Yes, he would insist that they go down to the mint. Why? For a moment he saw Martin's head in the big press that punched out the gold eagle blanks.

The massive press closing, the punches coming forward and slamming into not a plate of gold but Martin Jefferson's screaming, fear crazed face, smashing out double eagle sized punches of his face, smashing the life from his damned, selfish body!

No, that wouldn't work. They would have to sign in with the guard and write a report why they went there on a Sunday. No, he would wait until Wilma went to church, then he'd challenge the beast in his own lair.

"Yes," he said out loud.

The sound of his voice brought him more alert. He dressed, put on a jacket and pushed the revolver with the six inch barrel in his belt. The jacket would cover it. He moved it just in back of his side pocket, half on his side, half his back. Yes, that covered well.

He walked around and practiced pulling the weapon out of his belt and aiming. After doing it twenty times, it felt more natural, like something he could do quickly if he needed to. Then he loaded the cylinders, four of them, leaving the fifth open and under the hammer.

He pushed the weapon back in place to get used to it being there.

Down in the kitchen the cook was making coffee. He waited for it to boil, then took a cup out of the veranda and in the morning chill watching the fog start to flow back toward the coast. The sun would soon burn off the rest of it.

It was fully daylight now. He sat there sipping his coffee and watching the sleepy town start to stir on a slow Sunday morning. His thoughts kept going back to Redfield, his second son, the brightest, the most talented. Victor, his first born, was settled down with his wife Denise, the Knox girl. Victor was not working at the mint. He had wanted to try something on his own and was now in a big retail store downtown.

Redfield . . . Damn, but he missed that young man. For an hour he remembered Redfield. How he had took to his studies and did well. How he wanted to go to college but got wrapped up in the business world of the mint first. Redfield, a fine young man who had been wantonly murdered by Martin Jefferson!

Pickering couldn't sit still any longer. He buttoned his jacket hiding the weapon, took a walking stick, and strode down California Street toward the water front. A good walk would keep him razor sharp to confront Martin.

He got back just as his wife was coming down the drive in the back of their best buggy heading for church. She started to say something, then waved and the driver took them on past.

He went directly up the hill three more houses to the Jefferson place and rang the twist bell.

The servants here usually had the day off and Martin himself answered the door. He looked a bit harried, as if he hadn't had much sleep.

"Pickering? What do you want?" Jefferson asked sharply.

Pickering snorted and stomped into the house. "Damn fine way to greet a friend and associate. What's the matter with you this morning?"

"Worried about that damn Oakmarker. I guess we should have checked his body before we left. Now, what can I do for you?"

"Got any coffee?"

Martin frowned at him a minute, then nodded and led the way back to the kitchen. A pot sat on the wood cookstove. Martin poured one for Pickering and refilled his own, then they sat down at the table.

"I saw in the papers that the witness to Redfield's accident was murdered, and then the man who evidently murdered the man was himself shot down and killed."

Martin looked up. "Read that myself."

"Now what I want to know is why something like that would happen. The only way I can figure it is that the witness to Redfield's accident was lying, or he saw more than he was supposed to. Why else would somebody kill him?"

"The papers said the man was a drunk. Those people down there get killed all the time. The man who killed him might have been after his shoes or his hat or even the bottle of wine he carried."

"I don't think so, Martin. I talked to the police

about it. They think it's curious, too. In fact, they're starting a new investigation into Redfield's death. One man down there said that it looked like a case of murder to him."

Martin sipped his coffee. He had on a pair of casual pants and an open collared shirt. Slowly he shook his head. "I wouldn't pay much attention to what they say. The policemen are trying to be important, to make something out of nothing."

"I don't think so, Martin. I found out as well that this witness, Stoop somebody, was receiving money from someone every week. Cash, greenbacks in an envelope that he left with his landlady so he wouldn't spend it all in one day or give it away. Stoop had a lot of friends down there once he had some money. Folks down there say he didn't have any money, ever, until after that accident he witnessed."

Martin stood up, anger washing over his face. "Pickering, what are you trying to say here? Don't beat around the bush. Just come right out and say it."

Pickering sipped at his coffee with his left hand. His right hand reached for his gun below the top of the table. When he stood he had drawn the revolver and now aimed it at Martin.

"What the—"

"It's a gun that's going to kill you, Martin. This all started with the letter, Redfield's letter. I never knew what was in it, you said I didn't need to know. But now I know that Redfield must have found out for sure what we're doing, and have been doing here for 10 years, and he wrote the Director about it, knowing that it could hurt all of us. He was willing to make the sacrifice.

"You found out about the letter, exactly what

it said, so you, Martin Jefferson, hired someone to kill my son."

Martin stood without moving. His face showed concern, but no panic.

"Pickering, you have a fertile imagination. Your trouble is you don't temper that imagination with a little common sense. Why would I jeopardize all this by hiring someone to kill Redfield?"

"Because his letter could end all of this and put all five of us in jail and ruin our families, that's why."

Martin moved a half a step.

"Don't move again, Martin, or I'll kill you where you stand. You hired the killer who murdered Redfield, then told the killer to get a bum and a drunk and tell him what to say and who to talk to. But then Spur McCoy came into town in response to Redfield's letter. He talked to the police, and to Stoop, and his landlady, and you went into a panic and knew Stoop would break and tell all, so you had someone kill Stoop.

"My guess is it was the same man who staged Redfield's accident after he bludgeoned my son to death. But you weren't secure enough to stop with Stoop's murder. You hid back 100 yards with one of your hunting rifles, and after Stoop had been killed, you shot down your own hired killer, wrapping up the witnesses neatly. You just didn't count on Spur McCoy, and on me."

"I suppose you've told our whole little scheme here to McCoy," Martin said, his eyes showing his anger.

"Yes. He knew most of it. We're all going down anyway, so I wanted to be sure to drill you right into the ground where you'd never hurt another living creature."

"Good try, Edmund, but it won't work."

"Why not? I've got the gun."

"Sure, but you forgot to cock it."

Edmund Pickering shot a quick glance down at the weapon. In that instant, Martin lifted the light kitchen table and rammed it forward at Pickering. The table hit Pickering's legs first, jolting him back a half step as he fired. But he'd had no time to aim and he missed.

The sound of the gun going off in the kitchen sounded like a thundering cannon. The blast let out a billow of blue smoke and a roaring explosion that lingered for several seconds.

The table Martin pushed crashed into Pickering's body before he could cock the weapon again. The table hit flat in Pickering's hand. The weapon fell to the floor and skittered six feet away. A moment later Pickering sprawled on the floor with the table on top of him.

Martin followed the table and jumped on it when it knocked Pickering down. Martin's 220 pounds crushed Pickering again as he was trying to crawl from under the table.

"Oh no!" Pickering wailed. "You've broken my arm."

Martin saw the pistol and picked it up. He checked the cylinder, then cocked it. He squatted near where Pickering still lay under the table.

"You've become something of a problem for me, Pickering, do you realize that?"

"Take me to the doctor, Martin. My arm's broken."

"Now that's a shame, Edmund. You might end up broken up a hell of a lot more than that. Exactly what did you tell Spur McCoy?"

"Everything, from the first, right up to how you

must have killed Redfield."

"You're an ungrateful bastard, Pickering! I brought you in on this 10 years ago as a favor, remember?"

"Sure, so I wouldn't have you arrested. I remember damn well. I should have turned you in when I found that first short measure on the scales."

"But you didn't. You asked me about it and you came into our little scheme. Now you're stuck with it."

"Then take me to the doctor."

"Wouldn't matter. It's smashing apart, this carefully organized operation of ours. Ten years was too long. I'm getting out, tomorrow. But it won't matter to you. First we're going to your house and open up both of those safes you keep well stocked."

Martin lifted the kitchen table off Pickering and pushed it to one side. "Get up, unless you want to die right here in my kitchen with a bullet through your skull."

Pickering shook his head, got his feet under him and forgot and tried to push up with his left hand.

"Oh, damn!" he screeched in pain. He pushed with his right hand and stood, then held his broken forearm with his right hand.

Martin prodded Pickering toward the front door, stopped at a closet and found a hat with a wide brim. He put it on Pickering and pulled it down.

"No sense anyone recognizing you this morning. We'll walk down the street to your place and in the back way. If we meet anyone you look at the sidewalk or I'll shoot you right there, understood?"

Pickering shivered, then nodded.

They walked, Pickering shaking now and then as the pain from his smashed forearm hit him. Inside the house they went directly to Pickering's den.

"Open it," Martin said.

Pickering shrugged. It was all the government's money now anyway. It didn't matter. He moved a small bookcase and opened a panel in the wall behind it and then turned the combination lock dial.

Jefferson pulled the safe open and looked inside. "How much cash do you keep in here, Pickering?"

"Not much, a couple of thousand, mostly in greenbacks."

"That's a start. I'll take the stocks and bearer bonds as well. I'll be able to convert them nicely."

"Where are you running away to, Martin?"

"Why should I tell you?"

"So you can brag a little. So you can demonstrate how much smarter you are than I am because you planned ahead how to be a total bastard."

Martin slapped him across the face with the back of his hand.

Pickering jolted sideways a step and smiled. "You always were a bastard, Martin. I don't know why I didn't see it that first day I caught you light weighing scissel."

"Shut up, Pickering. Where's your other safe?"

"I only have one."

Martin hit Pickering's broken arm with the barrel of the gun.

Pickering wailed in pain.

"You have any servants working today?"

"Just the driver who's at church and Juanita who left right after breakfast."

"Good, we're alone. Now, where is that other safe." Martin held the gun over Pickering's broken wrist.

Pickering shuddered with pain. "In the bedroom."

From the bedroom safe Jefferson took $20,000 in greenbacks and another thousand in gold.

"Now, that's better, Pickering. Let's go back down to your study."

Once there, Martin told Pickering to sit down at his desk. When he was in the chair, Martin pushed him up firmly against the desk.

"Now, I want you to write something for me. Take out some paper and a pen and ink."

Martin frowned. "Why don't you just take your money and leave. You'll get away and I'll be in jail."

"Might be an idea. First the letter. Put down the date, then: Dear Thelma Mae." Martin watched as Pickering wrote.

"Now write: I'm sorry. I shouldnt' have done it."

Pickering looked up at him and shrugged. He wrote it. Then he put down the rest word by word as Martin said them.

"There . . . is . . . nothing . . . else . . . I . . . can. . . ."

Pickering surged up from the chair, dropped the pen and clawed at the gun with his good right hand. The chair pushed Martin back and he lost his balance for a moment struggling toward the wall.

Pickering leaped from the chair toward the much larger man, who threw out his left arm in an automatic defense. It hit Pickering's broken arm and stopped him a moment, then he charged forward tackling Martin around the waist, both of them crashing over a chair to the floor.

Martin rolled once, then smashed the butt of the gun down on Pickering's skull and the smaller man slumped unconscious.

Martin stood slowly, touching a bruise on his hip where he had hit the chair. He pushed the weapon in his belt, caught Pickering under the shoulders and hoisted him back into the desk chair. He pushed it in place and put Pickering's broken arm on the desk top. Martin's wounded shoulder hurt like hell.

Martin made sure Pickering was still unconscious, then eased his head back against the tall desk chair's headrest. He took out the gun and put it in Pickering's good right hand and lifted it to the right hand side of Pickering's head. He paused just a moment, then pulled the trigger blasting a bullet into the unconscious man's brain.

Martin let go of the gun. Pickering flopped forward onto the desk, the gun still in his hand beside his head.

Martin took the money in a cloth bag and slipped out the back door. He went down the alley to his own house quickly and inside. Martin sucked in a long breath and leaned against the door.

One more problem solved. Next, what to take with him? He went to his den where the briefcase sat. The gold he had was heavy, but not too heavy. He would take one small suitcase mostly for the money and stocks and bonds. He was building up a goodly fortune.

The bank would open at ten. He would drive near it in his buggy and wait for the opening time.

Nothing to attract attention. He would withdraw from his account the $50,000 he had there. In cash, in big bills, hundreds, he decided. Nothing out of the ordinary.

Then back in his rig and drive to pick up Bonita. She would be ready. Going to Mexico City had been a long time dream for her. The coastwise steamer, *Mary Anne*, heading for San Diego would be sailing about one-thirty, the first mate had told him. Martin had given the man $20 to hold a cabin for him. There were only three.

Now, what had he forgotten? The secret to a successful operation of any kind was in the planning. He could see no flaw, think of no problem. But he had not considered Pickering a problem until this morning. Pickering was just a bit smarter than Martin had given him credit for being.

Knox certainly was no problem.

Martin went into his bedroom and selected a small leather suitcase with a place for a small padlock. He packed the gold and banknotes into the case, with the gold on the bottom when it was carried upright. He put around the currency two clean pairs of socks, underwear, a clean shirt and an extra pair of pants and shirt.

He would wear his usual dark suit to work, so nothing would be out of the ordinary. He would wear the heavy lensed spectacles he had found and a hat with a drooping brim. With that and his full beard it would be hard to recognize him.

Then he thought of a real problem. Pickering would be discovered when his wife came back from church. Martin had another 20 minutes. If he stayed at the house, he would be involved with Pickering's "suicide." He quickly wrote a note to

Wilma that he was going fishing down at the bay. He used to do that a lot. He left the note on the dining room table. It would give him an excuse to be away. He took his fishing pole, changed into his black work suit, and his traveling suitcase/ treasure chest and went down and harnessed the light rig.

Martin had driven down the street just before his wife came around from the other direction in their good buggy.

Martin gave a small sigh of relief and drove directly to Bonita's house. He would stay there overnight, take her with him when he went to the bank, and then directly to the waterfront and the steamer. There was little chance anything could go wrong. His arm throbbed high on his shoulder where he had been shot, but he could stand it. He was almost away, free and rich!

· 22 ·

By noon on Sunday, Laura had gone back to her home and Spur had looked over his notes and reviewed what he knew of the case. He decided he needed to talk to Philander Knox. Spur had an idea that he and Patricia could talk her father into turning himself in to the federal authorities Monday, rather than let them come looking for him.

He had an uneasy feeling as he rapped on the Knox's front door just after one o'clock that Sunday afternoon. No one came for a while, then a tear stained Patricia opened the door and rushed into his arms.

"It's so bad, so terrible, not like him at all," Patricia blurted out then began to cry again. Spur held her as they went back inside. He let her cry for a moment.

"Patricia, what's the matter? Is your father ill or hurt?"

She shook her head.

"Your mother, sister, you? What's the trouble?"

"Mister Pickering. He's dead. Shot himself in his den."

"You're sure?"

"Yes. Mrs. Pickering came screaming over here just as we got back from church about 12:20 or so. It took us five minutes to get her calmed down. Then she told us. We sent our driver to get the police. I think they're still over there."

Spur kissed her tear stained cheek. "Which house is it? I better take a look."

"Third house down the hill. You'll come back, won't you?"

"Yes. I want to talk to you and your father."

"Is this . . . is this part of the whole thing?"

"I'd think so. But Pickering didn't seem like the kind of a man to take his own life."

"That's what his wife said a dozen times."

Spur opened the outside door. "I'll be back."

He went down the steps and could see several buggies and rigs three houses down. He ran down there and worked through a ring of people. A San Francisco policeman barred the way.

Spur dug out his identification and held it up to the officer.

"McCoy, United States Secret Service. I have an interest in this case. Is Inspector Daniel here?"

"Yes sir, just inside," the officer said.

He waved Spur through the line. Spur ran up the steps and kept his identification card ready as he worked past four more officers. They pointed down the hall to the den.

Inside there were ten people. Spur saw Daniel and waved him over.

"Get everyone out of here that you can," Spur said.

Daniel began sending people out until there were only three of them left. They closed the door. The body lay where it had been when Pickering died.

"I heard the name, guessed at the connection and came right over here," Daniel said. "This is the father of Redfield Pickering, the young man we figured was squashed to keep him quiet."

"True, but why this one? Pickering here gave me a complete confession and description of the gold theft and everything else he knew about the situation. He was going to get immunity from prosecution. He had a clean ticket home on this whole affair. Besides, he wasn't the suicide type. Has anything been moved?"

"No. We're waiting for Lieutenant Bostwick who is in charge of all killings. There's a partial note, tipped over ink well, gun still in his hand. Damn well looked like a suicide."

"It's supposed to. My guess is that Pickering couldn't take it knowing that Jefferson had his son killed. He could have called him over here, confronted him, but Jefferson got the upper hand."

Spur looked at the body, then closely at the weapon without touching it.

"No suicide. The man has a serious blow to the top of his head. About right for a gun butt. Bleeding, and I bet we'll find some of the victim's hair on the gun butt. Also, I'll bet that revolver has been fired twice. You find a second round anywhere?"

"No. The wall safe over there is open. Not much left in it. I want to ask his wife if there was another safe in the house."

Spur found Thelma Mae sitting stiffly somber in the parlour. She looked like she hadn't cried enough yet. She nodded at him, and when he gave his name she thanked him for finding Patricia Knox.

"Yes, ma'am. I was wondering if there's a second wall safe in the house. You know, perhaps robbers did this."

She nodded, rose and led him into the master bedroom. The bookcase had not been moved back and the safe door still hung open.

"Philander usually kept quite a sum of money in there and some stocks and bonds. I don't know how much."

He thanked her and went back to the den.

A medical doctor was there examining the body.

Daniel scowled as Spur came back. "No damn suicide, it's a murder. The doctor said that blow to the head would have left Pickering unconscious for ten or fifteen minutes. Might even have cracked his skull. The note could have been dictated under threat of the gun. When the victim realized what he was writing, he could have attacked, been slugged, then shot."

"Both safes are empty. What would that suggest to you Inspector Daniel?"

"Robbery, or one of these men is getting ready to take a long trip with all the cash he can grab."

"My guess exactly. I don't think I can do anything more here. Thanks for the help."

Spur ran back to the Knox's house. Patricia was on the steps waiting for him.

"Is your father home?"

"Yes. He's badly shaken. He was a good friend of Mr. Pickering's."

"Ask your father to stay here, I want to talk to him later. First, come with me to see the Jeffersons. They know about this?"

"I think so."

Patricia came back from talking to her father and they went up the hill to the Jefferson house.

Wilma Jefferson met them at the door. She and Patricia hugged.

"I'm just devastated about poor Edmund," Wilma said. "What on earth made him do such a thing."

"There's a good chance he was murdered by a robber," Spur said.

Wilma Jefferson looked up sharply. "Oh, dear. When I got home I found Martin gone. He left a note that said he was going fishing. Pooh. He hasn't fished for five years. Then I saw that his safe was partly open as well. It's empty."

She motioned to them. "Maybe the robber was here too, robbed us and took Martin as a hostage! Oh, dear! Let's look in the basement."

She showed Spur where the floor safe was and he moved a table and lifted the trap door under it.

When he opened the wooden box they found inside, Mrs. Jefferson gasped. "That's where he kept his big money, and some diamonds. He didn't think I knew about it. They're all gone."

"What about your jewelry, Mrs. Jefferson."

Upstairs in her bedroom, Wilma Jefferson broke down and threw herself on her bed. All of her jewels were gone, even the cheaper ones she had owned for 15 years.

"What about a carriage or a buggy," Spur asked. "Are yours all here?" They walked out and looked in the small carriage house.

"The light rig is gone and so is one of the horses. The robber must have made Martin harness up the rig and took it as well."

"That's entirely possible, Mrs. Jefferson. Why don't you come down to the Pickerings and tell the police what we discovered. It might tie in with what happened there."

They let Mrs. Jefferson walk ahead. Spur caught Patricia's hand. "If you had to get out of town quickly, how would you go?"

Patricia frowned a minute. "A boat to Oakland and the morning train east."

"Second best way?"

"Steamships up and down the coast. Most of them haul freight, but quite a few people go from here to Los Angeles and San Diego and Seattle by boat."

"When do they leave?"

"I have no idea. I heard once that the city wouldn't allow any boats to clear the harbor on Sunday. Oh, one of the ship company officials lives right down the street. I bet he would know."

They saw Mrs. Jefferson into the Pickering household, then went down the street.

The man who answered the door was sunburned and chunky. He saw Patricia and smiled at her. "Little Patty, you have grown into a beauty. What can I do for you today?"

She asked him about ships sailing.

"Be three setting sail with the tide tomorrow. Just after one o'clock, I'd say. You going on your honeymoon or something?"

Patricia laughed. "No such luck. We're looking for someone who said they were sailing. Thanks a lot."

As they walked back up the hill, Patricia watched Spur. "Is this the start of it? Did Mr. Jefferson kill Mr. Pickering?"

"That's my guess. The confrontation I spoke of. So Jefferson could be planning his getaway right now. What would he do? You know him better than I do?"

"Mr. Jefferson? I've heard that he has a mistress somewhere. I'm sure somebody must know who she is. He might go there for the night, then leave on either the train or one of the three boats tomorrow."

"Let's talk to Mrs. Jefferson again."

Patricia looked at him. "Oh, I don't think we should. She's had quite a shock already." Patricia frowned. "You mean you think she might know who her husband's mistress is? That's crazy."

"Let's ask her."

Back at the Pickering residence, they found Mrs. Jefferson talking to the police lieutenant who had finally arrived. She finished and walked toward her house. They caught up with her.

"Mrs. Jefferson, I need to find your husband. I'd wager some of his things are gone and perhaps a favorite suitcase, will you check?"

"Ridiculous, he went fishing," she said and looked straight ahead.

"Mrs. Jefferson, it's starting to unravel. Have you ever had a piece of yarn on a sweater and pulled it and soon the whole sleeve was gone? That's happening here, right now, to the huge embezzlement scheme the three families have been working for the past 10 years."

"McCoy, you can't talk to me that way."

"It's true, Mrs. Jefferson. We think Mr. Pickering was killed because he talked to the police about it. The police have a complete account of the operation. It's all going to come out tomorrow."

Wilma Jefferson's lower lip quivered. She stared straight ahead but now two tears spilled out of her eyes and slipped down her cheeks.

"Tomorrow? So soon? Oh, damn! Suitcase . . . cash gone. You're telling me you think Martin has run away and left me here to face the charges."

"Something like that. Do you have any idea where he might stay tonight before he catches a train or a boat tomorrow?"

"Is that his plan?"

"We're guessing, trying to think the way he'd think."

"I know how he thinks. After 24 years of marriage, I should." She looked at both of them. "Don't you dare tell anyone I said this, but Martin probably is at a house on Hankle Street. 319 Hankle Street. It's off Sixteenth up from the park." Wilma Jefferson sighed, wiped at her eyes. "Looks like he's decided to dump me and take Bonita with him. Yes, I've known about her for four years. Little Mexican girl who must do him the way he likes."

She stopped and looked at Spur. "Damn, now I hope you do find him. Promise me you won't kill him. He deserves better, like 50 years in some stinking, hot as hell prison. Yuma, maybe."

Spur thanked her and they hurried to the Knox place.

"First we talk to your father. I don't want him doing something stupid at this point."

"He was in the house, last I knew," Patricia said.

They found Philander Knox pacing in his study. He looked up and saw Patricia and relaxed, but when Spur came in he scowled.

"What are you doing here?" he demanded.

"Daddy, Mr. McCoy has some things to tell you. He's only trying to help you, to help us. Will you listen to him?"

"Everything else is going wrong, I might as well find out who you are McCoy and why you're here."

"You probably have guessed by now, Mr. Knox. I'm a Secret Service Agent from Washington. I came in response to Redfield's letter about the embezzlement of gold here at the mint."

"Oh, god, it did get through. We're all doomed."

"Probably, Mr. Knox, but now is no time to make matters worse. Let me tell you a few things you might not know. Edmund Pickering has given a deposition to the court detailing everything about your gold embezzling scheme for the past 10 years. We know all of it. We also know about the murder of Redfield. We're not sure, but we believe that Martin Jefferson later hired the same killer to kill the witness, Stoop Lackwalter. Then Martin probably shot down the scarfaced man, Felling, just after he knifed Stoop to death.

"Last night, Oakmarker must have demanded more money from Martin, kidnapped him and was running. We found them before Martin got killed, but then Oakmarker did a stupid thing and killed himself.

"Which brings us to today. Pickering knew about Jefferson, and probably your plan to kill his son Redfield. He swore he wouldn't do anything for two days, but he did. We're guessing that he called Jefferson to his house and accused him of killing Redfield and one thing led to another, they fought and Martin, being a much larger man, won and knocked out Pickering, then shot him and made it look like a suicide. Then Jefferson emptied the safes at Pickering's, and at his place and left home, set on running as far and as fast as he can, come Monday morning."

Philander Knox had sat down at his desk and slumped lower and lower.

"Goddamn, so what's left?"

"Just that you might be able to help us find Martin Jefferson. Any idea where he might be going to spend the night?"

"No. He never confided in me, not in anyone."

"We're going to try to find him. Now there's at least four murder charges to bring against him. I'm suggesting that you stay home tonight, inside, and not go to work tomorrow. There will be a policeman here for you sometime in the morning."

"I'm under arrest?"

"Yes, I'm putting you under arrest and confining you to your home. If you leave, you'll be in more trouble. Will you stay here?"

"Please, Daddy. I don't want Mr. Jefferson to hurt you."

He stood and hugged his daughter, then nodded. "I'll be here when they come for me."

Spur and Patricia hurried out the door to the back yard. "Do you have a buggy hitched up?" he asked Patricia.

"We came home more than an hour ago, but let's go look." They found a light buggy in the yard with a horse still hitched to it.

"Hop in, I'll drive," Patricia said.

"Sixteenth Street, driver," Spur said and they rolled down the drive to the street, turned downhill and then worked south toward 16th Street.

"What will we do if we find him?" Patricia asked.

"I'll arrest him and take him back to the scene of the crime, then down to the police head-quarters. We can't afford to wait for those warrants that won't come until tomorrow."

They had just turned the corner off California Street south of Powell, when a rifle shot snarled in the afternoon air and a bullet bored through the canvas back of the buggy.

"Get down!" Spur shouted, ducked himself and slapped the reins on the horse as the buggy careened down Powell Street.

"Who is it?" Patricia asked.

"Somebody with a calling card from Martin Jefferson, I'd imagine."

Another shot slammed just in front of them and Spur turned the rig into an alley, then quickly drove in toward a short building that left a large space in the alley. It hid the rig from anyone coming in the alley mouth. Spur vaulted out of the buggy.

"Stay here on the floor," he shouted to Patricia, then he sprinted for the corner of the longer building that hid them from the rest of the alley.

He saw the other rig turn into the alley and slow. The horse hesitated for a moment, then the reins slapped on the back of the animal and it moved forward.

Spur had taken to wearing his big six-gun Colt and now he lifted it from leather and waited for the buggy to come closer. These rigs had no protection on them at all for the riders. There were two of them in the buggy, one had a rifle, the other a hand gun.

In a second, Spur decided not to shoot the horse. Instead, he'd hit the man with the rifle, the biggest threat. The buggy charged closer and soon it came almost to the edge of the building that shielded Spur.

Spur looked up just in time to see Patricia wheel her buggy across the alley blocking the way. She jumped out and hid behind the bulk of the bay horse.

The driver of the other rig pulled up sharply and Spur fired. His round hit the rifleman in the side, drove under his arm and through his heart, dumping him against the driver who leaped from the rig and ran into the back door of an apartment house.

Spur raced to the building, dodged sharply as he saw a figure in the dark doorway and avoided a barking shot of a revolver. He ducked behind some boxes, then charged to the side of the building unscratched.

The other bushwhacker had left the doorway and darted down a hallway with half a dozen doorways. Spur didn't have time to check each room. He stopped still and listened. Stair boards creaked. He saw a stairway at the far end and raced to it and heard footsteps running upward.

It was a three story building. The man kept going to the top floor, then vanished down another hallway. Spur guessed this was some kind of low cost residence hotel with one or two room apartments.

Spur moved from one to another listening at each door. At the fourth one he heard muffled sounds, then a woman screamed.

"No, no. You get out of here!" The words came through the door.

He tried the knob. It was locked. He stepped back and kicked the door beside the knob and the solid door surged open and slammed against the wall. A shot roared from the room and the bullet ripped past Spur and and dug into the hall wall behind him.

He dove for the floor inside the room, blasting a shot at the haze of blue smoke he saw in front of him. Spur came out of a roll and squirmed behind a big upholstered chair. In his surge into the room he had seen the gunman thumbing back his gun's hammer. A woman fell away from him to the side.

Now the noise of the two shots faded. Spur looked around the end of the big chair and saw the legs of the man stretched out behind a heavy couch. He was about to fire at them when they vanished and he heard the bushwhacker running.

Spur surged upward and got off a shot as the gunman raced out of the room into the hall and vanished. Spur's shot missed.

He checked on the woman. She seemed unhurt.

Then he chased the gunman into the hall. At the stairway the man turned and fired and Spur felt the burn of hot lead as the slug grazed his left arm. He returned the fire but wasn't sure if it hit home or not.

At the stairs, Spur could hear the other man charging down the steps. Spur took them three and four at a time, racing down, risking a broken ankle to save a few seconds. At the first floor he saw an open door at the front of the building that led to the street.

Spur looked out, ducked back at once as he saw a gun come up from 15 feet away. The round blasted through the door where he had been. He dropped to the floor and checked again with his Colt ready.

The bushwhacker stood behind a post that held

up the second story of a building. Spur fired the moment he saw the man. His round had been aimed at the biggest target, in this case one of the man's legs which was at the side to give him better balance. The round hit his leg mid-thigh and jolted him backwards. He swore and tumbled in the dirt, rolled and limped toward the front door of a store.

Spur fired again. This round hit his other leg and broke one of the bones, dumping the man onto the sidewalk where he swore again and held his bleeding leg.

"Throw down your iron, it's all over," Spur called. The man fired at him again, but Spur still had the protection of the doorway.

"Drop it!" Spur demanded.

A three year old boy ran out of the store between the gunmen to see what the excitement was. His screaming mother stopped him just before he came into the line of fire. She snatched him up and rushed back into the store.

"Give it up, or you're a dead man. I'm a U.S. lawman working with the San Francisco police."

The man swore again, started to toss the gun aside, then lifted it and fired at Spur.

McCoy snapped off a return shot. Spur felt the wood splinters sting his face as the man's round came close. His own shot caught the bushwhacker in the right shoulder and slammed him back on the sidewalk spilling his revolver from his right hand and sliding out of reach.

Spur charged up and grabbed the weapon, then knelt in front of the man. He backhanded the gunman across the face.

"Now, you liver-bellied bushwhacker, you have 10 seconds to tell me who hired you or you'll never make it to jail alive."

"I'll tell you, if you'll take me to a doctor. I'm all shot up. You got to get me a doctor."

A scattering of people gathered to see the outcome of the shootout on the street, not a usual happening in San Francisco in 1874.

"If you live the next five minutes, you'll get a doctor. Now who hired you?"

"Martin Jefferson."

"Thought so," Spur said.

A policeman ran up with his gun out.

"Put away your iron, young man, the shooting is over. Get this prisoner to a doctor, then take him to jail and charge him with attempted murder. My name is Spur McCoy, I'll be down to sign the complaint later today."

The officer looked at him a minute, then nodded and checked around for the closest doctor's office.

Spur headed back through the building he had just left. He found Patricia halfway along the hallway looking for him.

"We got him. Now let's go see if we can find Martin Jefferson in his love nest."

· 23 ·

Patricia and Spur drove 20 minutes before they found the street, then they looked for the right number.

"Oh, how is Lucinda getting along?" Spur asked.

"Just fine. She's gaining her old confidence again. I don't think she'll ever be quite the free spirit she once was, but she certainly can live with normal people as well as you or me. She isn't crazy at all. She should have her baby in about a month."

"Did you ask her about the embezzlement?"

"The first day. She said she knew about it, knew precisely how they did it and when she told her father he almost killed her. He was furious. She told him if she could figure it out, someone else could as well. That's when he started spreading stories about her being crazy. Then a month later he put her in that clinic. I don't think they've reported her missing yet to the Jeffersons. They're probably afraid to tell Martin."

They drove slowly along the street watching for house numbers. Most of them didn't have numbers, but they found enough. A block later they found it, a modest little place with a small shed in the back for a horse. Spur parked four houses down from the residence, walked to the alley and counted houses down to it. Yes, there was a buggy in back, a light rig, and the horse had not been there all night. It had come in sometime this morning.

He walked back to Patricia's buggy out front. He could arrest Martin on sight now since he knew, or strongly suspected, that he was getting ready to run away. How could he get Martin outside without endangering the woman?

The idea came slowly, and he grinned, then talked to Patricia.

"I'm going to go right up to the door and see what I can do. If I yell, you drive the rig up as close to the house as you can get it. There's a buggy parked in back that probably is Martin's. But we can't be sure. He'll be armed by this time. Stay back if you hear any shooting."

He frowned at her. "I still haven't scolded you for blocking the alley back there and risking getting shot at. You made a fine target for about two minutes. It takes less than half a second to get off a pistol shot. From now on, don't get any bright ideas or I'll take you home, understand?"

Patricia grinned and swirled her red hair around her head. "I don't just have this red hair as decoration, you know. It gives a hint at my aggressive, wild and crazy personality."

"I know, and I want that personality to grow up and get married and have six kids and live to be 95 years old. So be damn careful!"

He left and crossed the street, then walked past two houses and up the path to the door on 319. He rapped solidly on the door with his knuckles. He thought he heard someone inside, then nothing. He rapped again. This time he heard footsteps coming to the door, soft footfalls.

The door cracked open and a dark brown eye looked out. He wedged his boot in so the door couldn't close.

He sang. "We shall gather at the river, the beautiful, beautiful river." She tried to close the door.

"Sister, give me a minute of your time. I'm with the First Baptist Congregation out making friendly calls on the people on this street on this the day of the Lord. God has moved me to come see you. I only need a few moments of your time. . . ."

She let the door open a little more.

"I'm sorry, señor. I am Catholic. Not Baptist."

"You don't have to worry none about that, sister. You can still be saved by the blood of our Lord, Jesus Christ."

The door came open a little more. He reached out slowly, then grabbed her arm and started to pull her outside.

Someone held her from inside.

"Not a chance, McCoy!" Martin Jefferson's angry voice bellowed. "You let go of her right now, or I shoot her dead. You want that?"

"Don't bother me much," Spur said, but he had

moved to the side against the house out of any line of fire. Suddenly a shot roared inside the house and a bullet tore through the thin door about where McCoy's head had been a few moments before.

"Oh god, I'm hit!" Spur bellowed with what he hoped was pain and anger. He knew he wouldn't win any acting awards, but he could try.

He dropped the woman's hand. The door slammed shut and he heard a bolt slip into place. Spur ducked under the window and around to the side of the house and toward the back.

It wasn't a minute later that he saw the two people come out of the house. Each had a small suitcase that they put in the buggy. They jumped in and backed the buggy out slowly.

Spur put a round across the front of the horse.

"Move another foot and you're dead, Jefferson. The girl, probably, too. Ease up and step down and this all will be over soon. You really didn't think you could get away from all of us, did you?"

Spur was bluffing. He didn't have a good shot at Martin because the girl was in the way. Martin might know it as well. He planned on shooting the horse in the head if he had to shoot. It was at least 40 feet to the buggy. Not the best odds for a head shot.

Suddenly the reins slapped down hard on the horse's back and the rig jolted ahead. Spur shot and missed. He turned and raced around the house toward the street.

Patricia must have brought up the rig when she heard the first shot through the door. Now she was almost in front of the house and headed in the right direction.

He ran, jumped in the rig and pointed ahead. "He's got the girl and luggage going in this direction out the alley."

They galloped down half the block and turned left to find the alley. Just as they turned, the black rig came racing out and turned away from them. The contest was on.

Sunday afternoon. Not much traffic in the streets. No lumbering freight wagons, no oxen drawn rigs, only a few buggies prancing around and in no rush.

Where could he go? The city of San Francisco is built on a peninsula, with the mouth of the bay cutting off any land travel to the north. That left only the route south around the bay. There were no roads or even paths along the bay itself, since there was much wet lands and salt marsh where the bay ended. On the beach side was the continuation of Greary Road that wound down along the coast and past more marshes and a big lake.

The south arm of San Francisco Bay was at least 25 miles long, with few roads and fewer settlers in that area. There would be no way to get back to commercial transportation which by all evidence so far, Martin must need.

Spur took the reins and urged the horse to run faster. He knew at the current pace both the horses would tire and stop or break down. The important thing now was not to lose Martin in the maze of streets and buildings.

They skidded around one corner and saw the other rig ahead just ready to turn. It careened up on one set of wheels but they came down just in time before the buggy tipped over.

Spur drove around that corner and saw the

black buggy stopped half a block ahead. Just after he raced to the buggy at the start of the chase, Spur had reloaded his revolver, putting a sixth round under the hammer.

Now he pulled up cautiously to the black buggy, but soon he saw that no one was in it. The pair and their suitcases were gone. "Stay here. If they come back scream as loud as you can."

He looked first on the near side of the street. He found only what looked like an unused warehouse that was in disrepair. Spur looked over Martin's buggy, went to the front of it and unhooked the harness traces from the buggy. The rig couldn't move until they were hooked on again.

He ran to the front of the warehouse and bent low and looked in. Nothing stirred. He picked up a rock and threw it inside the door into a shadowed area.

The moment the rock hit the wood floor a hand gun snarled from deeper in the warehouse. Spur saw where the shot came from but he couldn't fire back for fear of hitting the woman. What was Martin trying to do? Probably to kill Spur and then stay at a hotel until time for the boat or train.

Spur edged around to the side of the building. It was about 40 feet wide and twice that deep into the block. The lot beside it was vacant. Spur ran hard to the back of the structure and looked for a door. He found a small one that had been half torn off its hinges.

It hung there by the top hinge at an angle, allowing plenty of room for Spur to bend down and look inside.

It was dark. Only a shaft of light from the front door showed inside. It had no windows or sky- lights. Spur closed his eyes 30 seconds to help them adjust to the faint light. When he opened them he checked the area where he had seen the gunshot.

Now he could see inside well enough to decide that no one was in that spot. He looked around but it was too dark. He searched for another rock, found one and gave it an underhanded toss into the center of the building.

Two shots blasted at the sound, both came from the rear wall, down maybe 20 feet from where Spur crouched. He tested the old boards, then slid inside the building and to the right toward the gunshots.

He sat there, his Colt in his hand, legs in an easy position as he readied to wait them out.

Less than three minutes later he heard someone whispering, then a woman's voice, indignant, not trying to be quiet.

"Well, I don't care, I can't wait. I have to go right now."

He heard what could have been a slap and then the woman began to cry, softly at first, then a wail.

Spur waited. His patience had been trained and honed in the Southwest against the Apache. There you learned patience against the dry-land natives, or you died trying.

Another minute or two later, he could hear shoes scraping on the wooden floor as the pair moved toward him.

He waited.

The sounds continued, and grew closer. They were hugging the wall, working toward the doorway and its faint light. Spur moved an inch at a time straight out from the wall. He'd give them room to move past him on the wall.

Who would come first? The man, with the

woman following. Yes.

Spur waited.

Now they were so close he could smell them. A moment later the man outlined himself in the light from the door.

"Freeze right there or you're dead!" Spur barked.

The man roared and fired, but had no target. At the same time he pushed the woman away from him toward the voice.

Bonita stumbled into Spur where he crouched on the floor. She sprawled on top of him, her small soft body trapping him for a minute in a wildly flailing set of arms and legs. When they came to a rest he lay with his face pushing hard against her crotch, her dress billowing around her.

She moved off him and Spur scrambled for the doorway he had heard Martin scurry out of. At the door Spur paused, his eyes blinded. He shut them to slits and looked out. Even in the shadows it was a blinding shock. He saw no one waiting in ambush.

Spur slid out the half door and looked both ways. The buggy. He raced along the side of the warehouse paying no attention to the wails and screams of Bonita still in the darkness of the warehouse.

At the corner of the structure he saw the buggys. Martin was 60 yards away. He jumped into his buggy and slapped the reins on the horse. It spurted ahead, but the buggy stayed still since the harness traces were not connected. The force nearly jerked Martin out of the seat. He let go of the reins and swore.

Without a moment's hesitation, he leaped from

the stalled rig and ran to Patricia's buggy. She fought him a moment for the reins, then he pushed her aside but kept her in the seat. He slapped the leathers on the horse and the rig rolled away down the street as Martin kept one arm around Patricia holding her tightly.

Spur sprinted to the spot, saw the unhitched horse 50 feet down the street and ran for her. He led her back, hitched her to the buggy, got the reins and then drove quickly down the street after Martin.

Spur had little hope of finding him. Unhitching the buggy had backfired. Now the other rig could be a half mile ahead. The man had turned left at the first street and quickly drove out of sight. He could be several blocks away now.

Spur galloped the horse as fast as he thought safe, rounding the corner of the block with the inside wheels lifting just a little. Halfway down the next block he saw a rig stopped. It could be Patricia's.

As he rolled toward it, he saw a fight in the buggy seat. The horse had skittered around turning the rig sideways. It was Patricia fighting the large man for the reins. She bent and evidently bit him on the wrist.

Martin screeched in pain, then slapped Patricia viciously, Spur put a shot in the air over their heads, but Martin ignored it. He pushed Patricia, then hit her again until she let go of the seat. He pushed her out of the buggy. Patricia tripped and fell into the dust of the street.

At once her buggy drove away with Martin slapping the horses hard with the reins.

Spur charged up with Martin's buggy and

stopped where Patricia sat in the dirt.

"Are you hurt?" Spur called.

"No." She shouted, jumped up and scrambled into the buggy.

Spur charged after the other rig.

The two buggys created a small ballet as they slammed around corners, galloped down straight stretches, and gradually worked toward the bay side of San Francisco.

"Where's he going?" Spur asked.

"Don't know. He still has that heavy suitcase with him. It must be full of gold the way he puffed as he carried it. The man is getting tired."

"Thanks for fighting with him," Spur said. "If you hadn't stopped him, I never would have found you."

"He said some bad things to me. I got mad. I didn't even think about slowing him down. Dumb, huh?"

"Yeah, but it worked."

Spur concentrated on driving then, cutting down the distance between the rigs, but not enough for a revolver shot. They worked closer to the bay below the Barbary Coast section. The saloons here were dirty and dangerous.

Martin turned onto the narrow embarcadero right next to the wharves and piers. He drove to a spot he wanted, stopped and jumped out of the buggy. Then Martin rushed forward to a small pier, looked down and stepped into a boat. A man sat there with oars. He had been ready to go to a larger vessel somewhere.

Martin lifted his revolver and motioned and the man began to row away from the dock. By the time Spur left his buggy and raced down to the small dock, the boat was well out of pistol range.

Spur looked around the pier. There was only one other boat tied there, a sailing ship for gentleman sailors about 20 feet long. Two men worked on getting a sail up.

Spur ran to them.

"Gentlemen are you about to get under way? If so, I'm a United States lawman. I'm chasing that man in that rowboat out there. I'd pay you to help me overtake and capture the man."

The men looked at each other. One grinned. "I'm a lieutenant on the San Francisco police. Be glad to help. Hop on board. He motioned to Patricia who ran down the dock and stepped on the boat. They finished hoisting the sail, untied the craft and pushed away. A moment later the breeze filled the sail and they moved through the water after the rowboat.

Martin had the rower move south along the docks, just past the ends of the piers.

It took only a few minutes for the sailboat to come near the rowboat.

"Pull in to shore, sir," the policeman called. "I'm Lieutenant Newhouse of the San Francisco police force. You are ordered to row to the closest dock."

Martin fired at the speaker, but the round fell short. While Martin fired at the policeman, the man rowing his boat lunged upward and over the side into the water leaving Martin drifting. The incoming tide did little here but now it swept his boat toward the docks.

The swimmer surfaced 20 feet from the rowboat, took a breath and dove again before Martin could fire at him.

The policeman turned to Spur. "He's going where we want him. My advice is stay out of pistol range."

The rowboat bumped against a dock and Martin scrambled up a wooden ladder to the top dragging his heavy suitcase with him. Once on top, he ran for the street.

The sailing craft moved rapidly to the same dock and Spur ran after Martin with Patricia lagging behind.

Spur put on a burst of speed to come close enough to Martin to keep track of him. He ran up a street and down another lugging along the suitcase. All the gold in the case slowed him enough so that Spur could stay close enough to track him.

Then Martin ran into a street with dozens of Chinese signs on the buildings. All were closed now, but halfway down the block Martin vanished into an unmarked doorway pulling his suitcase with him.

Spur stopped and drew his revolver as he opened the door. There was nothing there but a set of steps that led downward. He paused. He had heard about the wild places in Chinatown. This must be part of it. If he didn't go ahead now, Martin might be gone for good.

He hurried down the steps, went through a set of swinging doors and into a brightly lighted basement room. The only person there was an ancient Chinese who looked at Spur with the same expression he had used for a dozen years.

The man chattered something in Chinese which meant nothing to Spur.

He held up his six-gun. "Police. Where did that man go who just ran in here?"

The ancient oriental pointed to the door to the right. Now Spur saw that there were six doors leading off the reception room. He hoped the old Chinese was telling him the truth.

Spur pushed the door open with his left hand, keeping his right filled with the Colt double action revolver, just in case.

On the other side of the door was another hallway. It led down a second flight of steps, these less well lighted. At the bottom and through a door he found a young Chinese man sprawled on the floor unconscious. If this was Martin's work, Spur was still on his trail.

Straight ahead was a green door. He opened it and found himself in a mass of humanity. Fifty or sixty people lay on mats on the floor. Here and there a Chinese opium water pipe sat with six or eight tubes extended from it from which men and women smoked contentedly.

Half of the people in the room were unconscious or sleeping. Everyone he could see was a Chinese. Martin was not there. A door swung softly at the far end of the room. He stepped carefully around the bodies. One hand snaked up and caught his ankle. He kicked the wrist and the hand's owner groaned and let go. At the far side of the room, Spur looked through the swinging door and saw a second level of opium addiction.

It was a large room with partitions six feet high giving semi-privacy. In each of the partitioned spaces was a thick mat with a naked man lying on it. Most of the men were being serviced by two naked, slender Chinese girls of no more than 14 or 15 years.

One man had four girls around him. Spur spotted two men who were not Chinese.

For a moment he could not see any other door.

Then at the near side he saw a panel that had slid open a foot, then silently closed. He walked to it, pushed it open and found a beautiful Chinese woman in her twenties bowing before him. When she ended the bow he saw she was nude and smiling.

"Me Ling can help honorable gentleman?"

"A white man ran in here with a suitcase. Which way did he go?"

"There is no other way out of the room of the Third Enchantment."

"He isn't inside. Where did he go?"

"Many small side rooms, like this."

She waved her hand around and he noticed that the room was decorated in Japanese style.

"Each room different."

"Show me each one, now!" Spur growled.

"Me Ling can't leave this room. Honorable one may look himself."

Spur shrugged, went back into the main room and saw where the side rooms were situated. He pushed aside the door panel to the first one and stared into the muzzles of a twin-barreled shotgun not a foot from his face.

· 24 ·

A high wailing laugh came from the naked Chinese girl who held the shotgun in Spur's face. She lowered it and he saw she wore a gunbelt with a six-gun in it and nothing else.

"Cowboy," she said and he guessed it was the only word of English she knew. Spur shook his head and moved to the next panel. He worked through eight more of the rooms and found each one had a theme and a minimal costume from Mexican to German and doctor to lumberjack. Nowhere did he find Martin Jefferson. Two more to go.

Just as he reached for the next sliding panel, a gun roared and a bullet slammed through the thin panel material missing him by inches. Spur dropped to the floor and with the barrel of his .45 pushed open the panel. Martin held a small Chinese girl shielding himself. His six-gun pushed into her belly and his other hand gripped the heavy suitcase.

"Drop your gun, McCoy, or this girl dies and then you. Drop it right now!"

Spur shrugged, and lowered his weapon to the floor looking for some defense. There wasn't much. When Spur put the gun down, Martin laughed.

"Well, the smart man finally made a mistake. His last mistake." Martin lifted the weapon from the girl's body and aimed it at Spur. The Chinese girl bent forward suddenly, her sharp teeth bit Martin's wrist to the bone and he dropped the gun and screamed, clubbing her to one side. He picked up the gun and ran for the door, the heavy suitcase slowing him.

A small knife darted through the air and hit him in the right shoulder. He screamed in pain as he charged through the room and toward the stairs.

Spur bent, scooped up his Colt and charged after Martin. In their rush to vent their anger at the round-eye, half a dozen naked Chinese girls clogged the room and Spur had to work his way past their slender nude bodies. When he got cleared to the room with the steps, Martin was already up them.

He sprinted after him, worked through the opium smokers and up the next flight of steps to the street. He saw Martin almost at the end of the block. Spur ran hard to the corner where Martin had turned. The fugitive looked back and fired a shot at Spur but he was too far away.

A half block farther and Martin had slowed to

a walk. The gold in the suitcase was dragging him down. Spur put on a burst of speed to catch him. When Martin saw Spur so close he looked around desperately. A couple heading for church pulled around the corner in a small buggy. Martin waved them to a stop, drew his revolver and forced the man out of the buggy, stepped in and drove away with his hostage.

Spur scowled at him, then saw a short cut through the block that had no buildings on it. He raced through the uneven ground and came out on the street just when Martin turned into it from the other avenue.

"No!" Martin bellowed. He pulled the frightened women to his chest for protection and began shooting at Spur. The first two shots were at too great a range, the third missed by a yard and then the hammer came down on the empty chamber.

Spur ran near the rig for a moment but Martin lashed the horse and began to pull away. Spur didn't want to, but it was the only way. He lifted his revolver and fired twice. The horse took the second round in the side of the head and went down in a heap in the traces, screaming in pain and fury in her death struggle.

The rig stopped suddenly, crashing Martin against the iron side brace that held up the roof. The woman stepped down from the buggy and held her skirts up with one hand and ran down the street.

They had worked out of the business section of that street and now several homes showed along the block. Martin raced up to one of them, tried the front door and found it unlocked. With his heavy suitcase he stepped inside.

Spur came toward the house slowly. A shot

whizzed past him and he ducked behind a tree that grew near the street. He waited five seconds, then ran for the back of the house.

A window crashed and a shot slammed close past him but missed. Spur gained the side of the house and edged toward the back door. When he got there he banged on it loudly, then hurried back to the front where he expected to see Martin come running out.

He didn't.

What was Martin doing in here?

A moment later Spur knew. Martin came out the front door, a shotgun in one hand and his suitcase in the other. He blasted one round of buckshot at Spur where he crouched near the wall of the house.

Spur saw it coming and dove flat on the ground away from the blast. He was far enough away that he felt only a few pellets hit the tough soles of his boots.

By the time he got to his feet, Martin had charged a half a block ahead returning to the business end of the street. He must have lightened his suitcase because now Spur noticed that the fugitive was running faster.

A block down, two policemen strolled along on a Sunday afternoon patrol. Martin saw them, sauntered down an alley to avoid them and then ran hard up the alley.

Spur followed. The police were too far away to be of any help. He spotted Martin at the end of the alley. It was blind, with no outlet, only stores and offices on each side and a building under construction at the end. Already, it was five floors of raw framework stairways and subfloors.

Martin stared behind him, hoisted the shotgun

but didn't waste the round at that range. He ran into the building under construction.

By the time Spur got to the front of the new construction, he had no idea where Martin might be. He could have hurried to the top floor and set a trap for Spur. He might be one door down waiting to bushwhack him with the shotgun. Digging a fugitive out of a building was not Spur's favorite job. There were too many places to hide, too many chances for deadly surprises.

He edged up to the door's opening, then in a run went through it at an angle and against the wall beside it so he would silhouette himself as short a time as possible. There was no shotgun blast or pistol shot to welcome him.

He listened but heard no movement. As his eyes became adjusted to the lower light level inside the building, he saw that there were few places to hide on the first floor. The walls were not in yet, just the framing. The steps leading to the next floor were a short distance to his right.

Spur moved that way, every sense alert, his ears trying to pick up some sound of movement, his eyes watching every hiding spot, waiting for the first sign of an attack.

Nothing happened. He made it to the stairs and took them three at a time silently until he could look over the last step into the second floor. It was a duplicate of the first, with only the support walls in to hold up the floors above it.

The pattern held to the fifth floor. He had to be on top. There was no place else to go.

Spur hesitantly looked over the top step. Here the walls were being finished. The framing for the roof was up. Some offices and hallways could be picked out. More places to hide from which to attack. Spur leveled the weapon in front of him, holding it with both hands as he moved toward the first hiding spot, a finished wall that had been plastered over lath.

The white plaster bulged through the spaces between the lath, holding the plaster wall in place and giving it rigidity and form. Spur darted around the first wall, but all that was in that room was plaster dust and a pair of overalls.

The next room was the same.

A laugh came, high and a little crazy. "Hell, McCoy, you won't find me that way. You'll never find me until I want you to, then I'll blow you in half with twin shots of double-ought buck from my scattergun here."

The sound bounced around the building so much he wasn't sure where it came from, but he guessed to his left. He worked back that way silently, then ran toward a pile of construction materials.

A revolver shot jolted through the afternoon air missing Spur by a yard but forcing him to dive behind some sacks of plaster. He looked around them. Where the hell?

Three hiding spots ahead. The stacks of lath, the plaster mixing machine with its big hand crank, or the small room that had been finish-plastered on the outside. He chose the stacks of lath. They were high enough so Jefferson could stand upright and still get good protection.

Spur charged to the side, parallel with the lath, and gained another square of plaster sacks set up so they overlapped each other and wouldn't fall down.

One more shot slammed into the quietness. This time Spur spotted the cloud of blue smoke that came from the black powder. The gunman was behind the lath.

Spur put a shot into the lath pile, saw splinters fly, and hoped some of them lanced into Martin Jefferson. There was no scream of pain, only a high wailing laugh.

"Damn, but you're stupid, McCoy. I knew who you were the first day I met you. Using that uncle routine about you and the Secretary of the Treasury was a time worn ploy. I knew right then you were from Washington, all right."

"Then why didn't you have me killed the way you killed all the others who got in your way."

"You knew nothing yet, just probing from Redfield's letter."

"But you did hire Scarface Felling to kill Redfield."

"Had to be done. I liked the boy. Smart, bright. But it turned out that he was just too damn bright for his own good. I had a talk with him and he wouldn't back off. So he died."

"And then you had your hired witness killed by Felling."

"It had to be done. He talked too much."

"And you finished the game by shooting Felling as soon as he knifed Stoop."

"It was a neat solution, taking care of two witnesses at once."

"Too bad you aren't going to get away with all that gold and cash. What I can't figure out is why you had to kill Pickering. Did he tell you that he made a complete confession to the police, that he was going to testify against you because you killed Redfield?"

"He couldn't wait. His testimony would have put a noose around my neck. But he got wild and tried to kill me himself, so he had to be eliminated."

"You're just a businessman looking after your profits, no matter how many people you have to kill or how many of your friends of 10 years you have to rip apart."

"You're getting the idea, and you're next, McCoy."

His revolver fired but the 40 feet meant the accuracy was poor. The round missed the stack of plaster sacks.

"One thing I haven't figured out, Jefferson. How did you arrive at the two percent figure for the skimming off of the gold?"

"Simple, in most smelting operations there's a one percent loss of metal volume due to the heating and cooling and cleansing processes. We figured that two percent would not be missed due to the smelting loss factor. Fortunately, we never had to prove that to the auditors. They never checked that far, and there was no obvious shortage when it came to the coins produced. It was foolproof."

"You should have left two months ago, Jefferson, as soon as you knew about Redfield's problem. That means you aren't quite as smart as you think."

"True, but now there's just one small problem between me and that boat tomorrow."

"So it is the boat. I wasn't sure."

As he said it, Spur darted to his next cover, a stub wall six-feet long that had been plastered on both sides and would give him an angle behind the stack of lath.

A shot blasted from Jefferson's six-gun and cut through Spur's left arm bringing a gush of pain and a stream of blood. Spur rolled behind the wall and checked his arm. Not serious and he wouldn't bleed to death. He went to the floor and looked around the end of the wall.

Jefferson had moved. The only way he could go was back toward the end of the building and the not yet completed outer wall on the fifth floor. Spur's field of fire commanded the stairs, the only way down.

"You don't have anywhere to go, Jefferson. You might as well give it up and take your chances with a jury."

"Not me, McCoy. I've been in court before. You've got too much against me. It would just postpone things. I'll take my chances with killing you and getting on that boat."

Spur decided that Jefferson had only moved around the corner of the lath stack. Spur headed for his next cover, the plaster machine. It was closer to the stairs, gave him good protection and moved him 20 feet closer to the target. If he made it.

Spur took the time to bind his handkerchief around the wound on his left arm, then surged toward the machine. This time there was no shot.

"Getting short on rounds, embezzler?"

"Only takes one round to kill you."

"That gold getting heavy, Jefferson? You should have taken it all in greenbacks, much lighter to carry."

"I'm doing fine. How is that arm where I winged you?"

Spur didn't comment. He was figuring the odds. If he stormed the lath stack, Jefferson could wait until the last second and then step out and blast him with the double-ought buck rounds, or even buckshot. Either one would chop him in half.

Spur knew he had to try something else. What? Drive the killer toward the open edge of the building. How? Near the big drum where they mixed the plaster for the men to put on the lathed walls stood tools and equipment. One box held dozens of hammers for the lathers to use. There were saws, clippers, nails, and a wheelbarrow that had a buildup of plaster on it. He looked at it again. It was a big barrow, four-feet long with a strong hard rubber tire on the front for easy pushing.

For a moment he looked at it and then he grinned. His movable fortress. The bottom of the barrow was rounded so the plaster would pour out easier. It was made of sturdy steel to hold the weight.

By upending it and holding the rear legs, he could bend over behind the barrow and wheel it directly at the man behind the lath. The revolver rounds would bounce off the steel or dig in part way and drop harmlessly.

The secret was to get to the stack of lath bundles before Jefferson had time to use the shotgun. Spur checked the distance. He slammed a revolver shot into the lath as a holding shot.

"You'll have to do better than that, gunslinger," Jefferson said. He sounded more confident.

Spur figured he was 30 feet from the stack of lath. It was not a stable pile, if he ran into it hard with the heavy wheel barrow, it would crash over on top of Jefferson. He wouldn't have to go around the side at all.

Yes. Do it, now!

Spur upended the big wheelbarrow, held on to the rear legs and bent over, yes, he could hide behind it. He rolled it to the edge of the big mixer, then surged around it and keeping the wheel at a small forward angle sprinted for the closest edge of the pile of lath.

He heard one shot from Jefferson, then the barrow hit the stack of bundled lath. Spur surged hard against the cross brace on the barrow, driving it forward that much farther until the whole stack teetered, then crashed over tumbling and spilling where Jefferson had been standing.

Spur grabbed his Colt and jumped around the side of the still falling bundles of lath.

Jefferson crawled out of the pile holding his left arm. There was blood on his shoulder where the Chinese knife had gashed him. It looked like the man's arm had been broken.

"Hold it, Jefferson. The game is over. You lost."

He no longer had the six-gun or shotgun.

"Where's the money?"

"Under there."

Jefferson stopped, stared at Spur for a minute, then shrugged. He stood, held his left arm and walked back to the pile of lath. With his good right hand he tumbled the foot square bundles of lath aside, digging down on the far end of the stack.

Spur let him do the work. After a few minutes, Jefferson grinned and picked up the heavy suitcase.

"This is what I wanted," he told Spur. He turned and walked away toward the unfinished outer wall of the fifth floor.

"Stop!" Spur barked.

Jefferson turned, a strange smile on his face. "Why should I stop? I have a boat to catch, I'll never get to the wharf over here. I have to get to the embarcadero."

He kept walking toward the open side of the

building 20 feet away.

"Jefferson, that's not the stairs."

"Of course not. Why should there be stairs? I've got the money. Thank you for your help. Now I really must say goodbye." He took another half dozen steps toward the edge of the building.

Spur fired into the wooden floor just in front of him.

Jefferson stopped. "Mr. McCoy, I told you I appreciate your help, that should be sufficient. Please don't bother me again."

There was a snap and command to his voice, but his face showed a pleasant smile as if he were on a Sunday stroll in the park.

"Jefferson, think what you're doing!"

"Yes, I have. I know. I should have waited for Pickering and Knox, but I'm sure they'll find their way to the boat. It's been all arranged. Best way to get to San Diego. Again, goodbye, Mr. McCoy."

He walked toward the edge of the fifth floor. The wooden beams rose to the roof, but there was no wall, nothing but a 60 foot drop straight down to the hard street below.

"Jefferson, no!" Spur bellowed.

He fired. The round tore into Jefferson's right leg dropping him to the wooden floor. He shook his head, stood and limped forward. Spur raced toward him, tackled the man from behind and brought him down hard. In the fall, Spur's head slammed into the wood between Jefferson's legs. Spur shook his head, dazed for a moment. His eyes showed him two of everything for a few seconds, then cleared.

He saw Jefferson almost at the edge of the floor. He had the suitcase of gold and cash. At the very edge, Jefferson turned and waved.

"Yes, I know. Yes, Wilma, I'm coming. We couldn't have enjoyed it more. Yes, next Friday at our house. Wouldn't miss it for the world. Goodbye."

Martin Jefferson's smile was bright, untroubled. He picked up the suitcase and before Spur could do more than come to his knees, Jefferson stepped off the fifth floor of the unfinished building.

Spur rushed to the side of the structure and looked down. Jefferson had hit on his head and shoulders, and slammed over. His head showed as only a large red mass. His body lay sprawled on the ground crumpled and broken.

The suitcase evidently had landed on the top and crushed downward. It had not sprung open or ruptured.

Spur remembered the angelic smile, the polite conversation, the recognition of who Spur was, and then the total fantasy of Jefferson during his last minute on earth when he thought he was at a party somewhere and stepping off the porch.

Spur took his time walking down the steps of the building. There was going to be a lot of sorting out and catching up to do. First, the police.

When he got to the ground, he found a small boy and paid him a quarter to take a note to the police station. The boy said he knew where it was.

Spur asked Inspector Daniel to come to the street right away. A man just died . . . Martin Jefferson. Spur was sure that the Inspector would be there quickly.

· 25 ·

Spur McCoy spent the rest of Sunday afternoon with the San Francisco police. Inspector Gale Daniel had been about to go off duty but when he read the note, he took three men with him to the street Spur mentioned and found the body and all the money.

"Glad you got here," Spur said as the inspector arrived. "I was about ready to pick up my suitcase here and head for China. Look at all of this cash."

Inspector Daniel took off his uniform hat and shook his head. "Never seen that much currency even in a bank. I want you there when we count it to be sure we get it all figured right."

Then he looked at the body. There was no reason to call a doctor. Martin Jefferson was carted

349

directly to the morgue. They took the money back to headquarters and began counting it. At last they agreed on the amount: $76,000 in cash, about 10 pounds of raw gold bullion and 37 diamonds up to one carat in size of undetermined value. One man estimated them at about $40,000.

The captain on duty, a sour faced German with a bristling moustache, sat in on the counting and signed a receipt for Spur concerning the amount, the size and clarity of the diamonds, with the guarantee the same items would be returned to the government's representative upon the determination of the case.

"Now we need your statement about how Martin Jefferson died. He had a stab wound and a bullet wound in the shoulder, was shot in the right thigh, and died of massive head injuries from a five floor fall."

Spur went over the story quickly, then a man was brought in to write down his statement and he went over it again, putting in more details.

He stopped to send a note to Patricia at both her new apartment and to her home explaining what had happened and that everything was under control.

When the session was over with the stenographer, they sent a message to the United States Attorney Charles Imelhoff. Spur asked him to come down to headquarters at once, the mint embezzlement case had exploded. When Imelhoff arrived, Spur brought him up to date on the developments that had moved so quickly. Imelhoff suggested they arrest the two men in the crime not dead or unaccounted for at once.

"That would be Philander Knox and Nance Sturgill," Spur said.

"We have no arrest warrants," Inspector Daniel said.

"You'll have them tomorrow morning," Spur told him. "Arrest them now to prevent any flight." Spur frowned. "I didn't see anything in the newspaper about a man falling to his death from the Telegraph Hill bluff. Why was that kept out of the papers?"

Inspector Daniel shook his head. "A suicide? We haven't had anybody go over there in three months now."

"You didn't find anybody out there today? I saw a man fall over there last night, one of the five in the scheme, Ben Oakmarker. If he didn't die in that fall, we've got a third man to try to find. We better send two men out to his place right now, and then check on the hospitals. He must at least be broken up. Check the admissions for his name."

Inspector Daniel sent two men to check the hospitals and the morgue.

Spur went along when they picked up Nance Sturgill, the weightmaster at the mint. He didn't seem surprised.

"Told you something was happening, wife," he said as he put on his light jacket. "I'll be in the jail for a while."

They checked at Oakmarker's house but the woman there said she hadn't seen him since sometime Saturday. She let them look through the house. There was no sign of him.

When they went to the Knox house on Knob Hill they did it low key. Spur and Inspector Daniel knocked on the front door. A servant said Mr. Knox would be right down. He came a moment later, saw Spur and the officer, and gave a big sigh.

"So it's to be now?"

Spur nodded.

"I'm glad it's over. I'll have to pay the price. It was an interesting 10 years." He looked at Spur. "Oh, about Jefferson. I heard you were chasing after him. Any luck?"

Spur told him about the chase. "Patricia helped me or I never would have caught him. At the end, I think he went over the edge into insanity. He thought he was at some society party. Then he stepped into space."

"Like father, like son," Knox said. "I always did think that Lucinda was the most stable one in that family. Patricia tells me that you released her from that home."

"Yes, she seemed normal enough to me."

"Yes, I agree. Well, I'm ready to go. Let's get this process started."

Betsy ran into the room and hugged Knox. "I'm so sorry, Philander, so sorry," she sobbed.

"Betsy, I knew the risk I was taking. I just wanted you to have nice things. You understand everything we own will go back to the government? The house, the mountain cabin, the jewelry, the horses, the furniture, the paintings, the rugs, everything."

Her eyes went wide for a moment, then she nodded. "I figured it might. I can find a job somewhere and work. I started out working, remember, before we were married?"

He nodded, hugged her again, then walked out the front door without looking back.

Down at police headquarters, U.S. Attorney Imelhoff said he was sending police guards out to the three Nob Hill houses to forestall any removal of property before the places could be formally seized in the morning.

"I also have freeze orders on all the bank accounts we can track down of the five individuals," Imelhoff said. "That should get things started. Does anyone have any idea how much money was stolen from the mint?"

Spur shook his head. "But I have an idea we will know exactly down to the dollar if we can find a certain ledger somewhere in Jefferson's desk at the mint. Let's go down and take a look."

Since it was a federal office, the local police could not budge the guard at the front door. But when the U.S. Attorney ordered the guard to admit them and to send a guard with them to be sure they did not violate any "sensitive" areas, the guard buckled under and opened the door. All three signed in putting down the time.

In Martin Jefferson's office they began a thorough search. They were not neat about it, and systematically investigated every possible file drawer, bookshelf and desk drawer where a small red leather bound ledger might be hidden.

An hour later they took all the drawers out of the desk. Spur found the short drawer and five minutes later they had located the key that opened the hidden compartment in the desk. Inside was a .45 six-gun, a box of shells, five one-hundred dollar bills which they confiscated, and an eight-inch high ledger bound in red leather.

Spur opened it to the first page. The initial entry was for June 12, 1864. The net amount was 8 pounds and 4 ounces plus. The dollar figure was for $2,874. He skipped over pages to the last entry Thursday, for 10 pounds 2 ounces . . . the dollar figure was for $3,348. The grand total sold to date in the far right column showed . . . $843,697.

"I don't believe it," Imelhoff brayed. "How could that much gold be lost and no one noticed it?"

"That's two percent of maybe ten percent of all gold coined here," Spur said. "That's two one-hundredths of a percent of all the gold minted. Over a ten year time it mounts up. But for one week, it's not a lot to be lost."

They took the small book, showed it to the guard and made a note that it was removed from the office by federal authorities, and signed out.

"Tougher to get out of there than it is out of jail," Inspector Daniel said.

Patricia Knox was waiting for them in the reception area of police headquarters. She ran and grabbed Spur's hand. "I was so worried about you when I lost you down at the dock. Sorry I couldn't keep up."

Spur remembereed the wild Chinese sex-games rooms and opium den he was in and laughed. "Just as well. The important thing is, Jefferson didn't get away."

"I heard, and you got hurt." She looked at his arm, untied his handkerchief and growled at Inspector Daniel until he brought one of the police-men who cleaned the wound and put on some ointment and then a proper bandage.

"Now," Patricia said. "What's next on our agenda?"

"Have you been home?"

"Yes, for a few minutes. Mother and I had a long talk. I told her I had helped you and she was angry for a moment. Then she stopped crying and started to figure out what we would do tomorrow. We both packed our everyday clothes, and we'll be out of there in the morning. The apartment I got for Lucinda and me is big enough for three. My mom is going to be just fine."

Spur told the policemen he'd be back in the morning if they needed him, and walked out with Patricia.

"Your mother is going to be fine. How will you be?"

"Just twice as fine, maybe even a little better. I feel sorry for Daddy, but at least he's still alive. He'll go to prison, I know, and it'll be hard on him, but . . . but he had to know this was the chance he was taking. He'll have to deal with that. As for me, I have a job until school starts. I'm going to help a friend in his law office. He said he'd pay me, and everything. I'll be a kind of stenographer for him and maybe do some research. Things like that."

"Good. How is Lucinda doing?"

"Better than I expected. She's working for a lady who has a small dress shop. Lucinda is helping fit dresses and picking out material. She's very good with fabrics and loves to sew and help the ladies who come in with questions. Evidently, they taught her to sew at the clinic. She might even start to design clothes. So you see, we have two working women out of three. That's not bad."

"Better than not bad, that's great." He kissed her cheek.

She turned to him. "I know a better spot than that. You never have really have kissed me. Is it dark enough here for that?"

"Plenty." He kissed her on the lips and then let up. She clung to him a moment. "I could really learn to like doing that . . . and all the rest that goes after."

"Plenty of time for you to learn to like that sort of thing, young working girl. First you find some young whelp your own age who is good enough for you. I'm still looking forward to your having those six kids."

Patricia grinned. "I guess you're right. But after knowing you, anybody who wants even to hold my hand is going to have to be so damn perfect!"

They both laughed and he called to a cab. Spur helped her step up into it and on the way to her Nob Hill home for the rest of this day, they talked about the other wives involved.

"Mrs. Pickering already knew that it was crumbling," Patricia said. "I guess Mr. Pickering had told her about you and that he confessed the whole thing. He told her they would lose everything, and that Victor and Denise would lose their house as well.

"Thelma Mae took it better than I thought she would," Patricia said. "She was calm and resigned. Then Edmund's murder this morning set her off. This afternoon I talked to her for a while. She's coming back around. Edmund had made her promise no matter what happened she would go back to her people in Nebraska. She has a lot of family there.

"She said she even told Victor and Denise. They decided they will stay here. He doesn't think it will hurt his employment, and Denise never was involved with the society things."

"What about Wilma Jefferson?" Spur probed.

"That's another case entirely. I went to see her after I got back this afternoon. She was in bed. Devastated. Absolutely in shock and crying. She should have been ready for something like this. I was there when a policeman came and told her that her husband was dead.

"That didn't seem to to upset her as much as the fact that she was going to have to move out tomorrow. Not the moving I'd guess, but the whole problem for her is what people will say. Her society friends. Rich people love to talk nasty about one of their own who falls. They just love it."

"What will Wilma do? Surely she won't stay in town."

"No. I told her about Lucinda. She shrugged as if it didn't matter to her that her only daughter was out of the clinic and entirely normal and eight months pregnant. That made me angry. Wilma just kept worrying about Wilma. At last she decided that in the morning she would start the trip back to Chicago and stay with her sister. She said at least there she can be poor with family."

The buggy had stopped in front of the Knox house a few minutes before and now they got out. Spur told the hack driver to wait. He walked Patricia up to the front door.

"Young lady, I'm glad we met, I'm proud to know you. I hope the next time I'm in San Francisco I'll find you married and settled down. You work on that, you hear?"

"One goodbye kiss."

He touched her shoulders and kissed her lips gently, then harder and she sighed and stepped back.

"Now I will remember that until I get a kiss that good to match it. I'm glad we met, Spur McCoy. You be careful, and the next time you come through this little old town, you say hello." She blinked and reached up and hugged him tightly, then hurried through the front door.

Twenty minutes later, Spur McCoy checked the Almont for any last minute messages. He found two from Laura Grandifar. One told him she would meet him later at the new hotel room. He grinned.

The room clerk at the Almont who Spur had told about his room at the California was not on duty. When Spur asked about the man by name, the new clerk frowned.

"He was killed Saturday night right here in the hotel. We don't know why. Nobody does. The police came and talked to us all. Nobody knows what happened to him."

Spur figured that he did. He'd give the police the details about the man killed in room 416 and that would be the end of it. Chances were he was the man who killed the Almont room clerk to get Spur's new hotel and room number.

Ten minutes later Spur came into the Pacific Hotel and up to his room. Laura sat on the bed waiting for him.

"Figured you would come home sooner or later. Is it true what we hear about the Jeffersons and the Pickerings and the Knoxes?"

"All true. Embezzlement. Gold from the U.S. Mint over a 10 year period. No rich relatives, no old money, all stolen money. Won't that tweak the noses of the San Francisco blue bloods?"

"Probably, not mine. I really don't like blue bloods anyway. I brought the midnight lunch this time. Champagne, blue cheese and crackers, bananas, peaches and chocolate candy. I figure that we're going to need a lot of good food to keep up our strength."

Spur sat on the bed. "This case is all over for me. Just the messy part to clean up tomorrow. The three Knob Hill houses will go on sale to help pay back the government."

"Unless it's a secret, how much did they steal?"

"You won't believe it . . . $843,697. Close to a million dollars."

"Damn! They did think big. So everything they own will go back to the government?"

"Probably. Unless we find some hidden bank accounts, most of that money was probably spent in high living. High Society living."

Laura unbuttoned her dress. "Money isn't that important to me. Oh, I spend it, but Daddy makes it honestly. I have more important things on my mind."

Spur helped her with the buttons, then watched with fascination as she lifted the dress over her head. The light, expensive silk chemise remained and delicately outlined her full breasts.

"Can you help me with this?" she asked looking down at the silk garment.

He pulled it over her head, tousling her shoulder-length blonde hair. Spur kissed her, then pulled her down on the bed on top of him.

A few minutes later he eased away from one of her breasts that had somehow slipped into his mouth. "You know I have to work tomorrow."

"Yes."

"You know I'll have to be sharp and alert and ready for anything?"

"Yes."

"And you insist on making love all night?"

"Absolutely."

"You win."

Later, he lay with her nestled close beside him. Tomorrow he would have to send a telegram to his boss, Major General Wilton D. Halleck in Washington D.C., the number two man in the Secret Service. He would report that this job was finished successfully, and that he was advising the Bureau of the Mint that it should send new people to San Francisco at once to operate the mint here.

They would also need to send in some lawyers to make attachments on all the property and monies that the three managers had and perhaps investigators to try to find any hidden bank accounts or assets. But that was tomorrow.

Laura and Spur had the midnight snack and again Spur thought about tomorrow. He would finish it up here and notify Halleck that he was ready for a new assignment. That might mean a day or two or three in the city by the bay, and perhaps Laura could give him a complete guided tour. Perhaps.

"Hey, quit thinking so much and come over here and show me exactly how that Around the World thing goes."

Spur grinned. He loved challenges. Especially the kind where a beautiful, marvelously built blonde was involved.

The hard-riding, hard-bitten Adult Western series that's hotter'n a blazing pistol and as tough as the men who tamed the frontier.

The hard-riding, hard-bitten Adult Western series that's hotter'n a blazing pistol and as tough as the men who tamed the frontier.

#26: LARAMIE SHOWDOWN by Kit Dalton
____2806-9 $2.95

#25: POWDER CHARGE by Kit Dalton
____2754-2 $2.95

#24: COLT CROSSING by Kit Dalton
____2728-3 $2.95US/$3.95CAN

#23: CALIFORNIA CROSSFIRE by Kit Dalton
____2674-0 $2.95US/$3.95CAN

#22: SILVER CITY CARBINE by Kit Dalton
____2649-X $2.95US/$3.95CAN

#21: PEACEMAKER PASS by Kit Dalton
____2619-8 $2.95US/$3.95CAN

#20: PISTOL GRIP by Kit Dalton
____2551-5 $2.95US/$3.95CAN

#19: SHOTGUN STATION by Kit Dalton
____2529-9 $2.95US/$3.95CAN

PONY SOLDIERS

They were a dirty, undisciplined rabble, but they were the only chance a thousand settlers had to see another sunrise. Killing was their profession and they took pride in their work—they were too fierce to live, too damn mean to die.

_____2620-1   #5: SIOUX SHOWDOWN
                              $2.75 US/$3.75 CAN

_____2598-1   #4: CHEYENNE BLOOD STORM
                              $2.75US/$3.75CAN

_____2565-5   #3: COMANCHE MOON
                              $2.75US/$3.75CAN

_____2518-3   #1: SLAUGHTER AT BUFFALO
                           CREEK $2.75US/$3.75CAN